DRACULA VS NIGHT OF THE LIVING DEAD

GERALD SIMON JAMESON

{Subgenre:Publishers}

CONTENTS

BEDSIDE MANNER

Nurse-and-union-leader *turned* homicide-detective, Eminence Gray, uses her gifts of empathy and emotional labor to catch the most vicious of West Brandon's killers. Em's ability to maintain this skillset will be put to the ultimate test when the highest-profile murder case her department has ever faced falls right into her lap. Add to Em's troubles a corrupt executive from her union days, back and up to old tricks, and it might just be Eminence Gray requiring a little *bedside manner*... or a lot.

INTERVENTIONISM

Roger Jech doesn't have any superpowers, but he has a super ability: harm him, harm yourself in equal measure. Hit him with a right hook, your jaw breaks. Shoot him in the head, your brains blow out the back of you. Drop him in a war zone, your enemies kill themselves killing him. Jech's a weapon to the wrong people and a savior to the right, but before he can become the latter, he must learn to harness his gift before it becomes his curse.

THE TAKING OF SHALE CITY

Shale City has seen better days. First, the dam burst, flooding out the town's iron mine. Then, local officials shut down the shipping and courier services, the only thing keeping Shale City hanging on... It was all the mayor of Shale could do to fight off the more 'legitimate' of sleazeballs trying to destroy her city, but now it seems as though some other kind of sleazeball force is encroaching upon her town, set on putting the final nail in its coffin...

{SubGenre : Publishers}
www.subgenrepublishers.com

❦ I ❦

THE OTHER VANIAS

OCTOBER 2, 1968

I vant to correct the record.

They never killed me when they pierced me.

They *never* kill me when they pierce me.

Of course, make no mistake, a skewering of the heart of a person of my disposition would certainly achieve this end. It wasn't because my heart was able to withstand such a piercing. It was because, though impaled, the piercing never occurred anywhere near my heart.

I am what is called a *Dextrocardiac*. What this means is, my heart and other internal organs are the mirror of any normal person's. You may have heard of this as *Kojima-LaMarr Disorder*.

My heart is at the right.

It's a condition that affects about one in every ten thousand. It doesn't affect *The Cursed* so, by the logic of this admission and the grace of my pen, you may now infer a little more of my origin.

Yes, a heart at the right. A thorn to the left. A happy accident.

I'd survived dozens of such encounters thanks to this quirk. My most famous was not my first either, mind you. Of course, each time my impalers insisted on excess. Merely abiding the ritual was what they told themselves. Fear becomes ritual over a long enough period but believe me, fear need not exit after holding the door for ritual. The fear remained and it was their only driver. Everything else was pretext.

It was fear that gave way to ritual that required, for each and every impaling, the cutting off of my head and my quartering besides—all while I feigned oblivion. They would send the five pieces *not* to the four corners of the globe but as far separated as was feasible according to the latest of their technologies.

Where did they distribute me this time?

Let's start with my head...

ii

Allow me to put something else to rest. In this case, a decades-long wives' tale. They never faked the first moon landing. In fact, they never faked it twice. And I'd know. I was there.

"I don't like it," the astronaut said. He was real marshmallowy in his pressure suit.

"Blame Russia then," said the other, looking equally marshmallowy. "Everyone else does."

"What the hell the Reds got to do with any of this, Gil?"

"Beating 'em to the punch ain't cheap, Sammy. Helsing Corporation's paying us a pretty penny for this. The reason we bumped the launch up eight months. Be a hammer and sickle down there if it weren't for HelCorp."

"I don't like it." Sam was grimacing at the company logo stretching across one of the ALSEP containers—near snarling at it. The logo said *HelCorp®*. There was a picture of a string of flowers next to the name. The flowers had purple petals shaped like moth's wings. He took the container from the top of the module's portable life support system, examined it. "We're turning what should be the most monumental achievement in human history into a mail call."

"We're achieving the most monumental feat in human history because of that mail call."

"Every gram counts. Anything extraneous and we won't get the lift we need to return to Mother."

"That's why we're leaving it, Sammy."

"What-a-ya think's in there?"

"Infamy. Now get your helmet on."

"I don't like it..."

"Splashdown in five." But Sam wasn't listening anymore. "Sammy, I said *splashdown in*..." He wasn't listening to Gil because he was listening to me. "Suit yourself, Sammy. You just sit and stew."

I did not talk though I communicated, clear as day.

Samuel.

And Samuel glanced, as was only natural, to his partner. Sam's expression was contorted as anyone would expect of a person hearing a voice *not* of the only other man present, but who was the only possible communicator. That is, his expression contorted only in the slightest. Maybe Gilbert had caught something in his throat, was the thought. Or, maybe he was attempting some caricature? Samuel's was a look of the mildest of annoyed anticipation: tilted face, lips flattening together into a perfectly straight seam, whites of the lower hemispheres of his eyes displacing his irises.

But Gil had since gone back to protocol. He was attending to the controls, paying no mind to Sam.

Understand me, Samuel.

In profile, Gil's face was still. No words were uttered. The uncanny sight brought out the smell, the old familiar. As I had hoped, Samuel's heart was racing. It wasn't racing to feed organs deprived of oxygen. It was racing to account for a pending depletion of oxygen, out of preparation of flight. It was adrenaline. He was scared.

Thirty-five, Samuel.

The stench was more powerful! I had Him!

Thirty-five and unmarried. Thirty-five and a scientist. Thirty-five, a scientist, and a peak physical specimen. I know what they think of you for this. You know what they think of you.

Samuel was shaking his head like he had risen too fast and was staving off a faint. He watched Gilbert's lips having yet to move. Maybe Gil had taken to ventriloquism? Romanian accent and all? Of course not, the phonetics were too perfect for a man of his soil.

Open the box and, along with the historical immortality granted a man first to set foot on the moon, I will grant you the spiritual immortality to preserve that historical self. They cannot besmirch your reputation in death if there is no death. Open the box.

"No."

"Sammy, you alright?"

Open the box, Samuel.

"Buggin' out goddamn it! Get the son of a bitchin' scrub-bers up!"

"CO_2 levels are norm... Sam?"

Sam was now in a panic. He was holding his hands to his

ears. It appeared as though he was trying to pop his own head like a melon.

Not hallucination, Samuel. A special accord. With me. With fate.

Sam ripped off his gloves and they floated gently to the bottom of the module. Gil put a jostling hand to his shoulder. Sam dug his index fingers into his ear canals.

Live forever. Write your own history. Rewrite it millennia later if you please.

"Shut up!"

Gil no longer entertained trying to calm Sam. He just got on the horn. "Mother, this is Falcon. Come in, Mother. Come in... Christ Sammy!"

"I'll shut you up!" and Sam's tearing open the ALSEP container.

The container was not locked though the twenty-eight centimeter by twenty-eight centimeter oak trunk inside it was: padlocked through hasps angled into each other to form the stipe of a brass cross. A horizontal flat brass bar sat behind the hasps, completing the icon.

HelCorp had ensured the latter protection, while NASA put all its trust in its selection processes. Neither Samuel nor Gilbert would open the container out of a commitment to duty. Theirs were supposed to be wills of steel. However, there are fewer people on this earth with true wills of steel than there are men with mirrored hearts.

"What the hell are you doing, Sam!"

"Shuhhhhtt!!!" He was shaking the trunk. In free-fall, it felt like the box was underwater.

Sam hadn't the key. He and Gil were to leave everything on the moon's surface, outer container and all. They never should have known there was anything without-key to even ponder the contents of.

Shut me up then, Samuel. Recapture your sanity.

"Mother to Falcon! Sammy's... Sammy!"

He was smashing at the lock with his helmet.

Gil wrenched the box away, but not before the latch-and-catch assembly on Sam's helmet caught the padlock, square. The lock body snapped free, separating from the chrome shackle. It floated down the capsule to join the hand coverings. Sam grabbed back firm to my casket as Gil pulled in the opposite direction.

What was their training for this, I wondered. Not much it seemed, as Gil was trying and failing to leverage against Sam as Sam failed the same in the opposite direction. Two beetles in amber, fighting over a ball of dung: my vile prison.

Just remove the shackle now. Don't fight to end my confinement, just remove the last of the lock. I will do the rest.

Sam made a swift grab for the left of the two leather straps running vertical along the trunk. He caught it, holding it firm in his left hand. He popped the shackle out the brass hoop and the bottom hasp swung downward on its hinge pin. The cross was broken. Immediately the straps burned away causing Samuel to lose his grip. Gilbert tumbled backward and I spilled out and upward, rotating in some sort of stochastic orbit for a moment before spiraling downward to the space between Gilbert's jaw and open collar ring, to his waiting neck.

Just a nick was all that was needed and I had his form.

He pulled me off himself, more curious, not even noticing the incision I'd left. He was immediately taken woozy as the turning had begun. He held me by the ears, close, trying to focus on my visage but I blurred on him. A taste was all it would take to complete the capture. My mouth went slightly agape and he could not tell in his stupor. A hissing, then the expulsion of my form into him. It was not blood, strictly speaking. We do not have blood in the way you would think, save for a clotted pool at our hearts. The chemistry of it, you'd have to ask that wretched Dutchman. What would he know anyway? It was almost certainly irreducible to science, certainly a violation of their laws. Order of form from decay, life from death. From my mouth to his soul.

I had him.

iii

Gilbert had recovered from his stupor, Samuel from his frenzy.

The two men marveled at what Gilbert held in his hands. He still had me by the ears as I feigned once more, a bit of repose.

"What in god's name is HelCorp up to?" Gil said. Sam just shook his head. "And, what was that all about, fella?" was the follow-up.

Gilbert was my valet, though he didn't yet know it.

"You wouldn't believe me if I told you," Sam said.

"Answer any weirder than this?" He raised me up a second to make the point, then lowered me toward the trunk below. He was mine. A flash from my eyes to his and he understood.

"Y'alright yerself, Gilly?" Sam noticed the flicker of silver in his partner's gaze. That would be his last awareness. "Gilly?"

A growl, was it? A swooping gesture, palm down, flat.

Sam's head came off clean. A lot cleaner than mine...

Gilbert twisted his palm inward to get a look. He did so without expression, no curiosity in the gesture despite it being an act of the curious. He saw that his palm's edge was bloodied though otherwise unspectacular: just another palm on just another hand. Yet, it cut through Sam like butter.

A spritz off the severed jugular caught Gilbert in the eyes. It shook him out of my hold. The first rumblings of *the thirst* would be more powerful anyway.

"What have I done..." He looked down to the lifeless eyes of his partner. The sight shook him. He should have felt the need to vomit but all he could think... "No..." He averted his gaze to Sam's headless trunk, neck oozing. "Oh god, oh Jes—"

Eat, my ward.

Gilbert's eyes flashed silver again. His pallor returned. More importantly, the thirst reared. This would be the first he ever indulged it, momentous, like a first orgasm: scary as though something had become broken in him, though once the process ceased: an event reminisced over more and more fondly, something always at the back of one's mind, desired always, never not, the desire's presence not a matter of *if* but to what degree. And the thirst that led to the feeding could not be fought off. It was like a tick for people with such a compulsion: one felt the urge to erupt, to indulge oneself. It would come on slow, it would grow. It felt like it wouldn't stop growing, like a pestering. One may stifle it, but it would only come back stronger, rampant. Stifle it again and it returned more fierce. On it went until the inevitable eruption: the tick, the emission, the *wanting to suck your blood!* and commencing to it! It would only be stronger the greater the iteration of stifling.

Gilbert buried his face into where he had severed Sam away from himself.

Drink until the calm arrives. Drink, my dear.

We smashed into the surface of the moon...

iv

He held me in his lap and we spoke face to face. He was out of his suit and cooling layer. He sat in thermal underwear, in lotus position on the surface. The lunar module sat about a dozen yards away, crumpled, where if we were to tilt at it it would appear no different than a swatted fly held to a window by its own burst guts.

I explained his new role. His bond. The nature of the thirst...

Pardon me if I make this all sound so trivial, like I'm onboarding a new accountant. There really is no ancient rite or ceremony about it. He was under my control. He had powers beyond his comprehension though nowhere near the supreme of mine. He would drink to sustain them, unlike my last valet who subsisted purely on creepy-crawly beasties.

"Now, my servant," I said in culmination. "I want you to get us back to Earth. Just us. Have you a way to do this?" I probed.

"I believe so, master."

He rose, shuffled to the crushed module.

Apparently, for situations like this a radio was kept next to the portable life support system. It was encased in indestructible material. Gilbert dug it out, flipped open the lid, and took the receiver in hand.

"Mother, this is Falcon. Mother, this is—"

"Receiving you, Falcon."

Gilbert's voice was cold and clinical, beyond that of us Cursed. It was like an airline pilot's. "Due to unforeseen events, our module has become unfit for liftoff. Will need EVAC immediately."

"Are you requesting Falcon II, lieutenant?"

"That is affirmative, Mother."

"Down in twelve."

v

The third astronaut's name was Roger. He wouldn't last long. He'd stepped out of the emergency lunar lifter to investigate. The first man to ever set foot on the moon as, strictly, Gilbert was no longer a man in his heightened state.

Bouncing over to the crashed module, Roger stopped at a curiosity. It was Gilbert's helmet, resting in the dust. He made his way to it, cautious.

The visor assembly was down. It was pure gold to him. He knelt. There was lament in his eyes. Nothing hopeful would follow from the facts before him: the wrecked module, now this lone cap on the ground. He knew this. He flipped open the visor. I glared at him.

He recoiled and Gilbert shot downward at him in an instant! He pinned Roger into the dust, pushing at his shoulders. Roger flailed. My servant tore the savior' suit off in two, clean like opening a party favor. No pop, just a gasping cold Roger standing in his cooling mesh, now frozen solid.

Quick, before the cryogenics!

Gilbert reached around from behind Roger's left shoulder, swinging a grasping claw into the frozen astronaut's chest. *Into*, deep down to the aorta. He pulled the vein out like a dispenser for one of his food packs. He sipped at the pulsing fluid like drinking soda through a straw. What little of the drink he missed floated away in shiny ruby orbs of an infinity of surface tension.

"Come, my ward," I said before he could finish. "We must leave for Earth immediately, to find the rest of me."

"We'll never be able to land this thing." He meant the emergency module.

"Can you direct it?"

He tilted his head at Eagle II. "Sure."

"Then fine. A soft landing isn't essential to our mission."

vi

We plummeted.

It was day where we were to land. I needed rest. So would Gilbert. Regardless of any dozing, I would be weak as I hadn't the earth of my nativity to sustain me, though I needed what little strength I could muster. An ill slumber would have to do.

"Entering the mesosphere!"

My servant held me in-helmet to his breast.

We hit the ozone and Eagle II flared to life, spinning like a gyro faster and faster as the air between it and the earth compressed to white heat. Centripetal force tore the module to pieces, flinging us outward at some angle of no relevance. We were plummeting to our lonesome now, the module just energy. Gilbert held me close. Closer, incidentally, the second the helmet vaporized. We began to cook, ourselves! But the Curse brought us back together faster than the heat could tear us apart! Our cremated remains left a streaking most immediate to us, like a comet, then dissipated to a gleaming aurora borealis as it spread from the tail. Through all this we continued our disintegration and reformation.

I could see the state of Florida and we were moving north. We weren't in much control, though I tried guiding us by telekinesis. Without Romanian earth and the remainder of my body, I was only at a fifth of my potency. With the sun at my back, it was a tenth.

Yet, I could choose the angle. I would need appeal to some bygone geometry of my youth, which was paltry even then—

"Landing at this speed is like spearing a fish underwater. You have to overshoot it by half meter of length by meter of height! If you wanted Washington, say, you'd aim for Baltimore."

Thank you, my ward.

We continued to burn away, then heal. Burn away, then heal... We were leaving our beaming essence all over the eastern seaboard.

Where we going? Gilbert asked.

Aid me.

And in his grasp, I was maneuvered to better assess the hemispheres. Darkness would come to the east in short order. Another happy accident.

I believe I left my heart in Pennsylvania.

2

THE DAY AFTER

OCTOBER 6, 1968

Let's get something clear.

They shot me in the face because they thought I was one of those stumblers. I wasn't. Never thought I'd be either since that blast pulped my brain, and you need a brain to stumble. I'd been thinking recently. About what? Doesn't matter. I was *thinking,* and as you need a brain to stumble, you need a brain for thinking too, right? But stumblers don't think last I checked, despite any brains.

Let's get it straight.

I think, therefore I am, so not dead. *I think, therefore I am not a stumbler,* so not a stumbler—yeah, no kidding. But, *I was shot in the brains, therefore I do not think... shouldn't be thinking?*

Strange.

Let's back up a few minutes and maybe *you* can tell me what the hell I am.

ii

I awoke to the taste of old pennies. Best I can describe it: the taste I used to taste for a second or two before my head would lurch forward and those coins would go flying, spitting. Really, all the pennies caused was my gramma to notice me about to choke on 'em and *that* caused a smackin' hand to wallop the back of my head to cause the lurch.

I woke to that same taste, but to a different wallop.

Never felt so alive, and it wasn't because I was brought back from the dead and thankful to be. I was full of vim and clear-headed like a high-schooler, with the wit and wisdom of an elder, and pardon me if that made me think I was something altogether different from what I had been seeing among the living, the not living, and the *inbetween* the last couple days.

It wasn't only my strength of mind—or having a mind at all—that made me sure I wasn't one of them. Whatever killed those stumblers in life, that left its mark, stayed with them after. Nothing heals on them. Stumblers got rot too. Everything just putrefies and falls away. I, on the other hand, was immaculate. I knew I'd been shot in the head because I saw it coming. Saw that twelve-gauge flash at me anyway. Heard one of them say *alright shoot him in the head, right between the eyes*. Maybe he was a good shot, maybe not. No matter because all he could see of me through that window was my face and he shot and I took to napping. Even if he were a bad shot, hard to miss with a *twelve* anyway. Should have had a hole the size of a bull chisel through my forehead and something out the back of my head the size of... No back of my head to speak of, really. Yet, here I stood, immaculate.

Should be burnt to a crisp too. Everyone else up there

on that pile was. Plus, I was naked as a jaybird, and I'm sure that sheriff and his men didn't strip us for the fun of it. Would they? Nah, they burned me. Should have a rotted-out melon for a head on a *marshmallow-fallen-off-the-stick* for a body, but I was back. I was back and I hadn't had skin this clear since the womb. Pale though. I'd have to find a mirror.

How'd I get here? Under this pile of burnt corpses? *Right between the eyes,* I heard, then pennies. Now I was looking up to the sun through the burned-out slats of some cellar, past the charred crusty limbs dangling in at me, reaching at me.

That's all I know *and* that about brings us up to speed *and* I bet none of you know any more than I do: I wasn't alive, wasn't dead, wasn't one of them.

iii

I couldn't see much down here, a spot of sunlight on the floor and little else. It was a spot about big enough for two people to stand in and have elbow room. It made me groggy when I did, howev—

Hell!

What was that?

It brushed past my leg. You could say it slithered past as it was low, but it was more just thumping and humping along. But fast!

"Who's there?"

Nothing.

I moved away from where I last sensed it. That only less-ened the feel of its thumping around in that dark. Closer, I could at least tell it was moving. If it was moving fast? What if it decided to creep?

Think man. You were only bragging about being able to do so just minutes ago!

I could get into the spotlight, though if I did, I'd have nothing but the dark around me and wouldn't see anything coming. If I stood outside it I'd only see that thing if it was stupid enough to come through the light!

Never been more clear-headed and that clear head told me I had no viable options. *Clear* meant able to be seen through, unencumbered, sure. It also meant free of contents, empty. My head was empty alright. I had not a plan in the world.

Then that thumping started up again...

By reflex, I jumped for the hole in the cellar ceiling and didn't even come close. Must have been a good nine feet up and I had to stand in the spotlight to try and in there it was syrup. In there it felt like something was dragging me in the opposite of anywhere I'd try to move. And even *if* I managed to catch hold I'd only have caught hold of burned slats happy to give out on me.

I kept jumping for it.

Couldn't reach the slats, though I could just tickle the crusty tips of the fingers of a roasted stumbler reaching down. *Grab on!* I hoped it would say but it was only the charred up old corpse some yokel'd taken the brains out of with a .30-06. I tried to grab on anyway, like a toddler lookin' to dunk a basketball.

I kept feeling for the thumping of that thing as I worked to escape. It seemed to be circling the perimeter of the cellar —not getting closer, yet—maybe sizing me up?

I collapsed.

Must not have rationed my strength carefully enough in the treacle.

I dragged myself out of the light opposite of where *what-*

ever it was was doing whatever it was, and I could drag myself just barely. But damned if I didn't get a good portion of my vigor back the very second the first part of me touched that dark. The rest of it returned as soon as I was completely out the light. I got some haste too and so I stood. I didn't *think* despite being able to do so just fine now. Instead, I got to my feet and I burst forward and upward, reaching for the reacher. I must have gotten all my strength back and some on loan because my head smashed right through the slats below the reaching corpse. We all fell down to the now-widened patch of light on the cellar floor, corpse right on top of me.

That damn corpse was moving?

No!

That Thumpy beast's thumping was growing. I could sense it moving toward me. I couldn't get out from under and it would have been nothing to push a waif of a burnt biscuit of a stumbler off me if I hadn't been making a habit of leaving the best of me back in that dark—

The thumping neared.

It was at my feet.

I tried lifting my head to see over the corpse that had me pinned. God grant me the muscle to do even that? Nope... There'd be no eyeing this thing yet I could feel that our thumper had thumped its way on top of the two of us. It was on top of the cinder corpse and the corpse lay prone on my belly, its face to my chest, buried in my heart in some weird pantomime of romance. Our humpy little friend maneuvering up my lover's thighs. Oh god you little tormentor! What ya doing down there? I worked my damnedest to lift the now combined weight of both the stumbler and the thumper. If I couldn't lift the one what could possibly make me think I could lift the two? My fully unpulped brain, that's what. Nope... My immaculate noodle was in syrup too, and even if it was in the convalescence of the dark, I'm sure it would only tell me: *what you can't lift now you can't lift heavier.*

My *couldn'ts* were vastly outnumbering my *coulds*. What could ya do...

I could sure jostle that's what. I could jostle because the thumper had changed our center of balance. It was tipping to the right and taking the corpse with it. I shimmied it as much help as I might in that direction.

I shimmied and jostled. Writhed and wriggled.

Shimmied more...

The monster duo listed just right and thumper lost its balance. It fell to the dirt beside, thoughtful enough to not let go of the cinder corpse as it went.

Free of the pair, I dragged myself to the dark as fast as the treacle would allow. I watched that mass of monsters, careful, on alert.

At first the corpse lay still. Damn thing looked contented with it all too, its waxen rendered lips receding in just the right way to affect some sort of crooked gaping smile at the sky above. I couldn't see the thumper.

Then there was movement.

The cinder corpse rocked leftward but rolled back to its original position. It rocked in that same direction again, only further over. It stayed tilted this time, like a sleeper reaching for a wake-up call. Only it wasn't the corpse's arm that reached out. It was the arm of whatever the hell that thumper was! And it was an arm alright... not reaching for any alarm. It was reaching and groping along the front of the corpse. It pulled. It tore away at the cinder chest, rending flesh, revealing the left rib cage. Its fingers wrapped around those bones and held on, dragging the rest of itself on top.

Good god! That humpin' thumpin' bastard was a half a torso, the right half, split down the middle—torn apart down the middle—headless!

It groped and twinkled its fingers across and upward along the cinder corpse's chest, up toward the mouth. It found its desired line only it was too low. It brought its fingers to a point and plunged into the throat right above the breastbone. It plunged, then grasped, held the top of the sternum like a handle. Pulled itself faceward now. The top of the torso's neck—the point of severing—appeared aimed at the cinder corpse's smile.

I said it was the right half of a torso, right? It had to be. The position of the arm dictated so. The orientation of the fingers palm-down n' away from itself had the thumb to the left, pinky to the right. That's a right hand at the right of a torso. Right?

Goddamn if I couldn't see a heart inside that thumper's ribcage, where the cage was split at the sternum and all it contained met the open air.

Was this guy's heart on the—

It began to beat! It began to beat and a pulse in the bisected neck began to… pulse.

A few drops of clotted blood seeped out, like an aspic. Each drop found its home in Cinder's mouth and no more than a second or two passed before the corpse began to move?

It was!

It twitched! It twitched and that Thumpy thing ran off.

Just a goddamn drop'll do ya?

The corpse rose, standing in the light, its back to me.

It took to crumbling, the char on its body fracturing. Beams of light emitted from out the seams as material fell away in chunks. The corpse wasn't falling completely to those pieces, only losing what of itself had been destroyed. Wasn't long before the whole of the figure was a gleaming trying its damnedest to hold on and losing and wherever any one ounce of that shine would fade, a pristine alabaster flesh was revealed.

More and more the corpse healed in that diminishing shine. Until...

It was a girl. A woman. Blonde. Slender. Naked of course. Hell, I was naked too I remembered. Spent all this time pondering my own porcelain pelt and I forgot? Didn't care I guess. I felt no bashfulness altogether. Felt the opposite: a sense of moorless pride. Why? Felt no cold neither, even in a pit in a Pennsylvania autumn. Though I ramble...

I stepped into the light behind her. I touched her on the shoulder. She turned.

"Ben?" she said.

"Barbara?"

✾ 3 ✾

THE MANIPULATION

OCTOBER 3, 1968

Darkness would come to the east in short order.

ii

Gilbert had taken several of their shotgun blasts to his torso and pelvis. The hunters had become spooked at my naked raving servant, the severed head of his master under-arm. He raved at them from the crater we made on our land-ing. We were in Maryland. We undershot our approach. He raved at the four men, all dressed like Elmer Fudd.

Oh yes, I had very much enjoyed your animated serials —before my most recent of executions. That's where they tracked me down in fact, a theater showing *Why do I Dream those Dreams?* The short was quite amusing. I especially liked when the little dreamer was in the sights of that dastardly spider. I digress...

Only one hunter shot at first—very hasty, very scared, judging by that familiar stench in-blood—while the others were somewhat more restrained if only for an instant. The three *did* quickly follow their reeking, fearful leader.

My servant would have to learn some restraint himself. Though I was not so sure how much courtesy a reasonable decorum would have earned him given the circumstances— what with his nakedness, pallor, and me at his hip—we will have many more encounters where his ravings won't just be the proverbial final straw, but a defect sufficient for provoking distrust in those who must obey. For his haste, he sleeps. He sleeps in the autumn grass, victim of a body of circumstances conspiring against him—beyond his control, yes—though his impetuousness was not of that body. That was what lit their fuse.

One kicked at him now.

If you thought these men were spooked by Gilbert's merely trying to flag them down, you should see them now.

The bird shot had begun seeping out of my servant's wounds. A pellet would emerge, coaxed out of a tear of flesh by, then carried away in, yellow bile. Immediately after its release, the tear would heal, leaving only that stream of bilium.

Had it been me, I would not even have lost consciousness. Gilbert was not me. He was only what you would call a *Quassy*. I would turn him completely once I was reformed. For now, I needed him free to move in the day. *For now*, he would heal though not be invulnerable in-total. Recovery would take time.

The sun was near-gone over the horizon, so their flashlights were on him and myself-feigning.

He began to rouse.

"Shit! You seeing this?" the leader shouted, handing his torch to the man beside. He re-levelled his gun at Gilbert.

"Wait a minute," said another of the hunters, pushing

the leader's muzzle out of aim. "I know this guy. He's some sort of space man for NASA or something." The sun was now completely under the horizon. "Was gonna land on the moon! S'posed to be there right now."

Leader wrenched his barrel back to true, smirked through his fears. "Gonna land in a shallow grave—"

But I opened my eyes at the men in a start! Near all attended to me in that instant.

You have seen nothing this day.

"We have seen nothing this day," said the leader and two of his fellow hunters. The fourth—the hunter who had recognized Gilbert—more marveled at the three's sudden stupor.

You will leave, remembering nothing.

"We will leave, remembering nothing."

"Whaah?"

You will leave, only not before...

"We will leave, only not before..."

"What the hell, guys!" And then the fourth noticed... "He's movin'! He's movin'! ...Who you talking to guys?"

Not before you ensure the fate of your strong-willed friend.

"Not before we—"

Make it look like an accident!

The leader and the other hunters in-stupor grabbed the fourth and held him in place.

"Come on guys! Guys?"

Gilbert rose. His nakedness revealed he was completely healed. He ambled weakly toward the men.

"Let me go fellas! Come on now! Come—"

But the leader had pulled the strong-willed's head back by the hair, taking his voice just as Gilbert would take his vitality.

Quassy fed to the hunter's screams.

iii

Again my ward sat in lotus position, me in his lap. He was wearing the hunter's outfit.

I must admit, prior to his dressing, I couldn't help considering his alluring pallor, his turn to Quassy having finished. Now he sat clothed, not a hint of blood on his collar—anywhere. I couldn't help considering this budding discipline as well.

We had deliberated over many things, decorum being one of course. Now our focus was on the conspicuousness of a man, slated to be the first on the moon, wandering around the east coast with the severed head of an ancient Count in-hands.

"If there was only a way for the world to see my conviction," I said. "To look into my eyes."

"There may just be, master."

Gilbert placed me in the wild oats, leaves a deep red of autumn—or so the first light of dawn suggested. I watched him through the blades. I grew weaker as the sun crept closer.

He had moved back to the crater, jumped inside. He began to kick in the dark and the dust. It seemed he wasn't going to find anything other than hole down there until... the distinctive *thunk* of a soft body hitting a hollow body! Gilbert had discovered another of those 'black boxes': indestructible for its carbon fiber reinforced carbon, or *carbon carbon,* oddly. In it was a flight recorder, a spare pressure suit, and the credentials of all men aboard Mother. He took his credentials and the suit's helmet, left the rest. Then, with his newly imbued strength, he tore off one of two square sides of the container.

With hands as powerful and fortified as hammer and

vice, he began folding the material at its corners, repeating this process on each new corner-formed until he had a circle so true only a Platonist could protest. He wedged that circle into the bottom of his helmet.

Dawn was breaking.

"Here, master. Sleep now."

He placed me inside through the viewport and lowered the visor assembly. From here, I would travel under-arm. It was no bed of my loam, and he wasn't exactly inconspicuous —what with his visage and now this accessory announcing his fame—but his helmet would keep me as hidden as possible.

It was time to leave. From these woods, we would fly for the south.

iv

We waited at the Northwest Gate. It was just past dusk. Whitehouse staffers were filtering out onto Pennsylvania Avenue. Night staff were filtering in.

The elected and the bureaucrats will give us no trouble. Maybe the occasional disillusioned staffer otherwise. It's the guard staff and secret service that concern me most, what with their likely military training.

"Leave it to me," Gilbert said. "I have been here before."

We walked up to the guard post. The uniformed secret serviceman eyed my vessel. Naturally, it was what caught his attention first. It should have. People rarely attack such forti-fied spaces with weapons held in-face. I say *rarely,* knowing full well I could have said *never.* Maybe some sort of dart blower? Anyhow... The guard, in all his competency, had not yet looked my servant in the eye.

"Lieutenant Gilbert Mandrake." Gilbert extended his

NASA credentials to the man still examining the helmet He was unable to see inside through the gold of the visor, though he sure peered at me like he could... "*Ahem!*" Gilbert directed at him. Guard snapped to it, bypassing any credentials and attending directly to my servant's ashen visage.

"Holy shit!" the serviceman said. "You're—"

"I'm here to see Dennis Rinevest. We have an appointment."

"I—I'll have to ring the West Wing. I—"

"Escort me."

The guard got a bit of his bearings. "I can't just—"

But the visor was lifted. I had his attention immediately.

"Follow me, Lieutenant."

v

From the Northwest Gate to the West Wing Corridors, we only met the resistance of a single Secret Serviceman. Luckily, due the agent's proximity to a security station consisting of three other willing apostles, he was subdued nice and quick.

On we progressed through these hallowed halls. It should be smooth sailing now as all of my intended puppets, from here on, are too mired in the machine to have brains—too administrative in one capacity or another.

vi

Two security agents, urgent in demeanor and hustling, moved swift to the office door of Deputy Chief of Staff Dennis Rinevest. One hammered on the aide's door. "Mr. Rinevest, this is call sign Signet. We're in code blue. Please confirm scramble protocol: four-D-Eight-F-Niner." There was silence. A few seconds went by. "In your blue passbook, sir—"

The door opened. "Gentlemen, come in," Rinevest insisted.

One of the agents entered while the second stood vigilant in the doorway.

"What is it, officer?"

"Just sit, sir." The agent's eyes darted around the small office.

The aide lowered himself into his chair, though uneasy. "Scramble says we've got someone unauthorized on the grounds, where?"

"Just stay still, sir." Agent reached for the phone on Rinevest's desk, tore the receiver from the cord.

"Now wait a minute..." Aide began to rise.

"Sit the hell down!" The agent put a hand on his holstered sidearm. Rinevest relented. The agent nodded to his partner. Partner waved us in.

"Jesus Christ, Gilbert!" Rinevest said in instant recognition. Instinctively, he rose to greet his friend. "I—" But the agent waved him back to seated. Quassy sat he and myself down in one of the guest chairs. The aide stared wide-eyed. "It's a bloody miracle," he assured. "Houston said you guys went dark moments before splashdown. We thought the worst. Prez was going nuts. We all..." He shook his head. "Bloody miracle..." He caught sight of my domed abode and reacted accordingly. "W—What's all this?"

My servant lifted the visor once more.

Take us to the Oval Office.

vii

The speed with which the president and his staff had

arranged for our address was truly astonishing. Within no more than a minute, the Commander-in-Chief, as well as the whole of his inner circle, were under my spell. Within forty-five minutes, his office was swarming with network news producers, camera operators, and reporters seduced the same. Only a single serviceman guard and a single camerawoman had the will to resist. They lay dead at the presidential seal now, both shot at center mass by a few of our more impressionable of armed attendees.

The room was abuzz with not just Whitehouse staff, network newspeople, and certain of their equipment. There was also what Gilbert informed me were video cameras and video monitors, utilizing something he called *tape*. For posterity, he said. Excellent!

Each monitor's screen featured a 'live raw feed' of its respective network's broadcast. One monitor for each channel was placed at the back edge of the president's desk. All but one was muted in order that he know the nature of the introduction.

A producer, holding onto an earpiece in his right ear, gestured for silence. He pinched his thumb and index finger around the volume nob of the unmuted monitor, began manipulating it accordingly. An NBC logo popped up on screen, then the presidential seal.

NBC News, said an anchor a half dozen miles away, *brings to you live from the Whitehouse in Washington, an address by the president of the United States, declared to be officially of the highest national urgency. The Commander-in-Chief met today with the National Civil Defence Council to discuss the status of the Apollo 11 lunar mission...*

The producer pointed to the man behind the desk as though to say, *You're on!*

Ladies and gentlemen, the president of the United States...

We were live only it wasn't the president helming the address. Facing home audiences was Gilbert. He and myself of course. Before anyone tuning in had a chance to react to the bait and switch, Gilbert lifted my visor. The gesture was quickly becoming analogue to flashing a passport to the universe: a key to man's will.

As the camera pushed in on my visage, I saw red. This was the standard, as intense seductions bring the shade to my irises. I felt a growing influence. My telepathic link was stronger than I'd ever felt it. I had all who watched. They were at mind's eye. They were glued to their devices.

Now Gilbert! and my servant spoke.

"Before we commence, if there are any near you who aren't paying attention, convince them."

It worked. The enamored were leading and the uninitiated were hopeless but to be led. More and more of them were under my control. Elderly all over were awakened to behold. Children were ushered into living rooms and away from their toys. I had them!

"For those who yet protest, persuade them."

This worked too! Wives held kitchen knives to the throats of husbands to coerce their submission. Barmen and bouncers held drinkers in place to sober and be sobered by my tale. A desk sergeant had ordered—not any criminal's, mind you, but—any patrolmen, still too incredulous, into his precinct's holding cells to watch. I had them all!

"The Apollo Eleven mission never took place."

The mission never took place, the room said.

"The Apollo Eleven mission will take place late next Spring."

Late next spring...

"What occurred to the east, what lit up the sky, involved the recent Explorer satellite shot to Venus.

Explorer...

"It was purposely destroyed by NASA when scientists discovered it was carrying a mysterious, high-level radiation with it."

High-level radiation...

I could feel any of their last apprehensions melt away as my Quassy spoke. There was no doubting the lesson.

"What you saw light up the sky was that radiation reacting with particles in the atmosphere."

The president believed it. Of course a man of his position would...

"It was a very high degree of radiation."

Mothers believed it. Fathers believed it. College kids and their professors believed it—even the philosophers!

"However, the chemical reaction that occurred in the atmosphere neutralized the radiation."

Most importantly, near all at NASA command believed it.

"There was never any harm."

I had put myself in all of their homes, their offices, their nightclubs and their honky-tonks. It was glorious, this Television. They were hopelessly inured. What a wonder!

Provide the last assurance, I commanded my ward.

"There will be a report tomorrow afternoon, from NASA, on the Venus probe."

Now our escape!

"Forget Lieutenant Gilbert Mandrake. No such man ever existed. Put him out of your mind. Spread this message you've heard this day. Enforce the message." Gilbert closed my visor. He held me back in his arms and we stood. "Enforce the message!" he shouted at the newsmen and women. Immediately, all relevant technicians began rewinding the film strip and videotape.

"Now we may walk among them," I said to Gilbert as we moved from out the desk.

"What about those of the strong will?" he asked.

"Their wills are strong to resist my charms though powerless against the multitudes. Enough of their friends and neighbors will carry our water. The strong-willed will not want to alienate themselves from those enforcing our message. They will deny what they can see with their own eyes. Truth be told, they would do it for a mere fifth of those we fooled."

Gilbert bowed at this, in trust of my assurance.

"Now, we must go. We have much work to do should I wish to become whole—"

But I was interrupted by a piercing wet scream of a sight most curious. Make no mistake, I don't mean *most curious* in the way of platitude, akin to the nonsensical, *most definitely*. I mean to say, my curiosity was maximal.

The serviceman guard and the camerawoman, moments ago dead on the floor, had come back to life. The source of the scream was of a secretary to Rinevest. The camerawoman had clamped onto her from behind and bit right through her neck to her jugular. The secretary bled out near-instantly. A tragic loss. Someone ought to have taught the camerawoman better discipline, wasting a good meal like that.

The guard was little better. He had his revolver out, though swinging it like a drunk with a cudgel, holding it half by the barrel, half with fingers run through the open cylinder well. Shells fell from that hanging cylinder in coincidence with the guard's stumbling creeping lurches.

What were these two? They were undead. I knew that much, as there was the slightest of accord, though they had not, strictly, The Curse. They were not perfection. Their wounds were not healed or even healing. They were ghastly!

All in the room were attending to the pair in some way or another. Secret Service had moved everyone to behind the desk and formed a barrier to keep the stumbling ravers from getting to any government people and civilians. Servicemen's guns were drawn. They were not sure what to do from here.

The guard stumbler inched around in a circle as the camerawoman lowered. She knelt next to the secretary and began pawing at her, digging into her neck as though famished. Despite a lack of grip due the clotting blood at the wound, the camerawoman managed to rip free a piece of neck muscle and took to gnawing at it.

Secret Service moved to aid the secretary and detain the camerawoman as though either task was anything but futile. This left the professionals and the politicians unprotected, a fact of which our stumbling guard was not unaware. He moved for the vulnerable.

Gilbert!

"Protect the address!"

Reflexively, the president, Rinevest, and a few producers circled around the techs holding the reels of film and videotape.

At this point, Gilbert had taken to hastening the two of us to the door. I suppose a good servant has such instincts: to shield his master like this. However, in time, he would have to learn to cater to *my* instincts.

"No!" I shouted. He halted. "I want to watch."

And what I saw was the guard moaning and lashing out at the bureaucrats. He did so in a way lacking calculation. It was his grasping, much like the camerawoman's, that I assumed would be his most effective maneuver—not this mindless flailing—but his pistol kept him from any serious holds.

Meanwhile, the camerawoman had been pulled off the secretary. She gnashed at the servicemen as they rolled her prone. One of them held her nipping visage against the floor. Two others kept her shoulders pinned. A fourth reached under his blazer, removing some handcuffs from a gear pouch on his belt.

Just then, Rinevest's secretary jumped up onto her feet, her head hanging from what the camerawoman had left of her neck.

Well, if you had any doubt these charmers were of some subclass of the undead...

"These creatures, master, they are able to turn the mortals."

Quite right, my servant. Though, this appears more a side-effect of their feeding less anything intentional.

Another scream! This one from the president. The guard had managed to drop his revolver and had the politician!

The handcuffing agent said *leave her to me* as the others got off the camerawoman and broke away in directions according to some sort of protocol. Two moved to the stumbling guard with the president's face now in his grip. The other drew down on the secretary, aiming his revolver at her head bouncing off her right breast. *Stop!* shouted a good proportion of them all over the place, not breaking with their pattern of futile posturing.

None of the three stumblers had any inclination to do as told.

The two agents attending to the president pulled the guard free. They launched him across the room, past the agent shouting at the near-decapitated secretary, to join that near-decapitated secretary.

The president screamed again, though not of any immediate threat. All other bureaucrats were panicked too but not yet wailing.

My hypnosis was wearing off.

Gilbert, raise your left arm. I will empower you.

He did as I asked, putting me under his right arm and wavering his left hand at the three stumblers. The accord grew stronger. I had Gilbert move as though he were puppet master. Just as I thought. The stumblers were under my control!

I commanded my servant and he drove them with a grace they could not muster themselves. Their stumble was more fluid at present. However, moving them was still like molding half-kilned clay.

Gilbert swooped to the right and this sent the guard stumbler leaping onto two of the Agents. Neither had the opportunity to fire their pistols as they were toppling. My ward half clenched the fingers of his left hand and the thrown guard began chomping into the face of the agent closest.

More screams.

In all this, we held the secretary still. I was not sure what use I had for her yet. The camerawoman was pinned fast to the floor, too, so there was no point wasting energy on her. As an experiment, I released the guard, leaving his next moves to his instincts.

Interesting.

The agent whose face was now dinner began prying the guard's lips from his. This only ensured two of his fingers be chomped off in his thoughtless grasping.

Screams renewed.

The other toppled agent was pushing and kicking at the guard, trying to get out from under him, careful to avoid his maw. The serviceman attending to the secretary holstered his weapon and helped his partner get free. Then they pulled the chomping guard off its lunch. A piece of the gnawed-at agent's lip came along in the lifting.

The chomper serviceman guard was once again thrown across the room. He bounced off the secretary who I now released to her instincts too. The cuffing agent rose from the camerawoman, removing his revolver from its holster. He and the other two erect agents took to unloading their weapons on the guard and the secretary while the gnawed-at agent lay in a pillow of his own clot. He moaned liplessly amidst the gunfire, unheard, by the very fact of this violence.

Guard and secretary were peppered with lead at their trunks. At most, this only made them jitter a little. This didn't keep them from heading back toward the crowd.

Now came the clicks of the revolvers. All standing were empty. The three agents gawked on in exasperation at the indefatigable pair. Pair were coming. Not stopping. The servicemen struck fighter poses. I attempted to retake control of the guard. Now, if only I could—

Bang!

Gnawed-at agent put one in the guard's brow—had to use his middle finger to pull the trigger.

Bang!

He did the same to the secretary where, due the proximity of her dangling head, shot out her right lung in addition.

The stumbling secretary and guard crumbled in an instant. Gnawed-at agent passed out from his injuries.

One of the erect servicemen knelt to attend to his passed-out partner.

Another decided to rush over to examine the two...
corpses?

The last returned to the cuffed camerawoman,
attempting to lift her up by those cuffs. Both her arms came
off in the attempt.

All bureaucrats were screaming now.

The hypnosis was gone, though the lesson learned.

*Now we may leave, Gilbert, but I'd prefer to take the power of
these men with us before we do.*

"These men?"

Not the men, my dear Gilbert, their power.

"Of their laws?"

Of their video.

❧ 4 ❧
THE PITS

I thought it best to leave that pit before sundown. I still do. Nevertheless, something kept us from leaving, kept us in that earth.

At first it was Barbara.

"We can't just leave," she insisted. "Somebody must know we're missing. Somebody must be on their way—to find me and my brother."

"Nobody's coming to get you, Barbara. Those things were all along the eastern seaboard."

"You don't know."

"*You* don't know. You were out through the whole goddamn show—catatonic. Tales of satellites exploding, radiation, stumblers from here to Key Largo."

"*Out's* an interesting way of putting it."

She rubbed at the side of her face—side where I slugged her. Didn't want to do it. She was in a panic. Shouldn't of... But... She rubbed at it in a way telling enough, though it was all healed. Course it was healed. That blood's gonna bring

37

her back from char-broiled but leave a bruise? Didn't want to do it. But...

"They were busting in. You were panicking. Remember?"

"You'll excuse me if the moments before my assault are a little fuzzy," she chided.

"Anyone ever tell you you're at your most helpful asleep?"

"You're ignorant!"

I stepped to the edge of the sunshine again to see what I could see. Dozenth time I'd done it. Hey, you got any *bright* ideas? "Know that much..." was my retort. I moved about the edge of that halo, careful not to disturb our thumpy little friend now seemingly spent and dead in the spotlight, curled into as much of a fetal position as a half a torso could manage. "Listen," I said, face to the sky. "I'm not in the mood to let those trigger-happy reactionaries take another shot at me. They don't think, they don't miss, and that's a bad combination. We're city ducks down here."

Light was doing its job on me again. I could only survey a second or two more or I'd swoon. I didn't hear anything up there. Had to get out or—

Crack!

She'd swung out of the dark. Clobbered me good. Halo made me woozy. The dark make her Hercules? She knocked me out of that spotlight and clear across the cellar! Second she did I felt aces of course, but the strength in her punch!

"How the hell, girl?"

"How the hell..." she muttered to herself, examining her fist. She did so walking toward me, through the light incidentally. Naturally, she weakened. Why keep walking into certain-sedative? We're gluttons for punishment I guess. Why do you burn yourself twice on the same pot?

Oh boy, now she's the one's gonna swoon. Before she tumbled I was under her, like a flash, scooping her up and out of the light, all the way to the other side. I held her a moment, examining her. What can I say, I really didn't want to manhandle her like I did the night last, and maybe, on some impulse I couldn't account for just now, I wanted to make it up to her—protect her a moment or two? Then I started to ponder that teleportation trick I just pulled. I was pondering as... Was it getting brighter in here—

"Get the hell off!" she said with a shove. This time the force was as mighty as last but I was aces remember? My recovery left me more than able to resist flight. But damn this dame could pack a wallop! Pried me loose with that maneuver like nothing.

"We gotta get up there," I said, my attention back on the escape hatch. I waved my hand through the halo. "This radiation be damned."

"It's not radiation, not like that."

"How do you know?"

"What'd you fail high school science?"

"Don't need high school science to drive truck."

"You really *are* ignorant..."

"What about the damn radiation?"

She reached out to the beam, put her hand in it like mine. "The electromagnetic radiation of this sunlight isn't what's turning us into those things. We'd all be stumbling if it were."

"What's doing it then?"

"Making us weak, or making corpses rise?"

"Hell, at this point I'll settle for either explanation."

"I don't know." I frowned at this. She noticed. "*But*, it isn't that shuttle's radiation affecting us because whatever that radiation is, it works in the dark too. It isn't the sun making corpses walk either because stumblers rise in the night as readily as they do in the day. Considering that sunlight is still just sunlight, and nobody ever came back to life before, stumbling almost certainly doesn't involve sunlight at all."

"Well, whatever the hell's raising them, and whatever the hell's in that light doing the opposite to us, it's nothing compared to this barrel of fish down here. We have to leave."

"Stumblers are up there."

"You don't know that. Those trigger-happy townies probably killed the score of 'em and half themselves besides. Doesn't matter anyway. Those things don't have any strength and we do."

"Not in that light."

"We're better off weak in the light than blind and bumbling in the dark. I bet we're a mite stronger than them, even in that sun. They're weak as hell, Barbara, and even if in them numbers, we're a better match for them if we can see them coming. Weak as hell though..."

"You can't even stand in that light!"

"We'll walk under a tarp."

"You don't know that'll work and you don't have a tarp."

"We won't know unless we try and besides," and I said this next part a *tad* condescendingly, "they're dumb and weak as hell."

"They managed to kill my brother!" she shouted. "*He* managed to kill—"

She moved off deep into the shadows. I couldn't see her, though I could hear her quiet sobbing. I knew why the tears. Everything in this condition just came so transparent. The answer: that bastard Harry, his wife—who was too patient by a dime—those teenagers: they had each other. I got my kids... Oh god, my kids! But they're up north. In the cold. Those stumblers would be popsicles up there and as far as I know, they only stumble on the east coast. Kids are fine. Bet I could get back to them in a half-day runnin' in this condition. They're fine. T—they gotta be...

"We all had someone's all. Either still got them or went with them—and not in the *dragged along and screaming* kinda way."

I didn't know if her brother was a good man in life or not. I had to try...

"It's trust Barbara. That's why your brother didn't make it. Think about it."

"W—what do you mean?" issued from the shadows.

I had to try. "I bet..." The thoughts came real easy in this state. Compassion didn't so much. It came, only it had to travel in the backseat to vanity now. I tried my damnedest anyway to put myself in her shoes and allay that feeling. "I bet more of us got run down by those damn things these last few days, not because we let them mob up on us or any such thing... It happened because... Because you just never expect it. You never expect someone, even a perfect stranger, to haul off on you like that—even in the bad part of town. We just don't do that but *they* do. Your brother only saw a man for all he knew. He just acted accordingly."

A tear rolled down her cheek. It wasn't clear, it wasn't milk either, or of any color or thick, but it wasn't water. It glistened like a gem. It must have created the light too as there certainly wasn't anything in her dark to bounce off of it. Ah hell! Who cares about the drop's constitution anyway? We're back from the grave here! She seemed touched is all. So I moved to her, lifted her, put my arm around her. She wept, wept in my embrace.

Her tears lit up the room.

ii

We just sat a while, felt a while. Guess about now we were a moment or two away from having reasoned a while. As I was explaining...

"We were gone, Barbara. Now we're not. Something about Thumpy's blood did that to us. Maybe if we could isolate it, get it to your brother. I don't know. Stranger things have happened... And all last night!

She laughed a little. I think she was heartened. I took her hand.

"If we could just get out of—"

"Ben?"

"J—just hear me out. If we—"

"Ben!"

"What is it?"

"How are you holding my right hand if you're sitting to my left?"

"Barbara, you know I'm holding your left hand—"

But Thumpy was gone! He wasn't in that beam of light, anyway. Barbara bolted upright. In the shadows, she heaved. Then the li'l bugger landed right back into that halo he'd been playing possum in.

We beat our feet to the torso now dragging itself in circles. It was propelling itself by its fingers, things just a motoring, like those *let your fingers do the walking* ads only in fast-forward. We surrounded it before it could make any long-distance phone calls.

It stopped.

It started... pleading?

It rolled itself onto its back—halfback?—its hand waving *no no!*

"Goddamn pervert," I said

"It's showing us its belly."

"It ain't got a belly."

"It's scared."

Was Barbara softening on this thing?

Thumpy started to waggle its finger at us. *Wait! Wait!* Then he... *he*? Jesus! Then *he* pointed to the wall behind, then up and out the pit. Then he was upright and thumped off! Off toward that wall.

"Sneaky son of a—"

He was scrambling along the ceiling and out the hole!

"He's gone."

"He left us."

"Barbara, he's a demon!"

"You don't know that."

"What's with you?"

"When we were talking. He was a good listener."

"Listener? He ain't got any ears cuz he ain't got any head!"

"Well, he squeezed at all the right times."

"Squee—"

He was back! At the opening! Thrusting that hand of his downward like we should take it. Barbara smiled. Smiled? What's with this girl—

Stumblers! They'd amassed over him. He hadn't noticed. He just kept imploring with that reach.

"Watch out!"

But it was too late. Three of them had him in their grip and were dragging him away. He was gone.

"No!"

"Barbara!"

She lunged, fast as lightning, more powerful than a shot from a howitzer. Girl burst through the ceiling leaving a second hole bigger than the first. She flew high up into the sky as corpses and half-burned tables and chairs rained down on me.

She was rising higher and higher, until... She went limp in the light.

"Barbara, no!"

She flailed a little, then went completely still. Gravity had her body now. The sun, her soul. She was plummeting.

And damn it, the girl in her haste had to fly so high the fall back to Earth would take her to pertineer terminal velocity. I couldn't leave the pit to help or I'd topple the same, right? Right? I had to try. I reared. Just as I did, her body angled past the hole it made leaving and out of sight. I lost her.

I don't mind telling you this hopelessness thrust on me for about the eightieth time this weekend can just—

Smash!

She fell through the ceiling not making another hole because she brought the whole goddamn ceiling with her. Brought all the dust in the county along to boot.

iii

I moved through the debris, calling her name as I went. The dust had settled but it had settled on my eyeballs. Didn't sting, it was like a curtain. Some sort of strange pull was guiding me despite the blur. It was pure sunshine down there too. I should have been a bag of wet bread but that pull was doing double duty moving me along.

I trudged on. I felt her strongest about two-thirds the way across. I closed my eyes. I was there by the wink. I can't explain it. I just can't. I just dug. I pulled off as many of those slats and fire remnants and charred stumblers as I—

"No."

"Ben?"

She said this weakly. Oh, Barbara girl... She'd fallen bad. The leg of the table had gone right through her. She lay there, impaled.

"Hold on Barbara." I grabbed hold of what had her. It was sturdy as anything, even after the fires. I couldn't budge it. The leg was solid oak. I kept trying. She groaned. I eased. "Hold on." She reached a hand out to stop me.

"Can't you feel it Ben? It's a fading..." And she went still.

"Barbara?"

She was gone. I just knew. Don't ask me how I did. Don't ask because you know it. It's in the absence and there was nothing there. Like the opposite of a sleep where someone's in the room and you feel their presence—know you're not alone. The opposite.

She was gone.

She'd come back and now she was gone. No pomp to it. A miracle snuffed. The cruelty in that. The goddamn cruelty.

She stared up at me with those eyes, fixed, like she knew it too and had to carry it with her.

"God girl, rest. Just..."

I reached out to close those eyes, to give her some peace in visage. I reached out and—

They rolled back in her head, a real unfeeling gesture for someone whose teeth were now tearing into my flesh. She had me. The son-of-a-bitchin stumble! I had son-of-a-bitchin forgot! I pulled my arm away and those teeth flayed more of me. She gnashed and growled.

I rose up and away only to tumble backward. I was syrup again. That pull was gone. To my credit, I managed to back up the exact distance the fall had granted. She gnashed on.

I tried lifting my arm to examine the bite. Couldn't.

Couldn't lift a thing. Why try for anything, trucker? Couldn't help but chuckle. "I get my life renewed too and now this..." My head fell back. I closed my eyes.

iv

There was a tearing. Some movement.

My eyes opened to her standing over me. Girl managed to do what I couldn't. She must have pushed against that oak just long enough and just hard enough to rip away whatever rotten flesh and bone was confining her. There was a hole of torn muscle and sinew from her sternum to her armpit. The flesh betrayed the angle with which it was torn, flowing in that direction. She looked like the worst of the stumblers: rotted out as though she'd crawled free of last year's grave. The body stood still, sizing me up as if it were the mind to do so in its condition. Weren't a mind. She started to move.

"God Barbara girl, no. No, please." But I was tired. Just... tired.

She lowered herself for her feeding but I was just tired. She could have me. Just ti—

Bang!

I felt the brains all over my face. Could taste them on my lips. Not like pennies... I could feel her having slumped over on top of me, her head once again on my chest. I couldn't quite see through the glare to what did this, not having attended to the brightness behind Barbara girl for a while.

Focus was returning, though.

More and more...

And then I saw.

It was the torso. He was holding the rifle I left in that old farmhouse. How close were we to it? Why do I care? Why would I ever want to go back to that place? Was a bit hungry though... No! Best thing to ever come out of that house was that gun and the gun was right here—in the hands of ol' Thumpy. How'd he... How'd he do anything he did?

I'd have a million questions for him but I'd have to come out of the light to think them. I'd have a million conflicting emotions over what that bastard did to Barbara but I'd have to come out of the light to feel them—

But he was gesturing again, wildly. Pointing down at me? At Barbara? What is it now, Thumpy?

I examined her as best I was able. Immediately I understood what that devil'd been raving about. Her skin: it had reverted back to the same pallorous and smooth complexion as before.

"Ben?"

I startled a little. "Barbara?" She raised her head from my chest.

She looked pleasant if only because she was opening her maw and that starts with a smile. Keep on, and the smile turns to grimace. Grimace widened and each of her canines grew what had to be a goddamn inch longer apiece. She sank them bastards into my carotid. It was all a vacuum pressure. There was that familiar pull again, not fading an inch. She was draining me.

It felt... Amazing.

THE MISS

OCTOBER 6, 1968

A bite for all my friends!

We had yet to exhaust the breadth of our control over these stumblers. We walked with near a gross of them, acquiring a few in addition here or there, repelling a great many more. We had our moat. Why be greedy?

And our friends provided more than mere fortification. They served as beasts of burden too. Three dozen would pull our supply wagon at any given time. They were tenacious about it if not mindful of the contents—even with Gilbert careful in his manipulation. Unlike an ox or a mule, you see, stumblers were careless over difficult terrain, falling frequently, where their falling would roughen the path further should they slip under the wheels. Our equipment would have jostled to bits if it weren't for yet a few others, themselves more than willing to serve as insulation, as though packing peanuts.

It was a true pilgrimage: our prairie schooner of a news production trailer traveling at the rear of the horde while

Gilbert and I travelled at its center, nestled away among these grotesque beasts.

Grotesque and *wretched* to boot.

Another dropped away on broken knees.

"Free this one, Gilbert," and my ward clenched a fist and the stumbler, now dragging itself by the skin of its fingers-shredding, stopped. It tilted its head at us, got an expression the closest thing to forlornness then, despite no obligation to do so, continued crawling after the lot of us. Curious.

Many more had become similarly useless along the way. They could only move so many miles, you see, before their integrity gave way to decomposition. Musculature would tear free from tendon, tendon from bone, bones would break like dry timber. A true grotesquery. They were not much for conversation either.

Popping and squeaking and cracking were as common an issuance from them as their groans.

"Two of those five, Gilbert," and he waved them over.

Gilbert was their puppet master and I his, at least when it came to controlling the multitudes. To turn them all, to mere Quassy even, would take me years. Here, between servant and master, we collected them like burrs to wool. He had brought me two of the finer specimens of the five as well. He was growing more and more competent with each passing day—more and more attuned to my instincts. I was his puppet master, yes, but his autonomy was something I was coming to rely on the bulk of each of our new adventures.

In keeping with *growth* and *attunement*, the stumblers were congregating in greater and greater numbers the further northwest we travelled.

"They are drawn to it, Gilbert."

"There is the accord, master."

"You are quite right in your derivation, though as a mere premise, it doesn't complete the theory."

"How do you mean?"

"There is more. More to them. You and I, we cannot sense it, can we? Despite our connection to them?"

"Surely *you* must be able, master?"

"That I cannot detect my heart without my heart is precisely why they butchered me, dear ward. This reunion was always the greatest hurdle of my many reformations." I lightened a little. "But now we have our friends to guide us. Another happy accident."

"Let them lead the way then, master?"

"Precisely."

ii

Pittsburgh was on fire. We would go around. Our friends were not tending toward the city anyway. My heart must be somewhere beyond the north of it.

Camps of survivors would be in greater concentration on our chosen path—the periphery. No bother, if we avoided them, they would avoid us. The self-appointed guardians would be our only problem, these glorified exterminators, these vigilantes. Keeping our friends from feasting on them long enough that Gilbert may have his chance would be our only problem. Last encounter with these men, all that was left for my ward was a German Shepherd. A paltry banquet to be sure: more energy spent in the feeding than was derived from the feed. It would have been a total loss if that beast hadn't made for such a good scout subsequent to Gilbert turning him. He would bark at any threat miles ahead of our sight and my ward would run off with him to hunt. They were hunting right now, as a matter of fact.

A servant for my servant. Good boy.

iii

Quassy held me over the crypt so I might see.

"What happened here?" I asked.

"A massacre."

There were the charred corpses, fallen to the bottom of the hoard along with the wooded debris of the pyre, then there were the corpses above, at ground level, surrounding Gilbert and me and our friends. Our friends were themselves corpses to acknowledge a technical point, though animated and never yet put to flame. That made them different, did it not? I digress... Now, I don't mind telling you that my night vision was immaculate. I would have no problem observing all that I've described in mere moonlight. In less. Gilbert's night vision was not immaculate. It was that of the Quassy, hardly better than mortal. How was it then that he could see? See this *massacre*, as he put it? He could see because the fires that fed off these forsaken souls still burned!

The burned and burning stretched on for a hundred yards easy in all directions, the strewn mounds of them angling to a point at the farmhouse, stopping just before the front door. The mounds had consumed the trees and the brush as well. The largest of the oaks blazed red at their exteriors, expelled steam from their boiling centers. Defiant, though they will succumb before the corpses ever cease to burn.

The light of the fires meant our chaperones could see as well, as much as they could see anything. However, these friends of ours didn't much seem to care about the plight of their brethren just smoldering away. Those wretched mongrels! Even a man as callous as I can't help feel a lament should I lose a companion of particular use to me. Not our friends, however. They just milled and shuffled amidst those of their unique disposition retired to flame.

So many, retired...

Whoever determined this teardrop crematorium would have been burning men, women, and children a great while. A great while where a great many men would be needed to ensure the task. Where were they? Overwhelmed by the mobs not able to be subdued but who came, feasted, and then moved on?

Yes, a great while, as the stumblers would have come in droves, beckoned by my heart. There were not enough bullets in the world—

Would have come?

Gilbert, they're still tending. Free some of the more tenacious!

He did just that, and our emancipated friends continued on north. I watched yet held no hope. They lumbered toward the farmhouse. If they continued past, someone had absconded with my heart.

Someone?

Fashion a torch for yourself, my ward.

"Yes, master." And he sat me at the edge of the hoard.

Near us was a collection of pulped stumblers not yet touched by the flames. Gilbert moved to them. He tore several pieces of the loosest fabric hanging from their bodies. He then moved to a pile alight. He sniffed. He peered closer. Some fat dripped and sizzled out of a tear in the belly of one of the more rotund of these poor devils.

"*Vita mutatur, non tollitur*," he whispered as he thrust the fabric deep into that belly! He let it stir some seconds, then pulled it out quick, soaked in makeshift tallow. "I'm sorry."

He wrapped the fatted cloth around a thin wooden slat and lit it in the fire. He returned to me.

Now venture into that pit, my dear boy.

He jumped down.

Feel for a cross. There will be an unpleasantness. The unpleasantness will grow as you near.

"I feel nothing, master."

Damn! It will be ornate. It will be broken and of the pieces, some will make up a cross.

"There are pieces of everything everywhere, master."

Find it!

But he was still. "Master, pardon me a thousand times. If there is no unpleasantness—and I promise you, there isn't —then if that means the cross is broken, then the seal is broken. Your heart is elsewhere, or they would not be tending elsewhere."

My god, he was right. I had been bested in this. What was my saving grace? That my desperation led me to not think? Well what then, other than this latter consequence, could have led to my desperation?

It mattered not.

I had been bested.

Your derivation is sound, my Quassy.

iv

We were at a loss. No happy accidents now, only what those with no sense of the cosmos would call a series of impossible coincidences, all converging to failure.

I needed to think. I needed to think and all I could focus on was their smell. It was no distraction in my previous state of desperation—a state possessing a rankness of its own. It certainly was now.

I needed to think.

"It is about time we leave this place, Gilbert." And he put me under his arm. He turned from the crypt, lowering my visor assembly. As the shade of that gold approached to dampen the flames, they appeared all the brighter. "Stop!" I shouted, and he did. "What a horrendous task," I admitted of the fires. "I can't imagine even the most diligent of the mortals having the temperament for this."

Our scout barked.

"I don't believe they have, master." Gilbert was pointing to an opening in the mounds.

v

It was a boy.

He couldn't have been more than twenty. He had backed himself into a ring of the burned. He sat on the ground. There was a pistol in his hand and a hollow at his crown. Skin flowered outward from it. Where the bullet entered, who could tell? There were no marks on his person other than the flower. Any answer would be by inference, therefore, a matter of deriving the unobservable from the observed. And I could see, from his mouth, there dripped blood.

"I believe you are right, Gilbert." And I did. And I felt lament at this. Lament! I was weary even in the night and it was bringing out the sentimentalism in me. But repose would have to wait—for me at least. I needed desperately to reckon and I couldn't do so under-arm. "It is late Gilbert," I coaxed. "You must get some rest."

"I can walk in the day."

"Day or night, you cannot walk without end. When was the last time you slept? Not since our landing."

"You are right, master." And Gilbert clapped so that the dog would come and we may leave. The animal did not budge. He sat vigilant next the boy.

"Ha, you have lost him, Dear Quassy. But I have some more bad news. Sleep for a thousand years and it will be a mere blink if not in the soil of your homeland."

"Do you wish for me to sleep in there?" He pointed in the direction of the crypt.

"No. In the house, at the ground, so we may flee at any moment. Our friends will keep vigil. Though Gilbert, my dear Quassy, you will need descend into the hoard once more to collect your loam.

vi

I awoke to the bombardment. Gilbert was at the window observing. I had indeed slept. I shouldn't have.

"Vigilantes?"

"No, master, something much more worthy of you."

Bring me to the window, Gilbert.

He rushed to me, lifted me as I commanded.

It was the National Guard. "They have killed our escort," I observed first, "all our friends." And they *had* killed them, every single one of them! Our moat was gone, no match for their heavy artillery. And tanks? Good god, they had tanks! They were still shelling off in the distance because, I assume, in the night my northern heart had brought more stumblers.

The military men closest to us were not shelling. They were finishing setting fire to our friends.

I could feel a rage building in me, unencumbered. For the moment, I was happy I wasn't whole. Happy to not have my heart. "We will have to dispatch with these invaders ourselves, my Quassy. But hurry! The sun is coming!"

He moved to the television equipment we absconded with. He picked up a video camera in one hand and put his other on an Eidophor projector.

"I think I have an idea, master."

"Ah, my friend, but wasn't it you who doubted the power of the video? Said we would only be encumbered by these tools, never served?"

"I was wrong, master."

"Ha! Let us commence then!"

vii

He flipped the switch and the projector came to life. It shone from the front porch across the flames of our moat. None of the soldiers noticed at first. They had their backs to us and were advancing south, fending off the mob chasing after my heart. The bright of the fires of our friends, as well, had annihilated the flicker of our projector. Flame was not fit for screen.

Would there be no late late show?

Gilbert moved to a spool of garden hose next the porch.

viii

Now!

He twisted the nozzle just so and a funnel of mist burst forth. In proper measure, he began wetting the embers of the nearest mound. He moved back and forth in deliberate swaths. Soon the steam was billowing, and from it, my visage emerged.

I loomed, fifty feet high! It was glorious! A marvel!

The tank commanders saw me first. They were on the other side of the crematorium, several hundred yards out, attempting to thin the horde at a tree-line bottleneck. Curious. One of the two tanks, the one at the southeast of the quarter, was repositioning its turret. Who were they bearing down on? They were out of reach of Gilbert and me, and would not fire in the direction of their men besides, and yet I was sure I had seduced at least— The turret had stopped! Its muzzle was fixed on the tank sitting one hundred yards to its west. I had the commander and gunner at least! But that meant...

Commander, do not fire. Commanders, I want those tanks in perfect working order! They are mine!

I must not have had both superiors! The tank to the west was repositioning too!

Do not let them fire! Detain those men!

All four of the crew of the easterly tank emerged and flew toward the westerly. They ran through the stumblers. They moved with abandon. They moved in an arc away from their own machine and it worked! The turret of the westerly was now moving in the opposite direction to track them. The four were too swift—for the turret and the horde. They were on the westerly tank and swarming.

They smashed the butts of their sidearms onto the commander's hatch.

Men inside that tank, open all hatches!

Those smashing at the hull stopped. Then there was nothing. All was still but the horde at their flanks.

Open all—

And the driver's hatch opened. The men outside reached in and pulled the driver out. They held their guns on him as the Commander emerged from the same hatch. He held his sidearm on the driver as well. I had him. I had them all. But the horde *had* the tank! The stumblers had surrounded the machine and were groping for the men atop it.

Gilbert! Send the wretched away—

But the tank driver had been playing tricks! He had a grenade in either hand. He flipped the spoons and dropped them into the machine! No!

Boom!

The guardsmen at the homestead were shocked by the explosion though helpless to see. The site of the driver's attack was obscured by the mounds. All that was visible was the mushrooming ball of fire. *Did those stumblers manage to blow up one of our tanks?* was their collective conscious. They would consider this unlikelihood for only a moment. The horde was ambling up the branching valleys of the crematorium and this renewed their interests. The soldiers recommenced advancing.

In all this, Gilbert kept swathing. He increased the flow a few moments to work up a good plume. Satisfied, he dragged the hose across the yard toward the rear of the platoon. As he approached he gave the nozzle another twist to narrow its outflow. He raised the stream at a trio of soldiers closest. Spritzed them at their backs. They turned, saw my conviction immediately.

Serve my Quassy!

And two of the three moved right for Gilbert while the other only stood still. He did so a second more until his wits caught up with him. He raised his M16.

Gilbert handed the hose to the first of the two supplicants to arrive and moved for the guardsman aiming. First supplicant went back to spritzing the ashes—real diligent, real apathetic—as the second supplicant stood behind him, patient.

Bang! Bang!

Both of the guardsman's shots hit Gilbert in the chest.

One of the slugs exited under Gilbert's right shoulder blade, the other was currently oozing from out his left pectoral. The shell that went through hit the first supplicant in the throat. He went down, bleeding out as supplicant two picked up the hose and continued the task—real diligent, real apathetic.

Gilbert was on the guardsman who shot him. He was feeding off him amidst silent screams and M16 rounds firing off into the air. Feedings sometimes bring out a twitch in the fingers and toes...

The shots alerted the others. All but the gunner manning the Browning fifty-caliber turned to face me.

I saw red.

Shots were firing from all over, aimed at my ward. Most shells were finding their target too. I take it the troops were merely obliging their training as I had yet to command them to do otherwise. *Stop!* I demanded and most did.

I have many of them, my servant, but they're well-trained. I'd say only three of five are mine.

Gilbert spun his dinner to be between he and the infantrymen still firing.

Men: all in uniform are your enemy!

I was right. Three of five turned to each other and fired. They were in-stupor so did so clumsily. A number of them shot several times into the ground before even aiming.

You three: aid in preserving my visage!

And three of those men in-stupor stopped firing into the dirt and came to stand behind the one who was minding the embers.

By now the soldiers blasting had each other in their notches. Beyond the wall of steam it was firing squad against firing squad against firing squad.

Of course, two of five didn't submit, and two of five of at least thirty men meant at least twelve strong-willed soldiers amidst the thoughtless slaughter.

They were the more adept of course, by the previous argument. The bulk of them scrambled as soon as the seduced turned on each other. Goal was to get behind something more substantive than burning corpses. All but two made it behind a transport truck and the Jeep with the fifty-cal.

Quassy ended his feeding prematurely. He raised his left hand, hastening the stumblers from the south. Hot lead oozed out of him as he beckoned.

One of the strong willed took up the role of scout, assessing the gunfight to the north. The rest opened fire on the accelerated horde.

Gilbert was walking through the fracas now, dripping bullets and bile as he went. He was heading for those strong-willed.

The scout saw him coming. Without a second's thought he threw away his helmet and tore off the blouse of his fatigues. He broke cover and jumped onto the hood of the Jeep, scrambling for the cab. The gunner there had taken a hit from one of my enamored. Got him in the aorta—at least it smelled like it. Scout moved the gunner aside. There was reverence in this. All due respect shown, then he had hold of the rifle's triggers. He opened fire on Quassy.

That fifty chewed. Ate its lunch. My ward was hobbled by this. He lurched ever forward nonetheless. Last of the soldiers in-stupor could see the scout-gunner tearing into Quassy. They assessed the fireworks a moment then went back to shooting each other. Gunner was extra careful not to hit those men.

This scout is a smart one, my servant.

And Gilbert was taken down to a knee. Yellow bile rained.

A burst of the bilium sloshed onto one of my enamored—the last standing incidentally. The lone survivor wiped at the site of the splash, observed the substance a half-second, then recommenced his search for any remaining hostiles. He caught sight of his own fatigues and had no choice but to address *this* man in uniform too. *Bang!*

My ward was on both knees now. All he could keep erect was that left hand, his palm up and flat to the moon. He fluttered his fingers in out in out.

And the southern stumblers ran toward. They actually ran! Who knew my Quassy had it in him! Despite breaking down faster this way, their numbers ensured enough were closing the gap.

"Coons!" shouted one of the soldiers in cover.

"*Sergeant* Coons," said the Scout-Gunner over his shoulder. He saw the sprinting stumblers about to overwhelm. He spun, started mowing them down.

The soldiers in-cover rose to get better aim. They stood side by side, taking sprinters out in an auxiliary capacity.

They were holding them off just fine. Sergeant Coons was holding them off just fine when the dead Jeep gunner grabbed onto his leg. Sarge glanced down to him, saw the soldiers behind the Jeep in the process. All were rising to stumble. He hesitated as though he knew what the greater threat was. Nevertheless, he returned to the wretched at the south and...

Gilbert was on him! Quassy buried his teeth into Coons' neck. It was over for the sergeant and without that fifty-cal, the stumblers were on the remaining infantrymen in seconds. It was over for them too.

The stumblers were not tearing into the men however—not feasting—merely holding them in place.

Gilbert held a left fist to the air at them. He did not feast either. He was pacing himself.

I beamed over all of this scene in my hologram. I was overjoyed at our victory. I let the stupefied idiots minding the embers free. They still looked confused, only now of a congenital source.

The hose fell to the ground.

I faded away with the steam.

❦ 6 ❦

THE COMPANY PART I

OCTOBER 6, 1968

We came up into the fire, the instant the dark come to free us. For yards them people burned, in piles *some* eight feet high, a city. We came up into the fire and the stench. It was overwhelming. It was like I could hear it coming through my nose, see it at the back of my throat. We came up into the stench and the sobs?

"Are you hearing that, Ben?"

"Like it's right next to me."

"Same for me."

Then Thumpy bapped at my leg. He was frantic, alternating between bap and gesture, bapping then pointing. The point was in the direction of the sobs.

"Ok, boy."

We obliged him, moved to where he gestured while he bolted in the opposite direction.

"What's he up to—"

A stumbler was on me! One of five coming at us! He wasn't grabbing or tearing. He was... nudging me aside?

Pushing like he was— And Barbara ripped him off me in that instant, tossing him into the nearest burn pile. Stumbler went up like a torch. Girl must have thrown the thing thirty feet up like it was an inch! No time to admire the athletics, the remaining four were stumbling toward. The two of us struck a couple of awkward fighter poses as they inched closer and closer... closer until... They split away and moved right on past us—a wide birth, indeed.

We turned in unison and of a mutual curiosity. Stumblers were heading for Thumpy. A couple nearer already had him. Strangest thing, they weren't tearing at the little demon either, just holding him, still. He seemed fine with it too, more concerned about waving over the other four stumblers too haughty to devour Barbara or me.

At first Thumpy's wave was one of a palm up with fingers fluttering in and out—a *c'mere* kinda motion. That transformed into a shaking fist meant for us—a, *listen you two* kinda thing. He pointed toward the sobs once more. Barbara and I nodded like we just learned a new language. Thumpy waved goodbye to us then he broke free of the stumblers pinning him, leading them off and away.

"Thanks little man," I said in all due appreciation. Hey! A good turn's a good turn...

ii

Turned out the sobs belonged to a kid, couldn't've been any older than a college freshman. He wasn't in a letterman jacket or anything, though he was well put together, like he should be off on a ball scholarship or something. But here he was on the ground, cross-legged, at the center of a horseshoe pile of corpses aflame. He had a pistol in his hand.

Barbara and I entered at the open end of that horseshoe.

Kid didn't even have the notion to raise the gun at us.

"They'll just keep coming," he said.

"Kid?" I waved my hand back and forth at him. It was like he couldn't see me. "There's no one here."

"I don't think they can smell me in here." He was tapping the barrel of the automatic against his knee, rocking himself back and forth. "Ever get hit by a ton of bricks?" He said this chuckling. "We started this on a mission, ya know." He gestured around at all the grotesquery. "To save ourselves from them. But that's Bobby burnin' over there, from middle school. Just came to me, ya know? *Just us chickens...* Like when you read the whole page but it's like ya didn't even. You read it again until ya understand it and it don't come until you set your mind to focusing." He stopped tapping at his leg. "A ton of goddamn bricks..."

He put the pistol muzzle in his mouth.

"No!" Barbara shouted.

Bang!

iii

I had to get out of this county. Things gotta be better anywhere ain't here. Gotta head north, where it'll be so cold those things'll be popsicles. Wife had the right idea. Kids'll be right as rain up there... Ha! *Snow!* Where those things'll freeze stiff. Now that's a living arrangement! I had to search the old farmhouse first for any supplies we could carry, that and clothes—we were still naked as jaybirds—clothes and food. I was famished. Then north.

I flew through the front door, b-lined it for the fridge.

Some beers in there, a Coke, moldy bread. The same stuff I left behind when I raided it the first time.

What we got in the cupboards?

Soup and beans—hafta do.

I had the can opener. I looked and the thing was right where you'd expect it! So goddamn hungry I could eat the can anyway. I got the opener's teeth over the inside lip. Cream of mushroom, here I come. I squeezed the tool and the bloody thing disintegrated! Broke into pieces. Radiation do this too? Felt solid in my hand?

I grabbed a steak knife from the same drawer. What ya gonna do with— But I slammed it into that soup before I could finish the thought, like I was on a mission and wouldn't ya know it, the knife sliced through that tin like butter, and fast.

I flopped the lid and drank that soup straight out of the can like it was paying me to. I must have gotten a third of the way through before I let myself even taste the stuff and I don't mind telling you, that slop burned! I spat what I hadn't yet swallowed onto a spot I was planning on puking up what I did. How does cold soup out of the can burn like that?

I tore into the living room, still in a state of astonishment.

"Barbara, you ever hear of cream of mushroom going bad in the can?" But she was in an upward fetal position on the couch. Thumpy was consoling her with a pat at the shoulder. "Barbara?" Nothing. I went to her, took her by the other shoulder, shook a little. "Come on, Barbara girl. We're not doing this again are we?"

But she leapt up at me, fierce. "No, Ben. We're not doing *this* again!"

"Then what is it?"

"*What?* What's happening out there... What we saw... And seconds after, you burst through that door, for what, lunch?"

"I—"

"You what? Feel nothing? Contentment in the face of all this? He blew his brains out! I— It shouldn't be like this, Ben. I shouldn't be feeling like—"

"Like you're five and it's Saturday morning?" She latched onto me again, nodding. She teared up. "I hate to break it to you," I chuckled. "But these ain't the actions of a woman contented."

She pulled back a little. "You know what I mean?" I mouthed a *yes*, though my words didn't seem to satisfy her. "You do, right Ben? You have to. You're the only one else on this earth who possibly could."

"I do, Barbara. But it comes. Just not like it used to. But it came to you in that pit, and it came to me."

"This— It's going to take some getting used to is all."

"Boy you're not wrong. We're standing where I died."

"That's not funny."

"True, and yet we feel the way we feel. That's my blood right there." I kicked my foot in the direction of the stain.

"My god!"

"That rifle blew your head off a couple hours ago." And I kicked my foot at the gun.

"Stop!"

I did. I set my eyes upon hers and she mine. We laughed.

We laughed a good half-minute.

"God, we're awful!" she guffawed.

And something came to me in that moment. It came easy despite my hunger making it so hard to reason. Real easy to laugh though, real easy to maneuver too, felt like I could lift the house. I couldn't put two thoughts together and yet, something had come to me.

"Barbara, whatever we got in us, whatever it is, it brought us back—you twice. We're not psychopaths,

Barbara. We've come to know death isn't the end. How we supposed to feel in the face of that?"

"That— That sounds like there might be something to it."

"Glad you think so. Now, how about that dinner?"

"Not hungry."

"Come on, I don't recall you sneaking any secret meals."

"I'm not hungry!" she insisted, pulling further away.

"Alright, alright," I relented. "It's fine." But she got fixated, put a finger to the sight of my neck where she had had her fun. It was all healed. Everything was. I pushed her away anyhow. She kept fixating. "If the beans are as old as the soup around here," I chuckled at her, a little uneasy, "*no one's* eating anyway..."

iv

She wasn't hungry and I couldn't keep anything down. We decided to focus on clothes and supplies. I'd found a suitable wardrobe, must have been the man of the house's: grey wool trousers, white cotton shirt, socks, loafers, good enough. Barbara was having some difficulty. It wasn't like she was suddenly fancying herself a fashionista. It was that the woman of the house was about four sizes bigger than *our little Barbara*. I called her that by the way, jibing her: *li'l Barbara*! She bobbed her head at that remark more than you'd think for a girl wrapped in nothing 'cept a bedsheet standing before an adequately dressed fella. Just bobbed... Just bobbed her head?

I'll never call her that again.

She pulled open the top of a chest of drawers in one of the kids' rooms. It had to be a boy's room. There were pictures of ball players everywhere, a guitar in the corner.

No toys, so maybe he was old enough his clothes would fit her.

Right about now, she was flipping through a stack of white undershirts. At the last of the pile her thumb grazed something hard, smooth. She ripped her hand from it fast like she'd touched the hot element of a stove.

"What is it?" I said, reaching into the dresser. She watched over my shoulder, her finger fine now. I pulled out the stack of shirts and under them sat a crucifix. Barbara recoiled instantly, fell to the floor and covered herself in that sheet. The thing irked me, I admit, made me feel the way you feel when your fingernails drag on a chalkboard—

Barbara was screaming.

"Get it away! Get it away!"

I picked the artifact up. It didn't burn, though it provoked something in me. Nausea? A pressure in my forehead maybe? Embarrassment? I was cringing. The girl was in torture.

I chucked the thing away. Tossed it out the door—or so I thought.

My aim was off. That damn cross had shot right through the wall and into the lath across the hall, dropping into the stud bay. I scared myself a little at this. I was flexing my throwing arm when—

"Get it away!" she said from under the sheet.

I stopped my figuring, crouched next to her. "It's fine," I said, uncovering her. "It's gone."

"Oh Ben, it was horrible."

"It certainly wasn't pleasant..."

"How could you bear it?"

"I... I don't know."

v

I thought I was famished before but the hunger only grew. Barbara's was creeping up on her a little now too. I didn't pack any of the nonperishables before leaving the farmhouse. I tried a few more items in that kitchen and they all burned all the way down. *Gyurp!* And up... Barbara enjoyed them little better. Must have been the radiation. We left after she found an ensemble that fit her. She looked like a miniature me actually: same type of slacks and shirt. We ditched the rifle too—no bullets and we had gorilla strength anyhow. We just stuffed our pockets with a few things of general use and hit the road.

Real paupers.

She was a little reticent to run off from that place, still. I managed to convince her to at least come with me to the nearest town. *If anyone were coming to find us, they'd go there first,* and all that... She said she had an aunt in a town called *Hevans* to the north. Good enough for me as long as I was heading Santa's way, and Hevans was just that way.

And we moved along just fine. Would you believe me if I told you, despite being on an empty stomach going all the way back to my resurrection, the strength and vigor I felt at the house had only grown? Barbara's too? Probably not. Would you believe we could see in the dark? Probably not. We were walking *now*. We *had* sprinted a good portion of the trip, I swear we did—through the brush and the trees—like little sound barrier-breaking all-seeing bulldozers. Hunger's costing us our wits a little, sure, but if I was standing tippy-toed on a pitcher's mound of brains prior to my resurrection and now I'm on top of Everest, what difference does it make my falling a few feet? I ain't no dummy yet. Like with our sympathies, the thoughts are coming a little slower with the hunger. But the strength! God, the strength. The only reason we're walking now is because Thumpy couldn't keep up. Come to think of it, where is he? Haven't seen him in a while...

Oh, don't go thinking I've grown attached to the little side of beef! It's symbiotic. *Now that's a big word for someone in my condition...* He keeps them stumblers away. He runs them off to the outskirts of these woods, comin' back every once in a while for a petting. Not a petting from me, mind you, from Barbara. Like now.

"Stumblers got a real hard on for you, little man. Why?"

You'd swear that demon just shrugged at me without even a complete set of shoulders to shrug...

I said *symbiotic*, so how do we serve him? I don't know but he damn sure acts like he needs us. Needs Barbara anyway. She was rubbing what I guess you might call a belly.

"Oh no, he's bleeding, Ben."

"He's two-thirds amputation, Barbara."

"This looks new."

"You're imagining things..."

But Barbara wasn't letting Thumpy go. She was examining him further and he was getting antsy, like it was past time he got back to his patrol.

"Not yet," she said to him. He heeled. She searched through the pockets of the duffle coat she'd taken. "Here." She held out a lighter and some firecrackers. "If you get into trouble, set these off and we'll come running." He gave a thumbs up, put those crackers... somewhere. He scurried off. "Be careful, Righty," she whispered.

"*Righty*?" I said. "It's *Thumpy*."

"I prefer *Righty*."

I stared at her as though trying to figure. She smiled

lovingly at that torso as it ran away—smiled and smiled and clasped her hands to her chest. I shook my head. "Everybody's got a hard on for something these days..."

"Crude," she said as we recommenced our walk.

"I'm ignorant, remember?"

"I should have given you more credit."

"Nah, that about fits these days. I haven't the foggiest what the hell's going on."

"I should give myself *less* credit then..."

"Well, maybe somebody out there's got the answers."

"Maybe." And she was quiet a second or two after that. Quiet until... "Ben?"

"Yeah?"

"I was one of them before I was put on that pile, before I was one of them *plus* whatever the hell it is I am now."

"I figured. I can still picture clear as day them taking you."

"There was something it was like to be one of them."

"Something it was like—"

"It wasn't nothing," she said. "They're not mindless."

"Aiming to start an anti-defamation group, Barbara?"

"No... Well, I guess if they could be made docile... That's not what I'm saying."

"What are you saying?"

"I know what it's like to be one of them. I know what it's like to be *this*. I know what it's like to be one of them as *this*. I know what it's like to be me."

"And that about covers it," I said. "I'd say you've taken a damn thorough inventory of all the creatures you've walked a mile in the shoes of."

She stopped, stopped me. "We're not so contented merely for the fact we're back, are we?"

"*Now* what are you saying?"

"Well, who's to say we'd keep coming back? Maybe at some point some one end's *the* end, and that's it for us. Maybe that's it for everyone else too."

"You're starting to bring me down here, Barbara."

"I bet I'm not."

"Oh yeah?"

"I was me," she reiterated. "I was a stumbler. I was a stumbler in that pit. I'm this. That's not the whole inventory."

"Then what else you been, girl?"

"Dead."

"Well, that... That's different."

"How?"

"Well, dead's not one of the ways to be. It's what you are when you're not one of those ways."

"*You are*? Who's the *you*, Ben?"

"Not *you*. *You* aren't anything. *You* can't be dead—"

"I never died?" She had a slight grin.

"Of course you did, but—"

"So I *can* be dead?"

"Not *you*—"

"You died."

I sighed. "That I did, Barbara."

"What was it like?"

"What was it like for you?"

"Nothing," she said a little coy.

"Nothing? You had your brains bashed, you woke up next to Thumpy, and that's all there is to the tale?"

"Hey," she protested. "I thought I was the one asking. What was it, Ben?"

"I don't want to sound crazy." And I really didn't.

"You were brought back to life by the blood of the heart of a walking talking half-torso—"

"Wouldn't say *walking* and *talking*..."

"He moves. He communicates."

She was right. I relented. "It wasn't nothing, alright."

"What was it?" she probed.

"It was like nothing I could possibly understand... not in these shoes."

"Ditto."

"Thought you said *nothing*..."

"And I wasn't lying," she insisted. "It was *nothing* I could possibly understand."

I chuckled at this. But it really *wasn't* nothing. It was *something*. Might even describe it as... as... "Think we'll get back there any time soon?" I asked.

"Be nice."

"How do you know? Thought you *dittoed* to knowing nothing. Now you know it's nice?"

"I don't know what it was," she said. "Though I suspect it wasn't reserved for just you and me. It's a nice thought in knowing there's a place... A place for all of us. Whether or not we ever make it back to them in this condition, it's nice knowing they're there. I'd say it's niceness all around."

"Ditto."

Then those firecrackers started going off.

"Righty!" Barbara turned in circles trying to catch the direction of those poppers. "Where are they coming from?"

I was turning too. "I can't place 'em— Barbara!"

The stumbler had her from behind and without a beat had bitten into the space between her shoulder and neck. She turned fast, clapped her hands against either side of the stumbler's head, narrowed it to half its width in a flash and blood and brain burst forth at her. Stumbler toppled as she bent over, spitting out his effluence.

"You ok?" I asked.

"Yeah."

"So much for anti-defamation..."

"Yeah—"

"What the hell's going on!" said the stumbler! He was upright and healed and smooth and pallorous!

"Holy shit!" Barbara and I shouted in unison.

"Tell me what's going on, man?" He had a twang.

"You tell us?" I said, confused.

"Where am I?"

"A little south of Hevans."

"Hevans? *Hevans* what?"

"Pennsylvania."

"Pennsylvania!"

"Not from around here?" I asked.

"Fella, I'm from North Carolina."

"What's your last memory?" Barbara asked him.

"Fish— Why do I feel so light? Fishing, I was fishing for chub and these hands pulled me into the creek. Bit me... Jesus! I drowned in it! You know what it feels like to drown? Jesus..."

"Anything else you remember?"

"Jesus!"

"*Easy*... Help us and maybe we can better explain what's going on. What do you remember?"

"B—bits and pieces. Hunger mostly. Got better when I'd eat... Oh Jesus! I ate—" He was pointing at Barbara's healing neck.

"It's understandable."

"I felt better when I ate, when I moved."

"Exercised?"

"Travelled."

"Where?"

"Shit." He looked around. "Wherever the hell this is."

"You felt better when you—"

"I gotta get home." And he took off in a flash to the south —already out of sight."

"This is getting weirder and weirder."

But Thumpy was pulling on my pant leg again.

"Forgot about you, little demon."

"Righty!" Barbara crouched to attend to him.

"Seems alright," I observed.

He shook his fist at me.

❧ 7 ❧

THE CONSOLATION PART I

OCTOBER 7, 1968

We surveyed. All told, we had procured one M551 Sheridan tank, one transport truck, and one Jeep with one mounted Browning fifty-caliber M2 machine gun. All infantrymen were either dead or captive to the stumblers. Those captive weren't talking. It was their training.

"Hold me up to them, Gilbert."

"Yes, master."

I looked at them. I did not seduce them. I knew they were of the strong-willed, though it was more out of reverence that I relented. I despised them for what they did and yet I had to begrudge them their competency. I should clarify. I begrudged them all save for the four jokers who were *not* among the strong-willed but who merely had the blind fortune to *not* die behind that wall of steam. They were diligent in maintaining my visage, however. Maybe that was something?

I wouldn't be influencing any of these men. I would

nevertheless speak to them without utterance. I wanted to be in their heads.

You. You so callously destroy. Though would you if they hadn't bused you in from three counties over? Silence, still. *You're not fools, so you know there are men like you, maybe even from around here, gone to where you're from, destroying all the same. They'll kill your stumbling wives, mothers, children over there so you can return the favor here?* They still weren't moved. *Is nothing sacred?* They wouldn't be moved. I could sense a good measure of fear in them. They were scared before their deployment, before the endless classifications of their quarry—the wretched bastards—as nothing more than *marauding ghouls.* They'd kill their best friends if called the same against the backdrop of these fears.

"Remove me from them, Gilbert."

My ward walked me away.

Next time, we will amass a truly insurmountable army. We are going to HelCorp.

"We must find your heart, master."

If it is not here, then HelCorp is where it will be.

"Can you be sure?"

I am never wrong when it comes to these matters.

"What then, in the immediate?"

I rest. We have a big night tomorrow.

"I will prepare for your slumber."

First, I amended. *I want you to deal with these men.*

"What would you have me do?"

They ought to know how the other half lives, they want to carry on this way.

"You wish for me to let the stumblers loose on them?"

They are not the only undead walking these lands, Gilbert.

"I see."

'A truly insurmountable army.'

"Even those jokers?"

"Oh, why not…"

He bowed in oblige.

A screaming comes across the sky.

"What was that?" I asked.

"An F-4, master. A Phantom."

"Can you fly it?"

"Yes."

"Table your dealing with these men for now. Our friends will corral them in the meantime. A *Phantom,* you say?"

"Yes, master."

"Go fetch it for me, will you?"

ii

I'd never wished more to have hands than I did currently —to be able to caress what my man Gilbert had brought me. The Phantom was sleek and stalwart and all mine. I may not have liked the taupe and olive color scheme but without my body I was a mere beggar, and beggars can't be choosers.

"Master, may I ask what you intend to do with this?"

"Run your hand along it."

He did and I was able to sympathize with Gilbert as vicar. The power of the impression was weaker for its mediation, yet it was still glorious. What a machine!

Gilbert watched me in anticipation.

"Ah, dear ward, you are wanting the true answer to your question. Well, to be completely honest, I haven't thought that far ahead."

"I'm not sure where we can refuel."

"As long as we will reach our target."

"That depends. Where is HelCorp headquarters?"

"Holland."

"Certainly not, master!" He said this astonished.

"Holland, Michigan."

"Maybe." He opened one of the map books he'd found inside my bird. "We certainly won't be able to rearm." He continued to peruse.

"We'll have to pick the right targets."

"It can't be landed just anywhere."

"Then why land?" I said. Gilbert raised an eyebrow. "Ha! All will make sense in time, my servant. How long will it take us to get to our destination?"

"As the crow flies..." He flipped to the relevant page. "Twenty minutes flight time."

"Good, then we have plenty of those minutes in addition. Tonight we will send the men and our ordnance on their way and we will travel to Cleveland."

"Cleveland?"

"For my reformation. For the ritual to be completed, I need an artifact from my homeland, something contemporaneous to my time as mortal."

And yet his skepticism persisted. "But Cleveland?"

"The Museum of Art—a Romanian exhibit. Now come, we will fly."

"There is nowhere to land."

"A turn of phrase," I chuckled, trying to feign indifference to his persistent defiance, "from the old country. We will move by land, though swift. We will send our men on their way and enjoy our little excursion."

"Are you sure about this?"

Sure? Were we to do this now of all times: the rite of confidance? "That is not a question for *me*, ever! I'm going to pretend you merely mistook me for the void that turns one's doubts to echo—that you were only ensuring the right creature be interrogated. Or, is there really such presumption in you?"

"I'd never read of any such artifact in the liturgy, is all."

"Do you dare doubt me?"

"Master, it seems a miscalculation."

"So you do!"

"These lands are overflowing with all manner of attackers."

"Enough! Think long and hard about your next words, Quassy—of how you handle this test you've imposed upon yourself: this proving of your use to me."

"Would you cast me out so easily, master?"

"It's in your very words, mere *servant*."

"You need me!"

"I need your function."

"There's no one else to realize it."

"We have a whole battalion of Quassy now. Coons is their best, I believe." He stared at me, crestfallen. I was in no mood to allay him. "Do you really think any of this was pre-ordained? I just as easily could have fallen into the lap of Samuel!"

"You chose me!"

"Accident."

And with these careless words, he stormed away. I had—ha, in what seems a million lifetimes ago now—failed this test myself.

iii

I travelled with Quassy and there was a general animus. Purposelessness—or, at best, an eternal precariousness to one's use—is a hard prospect to live with. Doubly so when it's the judgement of those held in esteem. I would ameliorate him in time, but this process—this simmering before the tasting, so to speak—was as much a part of the rite as the butchering. For now, it would be cold shoulder.

iv

Our horde overfloweth. We had gathered enough of them to fill the museum courtyard: a plot near fifteen acres in breadth. Many of our friends were in the courtyard when we arrived but they were ours now. Was there no limit to my reach?

We stood at the south entrance. We thought we would have to bash through, however the doors were wide open. You wouldn't take stumblers for connoisseurs, yet who else would visit a museum in the middle of a cataclysm of their own making and not possess the basic courtesy to close the doors behind them?

Inside, we moved swift to the rotunda and Gilbert turned us toward the armor court. Good instincts, though something else had caught my attention.

It was in the atrium. It was the whole of the stumblers in this place, all in one concentration. There was no accord anywhere else and the pull there was tremendous.

"Go left, the stairs."

He turned. On we plodded. All the way to the bottom.

I was right. All stumblers had congregated at the center atrium like bees in an absconding cluster.

"Move them outside," I ordered. But Gilbert was glancing upward and not to our subtle horde. "Gilbert!" I shouted, and his focus returned. He sent the stumblers marching up the stairs.

Curious. What the swarm had been gathering around was a discarded suit of armor.

"History buffs, maybe?"

Then the suit started to rock back and forth, right there on the floor! *De Anima!*

I could sense Gilbert's astonishment too.

"It can't be what we think. The stumblers have not such power. I don't even have—"

"Is it morning already?" The armor spoke! It rolled over, taking hold of a claymore next to it.

Easy, Gilbert...

The armor raised the sword vertical. It took the hilt in gauntlet and used the weapon to leverage itself upward.

"Who are you?" I said.

It was standing now, tightening its gauntlet around the pommel of the claymore. The other glove moved to its helmet. "They usually leave around morning, then the new ones—" It flipped its visor open. "Oh hello," said the man behind the mask. He was cheery enough, though otherwise your run-of-the-mill man. "I'm Alister," he said.

"Of course you are," I returned, a little deflated. "What are you doing here, Alister?"

"W—well, I'm the... I used to be the curator here."

"You mean you used to be *paid* to be curator here? Everything seems in sufficient order, still."

"Yes, that would be the more precise account."

"Old habits, Alister?"

"Listen," he protested, sensing my judgment. "If it weren't for me—"

"You didn't ask who *we* were."

As though I had jogged his good graces... "Who might you—"

"These artifacts are the only family you have left."

"Yes."

I wasn't working any magic on him, I promise you—no

telepathy. He was just... "You are just... happy to have company of a type that doesn't tear pieces out of you."

"It's been a long time," he relented.

"This is a lonely place, indeed."

"Why not leave?" Gilbert interjected. "Break free of your confinement? Take your harness and your chances out there?"

"Gilbert," I warned. "Such presumption..."

Alister chuckled. "These... These treasures didn't just become so dear the second everybody up and left me."

"Curator of civilization?" I said. "*Sir* Alister?"

"I can keep those things off the exhibits this way." He half lowered-then-raised his visor a couple times. "They'll stay on me, not the art. It's really not as bad as it sounds. Some nights, it's like they're rocking me to sleep."

"And the nights that it isn't?"

He lifted the claymore. "I have this."

"You are very resourceful, very useful." I uttered this under my breath.

"I'm sorry? I didn't catch that."

"It would certainly be easier for you," I redirected, "if someone were to keep your visitors at bay—permanently off these grounds. Wouldn't it, Alister?"

"Of course, but how—"

"Leave it to me. In return, I ask only for a mere trinket. Take us to your displays, to the Romanian artifacts."

"B—But there aren't any."

"What? Your predecessor was in the newspapers. He was joyous over his new collection of items of the Dragon Lineage of House Basarab!"

"That was twenty-five years ago—"

"So you've relegated my past to the trash heap?"

"T—There aren't any *on display*. Allow me to clarify. I—In the archives, in storage."

"Here?"

"At the lower level—"

"The basement! You keep such treasures underground?"

"Public interest—"

"Bah! Stumblers have more taste! Take me to them."

v

Gilbert was fixated not where he ought be. Again. He was folding some chainmail, rolling it over and over in his hands. He found it among materials of no consequence.

"Gilbert, I don't know what has you so preoccupied, but the daggers."

He picked me up and moved me toward the objects of relevance. He sat me down once more and took to the nearest crate, sorting quickly."

"It will have a steel hilt," I offered.

He filtered each candidate away, held it to me for my approval. They were beautiful alright, every one of them, though not suitable. He moved from crate to crate.

"These are the only ones?" I asked Alister, a little frantic now. "We've searched everything?"

"Yes."

"Bring me more than the daggers—"

"Except..." Alister said as though realizing. "...The stuff from 'The Impaler' exhibit."

I was disgusted. I'd sigh if I had lungs. Had Alister so little an awareness of my lineage? *"Then bring me the artifacts of the impaler."*

He gestured to a long shallow crate in the corner. Gilbert

brought it over. Inside was a harness. It was laid out in the crate as though, if the harness were filled, it would be a coffin.

"No dagger," Gilbert observed.

"The Basarab are a crafty bunch, my servant. The gauntlet."

More examination.

"It is just that," he said, rotating it.

"Under the lining."

He separated the lambskin from the steel—

"Careful," Alister urged.

"Gentle," I concurred.

And he was gentle now, though he wouldn't have to be for long. He could feel the hilt. He removed the tool.

"A-ha!" I barked in triumph.

vi

The three of us stood at the south entrance.

"You have been very helpful," I said to Alister. "As we promised, in return for this treasure, we will ensure you peace." Gilbert waved his left hand. "Look to the courtyard." And Alister did, and the hordes began to disperse. They, each and every one of them, moved to beyond the periphery, kept out as though by invisible wall."

"Whoa," Alister said, near pressed against the glass of the doors.

"This is a very important enclave, my friend. Take care of all treasures inside. Take care of yourself and all that falls within your domain."

He looked back over his shoulder, nodded, then... "Who are you?"

"I, my dear Alister, am Count—"

Schwip! Schwip! Two shuriken flew at us, both hitting Gilbert in the throat. Alister lowered his visor. Gilbert lowered mine. He pivoted around to the inside of Alister's armor, giving himself and me cover there.

Further of the attacker's shuriken pinged off Alister as we spooned inside him and against the door.

"What's happening, fellas?"

Gilbert was becoming woozy. He pulled out a star. He sniffed at its bladed tips and, before even a full breath, threw the weapon and its dual away, sickened, fearful even.

"Garlic!" I told him. I knew by the smell alone.

Though I couldn't see—I had no neck to turn nor shoulder to glance over, nor could I see through Alister if I had—I derived our attacker out of ranged weapons. The pinging had stopped, after all, and so now was our moment. We had to confront her. For that we would have to spot her. Would we even see this woman from any other vantage? She had evaded all of us the entire of our visit, even in her attacking, and now my Quassy was sapped. We had no choice. Continuing to cower in this harness would be our end.

"You must take her, Gilbert," I broke to him. "But you will be at only a fraction of your strength: little more than man at the first."

He stood, spun, held me out to Alister.

"Protect master with your life."

"*Life?*"

He put me under his arm a second more. With his free hand he relieved Alister of his claymore. He angled me closer to the knight, anew. "Take master," he implored, and Alister took me over.

Gilbert entered the fracas as we retreated to the corner of the south vestibule.

The atrium, Gilbert. That's the direction she was heading before I lost her scent.

He moved swift, sword raised in hands.

❧ 8 ❧

THE COMPANY PART II

OCTOBER 7, 1968

Hevans City wasn't the kind of place you just walked into. Nowhere around here was the kind of place you just walked into. Anyone walking, not running, was as good as a stumbler to anyone not a stumbler, and anyone running was only bringing more stumblers. How were the three of us to make a good first impression on a wall of trigger-happy city fathers watching us emerge from a monster infested wood like a matinee of *Mary Poppins*? We wouldn't, that's how. They'd shoot us all in the head the second they saw us. And even if they took a second glance before the execution, they wouldn't exactly be thinking *aristocrats,* what with a bleeding crawling right tit at our hips!

All due respect, Thumpy...

You didn't just walk into a city like Hevans for another reason: the National Guard wouldn't let you. See, it wasn't just gun-toting townies out there anymore and it wasn't just gun-toting townies *fast*. The guardsmen got to Hevans before the dawn of that first night. Us three travelers were watching them right now. We were peeking out the bushes at them. They sat across a hundred-fifty-yard swath of alfalfa then a highway. Had a guard post set up at a Diner that way.

Excuse me... Two of us travelers were watching now. Thumpy'd left to divert the latest stumbler horde of all hordes seemingly forever on him or coming for him.

We'd skulked around these bushes the whole of the south side of Hevans and a good portion of the west. There was nowhere there wasn't a soldier, a copper, or a deputy. And I say *deputy* to be nice. These assholes were vigilantes, plain and simple.

I guess I'm not so nice...

There wasn't a path through in that third of the city so I'm guessing there wasn't a path through anywhere else—no path a bullet couldn't cross, anyway.

What? *Maybe I'm exercising a prejudice?* you're thinking. *Maybe I'm fearful for nothing, and all we need do is step out of these woods waving a white flag and those kind servants will welcome us with open arms?*

Well...

In all our skulking, every mile or so, ol' Thumpy'd attract a few too many friends and *a few of those few* would stray and get too close to the city line. Thumpy'd be lying low of course, as though there was any other pose for the li'l demon, but the form of the stumbler'd be there in the moonlight for all to see: as plain as... moonlit night. Guns would start popping and some combination of *federal*, *state*, and *local* would mow the stray down. It always went the same way: a few pops from the first to see... a couple more from 'em... then the cacophony. And for all those gunmen knew, stumblers could've been fleeing farmers, campers, county by-law officers, didn't matter. They shot the brains out of all of them, and then some, and of course none of those stumblers looked like county by-law officers because stumblers actually got brains to shoot out!

Sorry about that. I havn't eaten in days.

"I'm going to storm that diner if we don't figure something out soon," Barbara said.

"They'll shoot us."

"Never stopped us before."

"Yet," I said. "You forget our conversation?"

"Yes, I'm starving."

"What makes you think that radiation hasn't ruined all their food as well?"

"Because I can see people in that diner eating it right now."

"They're soldiers, Barbara. You ever see what's in a K-Ration? Irradiated meatloaf's a delicacy next to that. Besides, you see that truck? That's a fifty-caliber light machine gun in that truck. It'll rip you in two before you even get to the highway. I don't know if there's any coming back from that."

"Why're you an expert on military-grade weapons all of a sudden?"

"I don't know how I know what I know. I mean, 'I know' because whatever's in me's turned *Ulysses* into *Fun With Dick and Jane* and 'I don't know how I know' because whatever's in me makes me dumber the longer I don't eat... As far as how I know that gun stuff in particular... I don't know."

"Don't I know it... Don't I?"

"We're getting dumber by the minute."

"And stronger. I'm getting some coconut cream pie if I have to knock the coconut tree over with my face."

She started to rise. I pulled her back down.

"Hold on," I said. "Look, I want a slice of that pie as

much as anyone, more, but those guns—" Then something came to me. It was Thumpy, back from his stumbler drive. Then another something came to me. "Wait!"

"What?"

"What if we had Thumpy—"

"No!"

"Hear me out. What if we had Thumpy lead a pack of stumblers—"

"*No!*"

"Damnit, let me finish... Lead them out past those guardsmen? Thumpy'll stay real low, like he always does. He'll be fine. Then they'll all give chase and we'll sneak into that diner without anyone taking a single shot at us. Hell, we'll dance into that diner if all goes to plan!"

"You see any civilians in there?" she asked.

"We'll stop by one of the trucks. They're bound to have a couple of spare uniforms."

"You see any women in those uniforms?"

"You'll be a secretary to the general."

"Which general?"

"George Washington. Are you ready?"

"Those stumblers have life in them."

"*Rrrrr*, girl!"

She looked out to her oasis, "Damnit, I'm so hungry!"

"Well what are we waiting for? It's my plan or we're eating *mud* pies."

She flashed a face at me, defiant. "Then my name is *mud*."

"Come on!" But she wouldn't budge. "Come on, Barb—"

"Shut up I got something!"

"What?"

She turned to Thumpy, gave him a rub or two on the

back. That guy just purr? She stared at him imploringly, held out her cupped hands to him, "Can I get a refill?"

ii

I hadn't yet any idea what her plan was, but there she stood, a half-cup of Thumpy's coagulated blood pooled in her hands.

"Righty, do you think you might do me one last favor?" He gave her a thumbs-up. "Wonderful! Righty, bring me a single one of your friends. One of good humor."

He took off into the woods in a flash.

"Ok, what do you have planned here, Barb—"

But there was already a rustling. Li'l guy was back, back with a single solitary stumbler!

"Ben, you and Righty pin him down."

"Barb—"

"Do it!" she barked. I hesitated. "Coconut cream pie?" And she said this sweeter than that pie.

Oh what the hell? I went to that stumbler doing nothing other than squatting next to Thumpy, holding onto him. Still as strange a sight as anything: that little demon's neutralizing those things. I took the stumbler by the shoulders, lifting him. Guy got agitated right away.

"Lay him on his back," Barbara ordered.

In for a penny... I put my leg out against the stumbler's calves. I braced him, neutralizing most of his thrashing, and leveraged him backward. Real gentle. As he tipped, I pivoted to his other side, easing him down like a baptism."

"Hold him still."

I put my knee on his belly and kept his shoulders pinned. Thumpy put a hand to his forehead. Barbara knelt down, careful not to spill any of that soup in her hands.

"Here goes nothing..."

She dribbled the blood into his gnashing maw. He was resistant initially, then after the first few drops got through he went real still. Then he practically gulped the stuff.

"Okay, let him up," she said backing away. We did. He went back to minding Thumpy, paying no more *mind* to us at all! "Are you ready?" she asked me.

"Your show, Coconut Pie."

"You ready?" she said to Thumpy.

He gave her another thumbs up. She raised her hand, poised. *Wait for it...* Hand hovered a moment...

"What's *Ulysses*?" she asked.

"I don't know," I said.

And she whipped that hand downward, gave Thumpy a playful spank on the bum to start the proceedings.

"Go, boys, go!"

Bum?

But that little demon took off with the stumbler not far behind. The second they got clear of the brush, we heard the popping. The second we heard the popping, the stumbler started to jitter with the lead. Then his head exploded and we heard a crack of a higher calibered rifle.

"Wait for it..."

And that stumbler was back up, running in circles, looking like porcelain!

Holy shit! I gotta get home!

And he was gone for the south despite those pops still peppering him!

Barbara turned to me pleased as punch as Thumpy's spawn ran past us and on to the panhandle for all we knew. "Now we try it your way."

iii

We had a good two dozen of the cursed stumblers. And I'm gonna call them *cursed* since what else would you call a person full of that little demon's blood? Anyway, a good two dozen and Thumpy was keeping them at bay. All was ready except Barbara.

"And as soon as the last of 'em're turned, you come right back here! Right back here, Righty..." She shook the bush we'd been hiding in. "...Right here." She knelt down and gave him a good patting. He rolled over. "Now, you be careful."

"Barbara."

"Right here..."

"Barbara!"

"*Extra* careful." And she joined me at the edge of the tree line. "Send him," she said.

"You really sure? It's just dinner."

"No, it's not, Ben. It's the north."

Good enough for me.

I turned to the little man. "You have to get close enough they give chase with that fifty-cal but not so close they use it. Got it?"

He thumb'd up.

"Good." I chopped my hand in the direction of the diner and the demon hit it.

Stumblers followed, as we hoped they would.

And then came the popping, as we hoped it would.

So far, Thumpy was leading them through the alfalfa at the exact angle we needed: toward town then toward its southeast flank—making it appear like they were looping around and back in over that way. He was driving those things as hard as he could too. For stumblers, they were flying.

And so was the lead. We even heard a few of the high-caliber cracks. Nothing was connecting, not yet.

They were getting closer. Despite that, the fifty-cal wasn't budging. Thumpy needed to let the gunner see the whites of those stumblers' eyes but if he didn't turn 'em soon he'd hit that gunner head-on for the shredding."

"He's too close!" Barbara cried.

"A little closer..."

"No!" she hugged onto me. Buried her face in my shoulder.

A couple cracks and a couple of the stumblers turned to cursed.

"Little closer..."

More and more cracks. More and more cursed. I figured maybe they'd cooperate, stick with the herd? They just ran back to us and on to the south—maybe in a few circles first, then south.

Where am I?

I gotta get home!

I think we still had enough stumblers, right?

"Little closer..."

And Thumpy was there! The gunner was racking that fifty.

"Crank it, buddy!"

But he kept on, little bastard kept on.

"Turn, ya bastard!"

But he wouldn't.

I squeezed onto Barbara like she was squeezing onto me.

And she pulled back, looked over her shoulder, saw the motive behind my pressing into her. Then she broke away completely like she was gonna head out past that line.

Gunner had those triggers.

I reached out for Barbara.

But before I could restrain... "Turn, Righty, Turn!" she screamed. And he veered! Spun the horde so sharp a few at the tail couldn't hold on and broke from the group. The fifty shredded them though quickly had to prioritize. The horde was looping around the southeast side and all other Jeeps had tore after it. They were useless without the heavy artillery, though. The fifty had no choice but to follow.

"That's all of them. Let's move."

Gotta get home!

What is this place!

iv

Gonna dance into that diner...

We were in the back of a transport, rooting through supplies. That fifty was blasting on the other side of town so it was a safe bet we were still in the clear.

"At least we know we'd stand up to their cannons," I said. "That pile of mincemeat got right back up and mailed himself to Georgia— Barbara?"

"Nothing fits." She kept rooting.

"He'll be okay, Barbara."

"We could have walked in after all."

"We didn't know that. Still don't. Think after we walked through their hail the army'd just stop? Like, *hey, gotta admire their spirit* or something?" She kept rooting. "He'll be ok."

She picked up a top that looked to satisfy her. She pulled it on and started buttoning up.

That was my cue. I moved to the rear of the transport box and hopped out. I reached back in to help her off. A hand reached out and took me. It wasn't Barbara's and it didn't take me by the hand. I was held fast at the wrist. Some infantryman we'd missed?

Nah.

"Righty!" the girl exclaimed. And she jumped out of the truck to greet him.

Danced out of that truck?

Thumpy let go of me and latched onto her. She carried him up into her arms, held him—a real grotesquery.

v

We sat ourselves at a couple stools near the back—where the counter bent. The hope was to stay under everyone's radar but the cook's. We sent Thumpy back to the bush of course. Not a diner stool in the world isolated enough you could hide that bloody stump!

In keeping with hiding...

I wanted to know exactly what we'd walked into but I didn't want to get caught gawking around the place. I glanced over-shoulder therefore. What'd I see?

The diner was well-populated considering most of the guardsmen were out chasing Thumpy. It was mostly uniformed cops and vigilantes. A waitress of about twenty-five was behind the counter in addition. She approached us.

"Hi y'all. I'm Janie and I'll be your host, waitress, dish-washer, janitor, and half yer short-order cook! What can I getcha?"

Barbara picked up a menu.

"Do I sense a little sarcasm?" I asked Janie.

"Do *I* sense a little sarcasm?" she shot back.

"Fair enough. Are our boys giving you a hard time?"

"Your boys?" she said quizzically. Was she onto us? Did I

lay it on too thick? Give up the ruse? "Nah—" she started to assure me and I exhaled at her in relief. *Super smooth, dude...* After eyeing me funny a second, she continued. "It isn't you." And she angled her head down the counter. Vigilantes that way and little else. I nodded. She commenced with some cheer. "For real and for true, can I get you two anything?"

"What'a'ya' say, Barbara? A couple of T-bones and pie *à la* mode?"

"Sounds about right." She put her menu down.

"Oh, jeez," Janie said in a way contrite—in a way to say we weren't getting those steaks. She took the menu off the counter and put it underneath. "I'm so sorry. We kinda got taken over after the takeover, if you know what I mean, and all the real stuff went by lunch today."

"*Taken over*? Us army can sure eat."

"Again..." Janie intimated. "...Not your guys." She gestured down the counter once more.

"Well, what do you have?"

"We got tuna salad, egg salad, ham salad... Oh, and chicken—"

"Salad?" Barbara guessed.

"Cordon bleu."

"How is it?"

"It ain't French."

"What'a'ya say, Barbara? A couple of tuna salad sandwiches?"

"Sounds about the default."

Janie smiled once more, though in a wincing manner. "Sorry again, you two. I'll have it right out." And she moved on to warming up the coffee of a vigilante down the way, leaving Barbara and me to our self-imposed lonesome.

"So..." I broached, "This'll be our last meal together, I take it."

"I guess so..."

"Who gets Thumpy?"

"Ha! *Righty*."

"He gonna live with you and your aunt?" I guess my saying this is what gave her the sullen look—like me when I think about my kids. "This place is well-secured," I tried. "I'm sure she's safe, Barbara."

"And she's going to want to live with *this*..." She waved a limp, ostensive hand across herself. "She's sweet. But she's chaste. But she's *real* chaste. As kids, she thought us hellspawn for dancing to Ed Sullivan. I don't know if I could do that to her again... *worse*."

"She should know about your brother at least."

"Now Johnny's someone could've used a taste of these powers." She said this pantomiming a left hook. She immediately cupped her hands over her mouth. "I don't know why I said that."

"Barbara, you've never really spoken fondly of Johnny, just spoken of him."

"That's none of your business."

"I don't want to push it, I don't, but nothing about him up to now was my business, and you spoke of him all the same."

"I—I don't want to talk about this."

"Alright, Barbara, I won't push it. Just know—"

'Alright, Vince,' I said. 'Hit him in the head. Right between the eyes.'

And I stood straight, listening down the row of stools. That voice, those words, last ever and eating at the inside of my ears, trying to chew through to my soul. I looked and there he was, like a dime store Ralph Kramden in a bandoleer'd gone popped off his belly. And right next to him was *Vince*, the man who'd done the deed!

"Ben?" Barbara said, putting a hand to a shoulder I didn't care to have company. I moved free of that hand. I couldn't help moving toward those men, like floating.

And, bang! Old Vinnie missed by a mile!

Oh no he didn't. Not when it counted.

That's why we gave him the twelve-gauge!

I was next to these fools. They hadn't seen me. The chief was facing Vince, his back to me, and Vince was facing the counter, staring into his soup. I wasn't sure what I was gonna do to these men who killed me but I was damn thankful my tuna salad hadn't come so I'd be good and dumb and strong doin' it. I wasn't sure what I was gonna do, but something less mindful in me musta been.

My hand was reaching out for the Chief...

❦ 9 ❦

THE CONSOLATION PART II

OCTOBER 8, 1968

He stood direct center of the atrium, waiting.

She's no closer to us than when I sensed her last, Gilbert. She must be nearer to you.

The lights were on. She was nowhere.

He was scanning, tip of his sword in the tiled floor. The garlic was still at a good force, damned weed! He'd overpower her despite this, as he was still more than man in terms of strength, though her likely skills would be the equalizer—

He moved! He picked up the claymore, hilt in his right hand, upper end in his left, like a ball player bunting.

Ping! Ping!

The shuriken deflected off the strong of his blade. They came at multiple trajectories but he moved swift.

Guess she wasn't depleted...

But where was *she*?

As bright as could be in there. Even the moon was contributing through the glass above. He could see it, ahead, refracted through the ceiling and shining off the barrier before the escalator.

But the reflection faltered. There was to be no eclipse this night...

He twisted, bent backward at the waist, damn near perpendicular, threw the sword up like a javelin. It crashed through the glass panel above him. It didn't come down...

But she did.

She plummeted. She wasn't flailing. She was throwing more of those stars!

He dodged successfully but, in his haste, he lost her. He lost her? Was she a bird? He spun. She was gone once more. He looked up. There was no way she made it to that roof already! Begrudge yourself your illogic later, my servant—

But two feet struck him mid-back, so hard they sent him flying—made him feel like he'd been folded in two. He flew forward and she pounced on him before any landing. She sliced and stabbed into his back with the blade of her ninjatō before getting to her feet and over him, readying the sword to plunge.

The wounds were healing though not fast enough. He felt every inch of the pain. Yet he wouldn't bemoan this. He'd bemoan the squandering *not* the torture. Pain ought be put to work. He planted both palms to the floor and lifted himself up and right through her stabbing sword, stealing it in torso. He spun, scissoring his legs around her's, toppling her sideways. Her head hit the ceramic with a clack.

He stood, loomed. In all his maneuvering he had driven the ninjatō further into his back and, naturally, out his front.

She lay watching. She took all of him in as though nothing was new under the sun. Unimpressed, she rolled, did a kip-up feeling the daze the tile had put in her. She stood before *him*, wobbled in the slightest. He remained fixed. Wobble might have been a trick.

Now he assessed her. She looked as one would expect: covered in dark flexible fabric, masked, her shoes modernized Jika-tabi. *Juuust as one would expect*. She was out of weapons at present—at least those she couldn't hide in her uniform where, considering the form-fit of it, meant most.

They circled each other. He took the butt of the sword through him in-hand. He cracked at the blade with his other. Blade snapped and slid across the floor. He ripped what remained from his back and lunged. She dodged and he fell past her. She spun and wrapped her arms around his neck, then jumped to wrap her legs around his midsection. He wrung himself, twisted, did so faster and faster. He couldn't shake her. She reached onto the front of his throat and tore out his adam's apple. Bile splattered and he began to gasp of pure instinct—forgotten he was undead.

Ah, but my servant, in that instance of fear, gave her the ultimate opening. She didn't hesitate. She tore out his eyes. She let herself off him. She ran to the south.

I smell her, I assured him. He was still in too much shock to register. *She's nearing, coming for me!*

But she came in silence. He couldn't hear. He was running, though in the wrong direction.

Not that way! She's behind!

But he kept going!

Behind—

He was leaving! Coward! *How dare you—* And the link was broken.

ii

Alister crouched, hunched over me in the corner of that vestibule.

"You must flee," I said. The stench was strong. Both of her adrenaline and his. "You are fit for flight. You must go."

But he stood. He positioned me behind a refuse bin. He turned and walked to the interior doors to face them.

"This is my domain."

"Alister, she is no mere stumbler!"

He was not listening. Double doors were propped open now by their stops. He was on watch, looking out into the rotunda...

When she clobbered him! Both feet kicked at him like what had hammered Gilbert. The weight of his suit didn't send him flying, just crumbling against the other side of the vestibule, against the exterior door.

He tried to move, only tipping himself to the side. "Can't... Can't get up," he said, stunned. He was reaching for his claymore. He must have forgotten. There would be no leverage for our dear Alister.

"Where is he?" She asked, rolling him back supine. His head was propped up against the door. She flipped open his visor.

His eyes narrowed at her. "You shall not pass," he scoffed.

She looked up and out the exterior doors, saw nothing. If that's where Alister had put me, that's where I'd be. She turned, went back in the direction of the rotunda, taking a right at the armor court. Good instincts.

Alister started to wobble again. "Gotta get up. Gotta get up."

But she was back in view near-immediately and carrying a rapier. She skipped silently toward our fallen knight.

He flipped his visor back down.

She flipped it back up. She brought the rapier to the opening there, resting it on her forearm. The point was directed at his eye. She drew the weapon across her arm like a violin bow—a crescendo.

She leaned in.

He clenched his eyes shut. He was so afraid.

Now for the coda...

She thrust—

"Stop!" I shouted, and her sword did just that: a halting before I could even get through the command.

Alister's eyes shot open. There was no puncture but he wasn't so much more relieved: that steel tip next to his cornea, and she, not even attending to where she was pointing it! She was facing in the direction of my utterance.

"You may have me," I offered.

She eased, stood fully erect.

Like with Alister, her eyes were the only thing visible. I could know little of her intension by expression therefore, though there was a confidence *cum* arrogance in her swagger. She kicked the bin away, revealing my cover. She lowered, opened the visor assembly on my cap. I had her in my glare immediately! She tilted her head, leaned in closer, tapped the top of my helmet two times as though to say, *Nice try*, and hopped back up to recommence her attack.

"No! No!" he begged.

"I am sorry, Alister," I tried.

She raised her rapier to his eye once more. She glanced over to me for a second in what I could only assume was gloating—damn her will!. She refocused on our curator.

"Please..."

She shook her head at him, drew back her bow...

Now, as I had said, I could glean little of her intention from her eyes alone. But *little* wasn't *nothing* and the cast in them—the instant she wrenched upward to see what was coming for her opposite that door—betrayed her. It was pure terror.

Gilbert smashed through the glass like a missile, sailing over Alister, catching the ninja by her shoulders and dragging her rolling on into the rotunda. He did it still without sight. Damn that weed!

They were flailing at each other using hand-to-hand. She was connecting more frequently, to little avail as he now had the strength of the strongest man plus half. They spun into the armor court still flailing. They were now spinning and thrashing *around* the armor court! There was no reverence in her, though Gilbert was careful of the artifacts—to the extent that his handicap would allow, anyway.

They went round and round.

Then she was off him. The hand-to-hand was only her grace. She could have ended it whenever she had wished and *now* was her will. He tried to sense her location.

She's no closer or further, Gilbert! She's right there with you!

He tilted his head to hear at any relevant angle.

A movement. A weak gust of air. She must have just brushed past. He backed himself up. He moved until he felt the sturdiness of something behind. She whooshed by his front now! He was up against a knight smack at the center of the court. Knight was on horseback, reins in its right hand, longsword in its left.

Gilbert heard a slight jangling behind the steed, from the right rear of the room. *Whoosh* again, and she was clearly toying with him. He tried reaching out for her. She merely silenced her steps. He still groped, desperately.

At this, she swooped in and put the wrist of that groping hand in an antique shackle. His right arm went up with a start. Before he could pull away, he heard a fastening. The arm fell, though no lower than his belly. The other end of the shackle was held fast to something of the exhibit above.

He could only move to pivot now. He turned to the right of the steed. It was silence there. He spun back and angled his head to its left. It was a similar absence.

She hasn't gone, Gilbert. She's calmed! She's culminating to something.

He put his back to the steed, square. Was he resigned?

No, Quassy! It isn't over. The dagger!

The dagger! He reached to the sheath at his ribs. He had it! He held it close, waiting for his moment.

Swoosh!

He slashed. Way too late.

Swoosh!

Another miss.

"Ha! Ha! Ha!" And she was laughing in his ear.

He jabbed in that direction and she just took the dagger away. Stabbed it high into his right outer hamstring. He winced in a pain not as acute as human, nor even a human and a half as the garlic was running its course, yet it was still a horror. He tried for the weapon and neither arm would reach. The fingertips of his left hand only tickled at the pommel.

But she wanted one hand bound and the other behind back! She raced at him with a wooden jutte in-hand, its end sharpened to needle. She plunged. She buried it in his chest.

His mouth suggested less pain at this, more shock, as though he never had a clue what was coming, as though he'd failed. *This* was her culmination. As mortality reared, he would look upon her with eyes healed just enough to betray desperation. To this, she gave the needle a twist. His head fell.

Gilbert? Gilbert?

"Gilbert!"

In an instant she turned. Turned to attend to my wail and that was the opening! That's when Gilbert reached out to snatch her jutted hand in his shackled own. She startled, pulled. He had her true! He reached up and back with his other hand—found what he needed in-grip. She pulled again in futility. His half-healed eyes flashed silver. Hers widened. He let go of her at the exact moment he brought the longsword down. She stumbled back just in time for the strong of the blade to catch her crown. She split all the way to her diaphragm.

Quassy gave the sword a twist and let go of the hilt. The ninja's left quarter peeled away from the right, drawing the rest of the trunk forward and across on its way to the floor. The process was slowed due the thorn. It tore back into my servant's shirt as the body fell. It was as though the hand of the ninja held that weapon tighter than when she'd lived. The tear it left revealed a chainmail—that garment Gilbert had been playing with. *Of no consequence*, indeed.

As the whole of her toppled to the floor, there was another reveal. Her left hand had opened. An amulet was held in it. It was of platinum, shaped like an eye with a red iris.

iii

We sat on the steps at the south entrance. Gilbert was attending to his wounds. Alister was observing things off in the distance, admiring the effectiveness of my forcefield.

"How is your vision?" I asked Quassy.

"Blurry," he said. "Like I have smoke in my eyes."

"It will be better by morning. All will be better by then."

"It was nice to feel *that* once more."

"There will be more battles, with more exploitation of your vulnerabilities."

"I take it there will be... That warrior belonged to HelCorp."

"Indeed."

"She had been following us? For how long? From where?"

"*No, never,* and *nowhere*," I assured. "She had been staking out this location. They know the ritual well. They knew I'd come."

"Then why send only one?"

"Because, despite knowing the ritual well, they do not know the ritual as well as I. I promise you, they are everywhere there are artifacts of my homeland."

"And spread—though thin—all over these lands, master."

"Correct."

"I told you this was a bad idea—"

"Not this again, Quassy—"

"I told you this was a bad idea in my haste, in my error. I may have missed the rite in the liturgy, but obviously HelCorp didn't or else why would she be here?"

"An art lover, like our friend Alister?"

"Ha!"

"Yeah, *ha ha*," Alister said, ambling over. "Can I get my claymore back? Last I checked, six-hundred-year-old swords are antiques..."

✦ 10 ✦

THE COMPANY PART III

OCTOBER 7, 1968

My hand was reaching out to the chief's shoulder...

Just tap him on that shoulder then start a friendly conversation then lull him then rip his goddamn throat out. Simple as that. Then make Vince eat that twelve-gauge. Simple. Ol' Chief Conan's about done busting Vince's balls, so I'll just—

"Hey, why don't ya shut up, eh Con?" Vince said this turning.

I withdrew.

"Now, Vin..." Chief's opening played at apology though its tone suggested, *watch it, underling...* "I'm only funnin' with ya. Ya know, *funnin'*?"

A couple of the chief's guys got up from their stools and stood behind Vince.

"Ah, hell!" Vince bellowed, unaware of the men looming. "Ain't angered at your wind ya gas bag! Nobody can shoot with you whispering in their ears cuz all yer good for is blowing hot air. Ain't that. Show some respect for Christ's sake. There're people in here lost their families."

But the chief wasn't hearing any point about any grief. He only cared about the talk of his hot air. He leaned back at Vince's culmination, grinning, as though to show it was all in good humor. To maintain dignity. That facade lasted about as long as you'd think. He lunged, pulled Vince up by the lapels.

"You think I'm lacking respect?" he said. "They're people *still got* their families because of me!" And he shoved the vigilante back onto the stool.

Vince wasn't taking it so he stood back up, was about to lunge himself when the chief's men grabbed him from behind. He struggled to break free. More of the men moved to the confrontation only they were grabbing at the guys grabbing at Vince.

"What's this, a mutiny?" Chief chuckled. The men had pulled each other off of each other at this point and had half-fists raised in an uneasy standoff.

"It ain't a goddamn party out there!" Vince charged.

"Coward can't do what's gotta be done." Chief said this to the room like he was some sort of orator.

"He's blood simple!" Vince added. "Like one of those things 'cept'n' if he had the balls to use it he'd be blood simple with a gun!"

Chief shoved Vince. Vince shoved chief. Immediately chief's men were shoving Vince's men and Vince's men were shoving chief's men and at this point I had backed up almost all the way to Barbara. Let 'em kill each other, I thought. Then the uniformed cops got involved. Then I almost got my wish as the chief grabbed for the pistol in his belt—

"Officers!" shouted a man in fatigues half through the

door. "McClellan!" he reiterated for the chief and the chief eased his hand off that gun still holstered. The soldier pointed to the south. "The matter's out there, or did you forget?"

Chief lifted his hands up like a kitty-cat pawing. It was one of those *easy now* gestures, as though anyone other than he was the loose screw. "Won't get any problems from us, Coons. It's your circus now..."

"*Sergeant* Coons," the soldier reminded. He glanced over to Barbara and me and saw all we were hiding—had to—though he kept on with his reconnoiter, cold. He finished and inched up to the counter to put his helmet on it. He acknowledged Janie who was waiting attentive, said to her softly, "Ms. Janie, those technicians I mentioned are back. They can have a look at that circuit panel of yours if you'd like."

"Yeah. Sure, sarge. Absolutely." She started pouring him a cup of coffee. "Much appreciated."

He put a hand to his brow and tipped a hat that wasn't there. Janie smiled at this. He turned to the chief, chief slumped back onto his stool, faced his soup. Then sarge sat next to us, took to his coffee while eyeing us up and down again.

"Them woods are a real *frying pan/fire* situation, aren't they?" He said this between sips. He rotated in his seat to better see the south, talked to it not us. "We got people in there needing liberation or else those things'll have their way with them, so those people cry out and their liberators go ahead and have *theirs*."

"Surely that will change—"

"*And then* there are the people in them woods just want to send their liberators running around in circles the last half hour." He let those words stew a little. His head tipped and turned real casual to get Barbara and I in its sights again. Saw all we had to hide, I swear to god— "But I digress," he said. "What were you saying about change?"

"S—surely that will change now that you and your men are here?" Barbara suggested.

"*My men*?" he said, pointing at our fatigues.

Our collective heads lowered.

"Relax," he assured. He tilted back at the south. "But take off those tops. Not everyone around here turns a blind eye so easily." We started to unbutton like obliging a school-marm for some reason. "No, I don't much imagine things will," he said.

"Things will *what*?" I asked, dropping my blouse onto the counter.

"What you said, ma'am." He meant Barbara. "That we'll change much. Most of my men are green as grass but it ain't the years that matter. It's something else." He leaned in, said in a bit of a hush, "Take the chief and old Vince there. I'd bet that dividing line I'm talking about is the same that runs between the chief and *old* Vince—chief's men and Vince's too: *dudes* and *farmers*."

"Dudes and farmers?"

"The dudes: the zealous hangers-on who can only ever try to look the part. Where lord help you if they ever realize their performance is lacking... Like that peacock with the ammo belt hanging off his shoulder, never a single shell of it ever moved to justice. Then there's the farmer: the man with a little corner to work who works that corner happy and who wants to be left alone doin' it and who'd never leave if not for some sort of duty calling—some charge. He leaves to meet the charge and he meets it head on and he meets it true because he's faced far worse in his little corner and he's still farmin' ain't he? Worse problems get solved down on the farm everyday so you damn well better believe they'll get solved where the dude's gone and caused 'em.

"Some of my men are the farmers and some of my men are the dudes. Let us pray a dude can change and let us pray I can tell them apart until then."

"How many of your men are farmers?"

"I'd say... a good third."

"Only a third?" Barbara said, shocked.

"A third..." I was gonna concur, but... "A third... That's... That's hundreds of thousands nationwide. How many farmers you got enlisting? Who's doing the farming?"

"Oh, I don't mean to the letter," Coons said with a slight chuckle. "Take McClellan and Vince over there. Both those guys were born and raised in Fox Chapel. Yet, McClellan's a dude and Vince a farmer. One only looks the part, and barely, while the other... well... the other doesn't *only*."

"What if I told you," I said. "Vince ain't no prince. He's put men in the frying pan."

"Yeah, with the devil whispering in his ear—"

But another soldier had rushed into the diner.

"Sarge! More on the move!"

"Numbers." sarge demanded, standing.

"Big. Bigger a horde than we've seen."

"Heading to the house?"

"Yessir. Roving north."

He grabbed his helmet and rushed to the door. He paused halfway through it and turned to us, still eyeing Barbara and me like we had everything in the world to hide and he knew it and I swear to god he did and— "You two watch yourselves in these parts."

And with that, he was gone. He and his men tore out in seconds, mobilized, gone down the road. I turned facing the south like I was sarge. Janie dropped our sandwiches off at our place settings. I reached behind and grabbed mine, took a bite. "I wonder how big a horde they were talking—"

I choked.

ii

The gob of tuna was too far down my gullet to not swallow. It didn't just burn this time, it sapped me. I was drunk or something, dizzy as hell. I reached over to Barbara to warn her. She had her head on the counter like she'd sipped from the wrong hippie's cup.

"W—What's in this?" I said to Janie. Her back was to me and she didn't hear. I pushed a carton of coffee creamer off the counter. It hit the floor with a dull thud. She didn't hear that either though she sure felt the half-and-half splash at her ankles.

"Oh my god!" she said, spinning.

"What's in this?" I tried again, holding the sandwich out to her.

"T—Tuna salad," she assured. "Mayo, mustard... Used to have onion and peppers before the chief's men ate 'em all. Spruced up though, with a little garlic toast. A—As a consolation for not having anything fancy." She caught sight of Barbara napping. "Oh my god! Y'all aren't allergic, are you?"

I stared at her crooked in my stupor getting crookeder. How long was this going to last—

Bang!

I spun from Janie. I saw Barbara was standing, wobbling and woozy. She held a trembling hand to her mouth. I spun again, one-eighty. This time the spinning didn't stop. Everything was rocked by vertigo but I could see Vince was dead on the floor and the chief had his pistol on him. Chief's men had guns on Vince's men too, detaining them.

People were shocked-still. Stillness would turn to panic soon enough.

The Chief put his gun away for the moment and backed up toward us.

I backed up too, slid into my seat. I gestured for Barbara to do the same. She was already sitting, gesturing similarly at me.

Turns out the chief wasn't moving to *us*. He was trying to get as many of the patrons in view as possible. "Now folks," he said dipping his hands at the floor, palms facing it, "calm down. Just calm yourselves."

I wasn't Sherlock Holmes. Not in my stupor. I wasn't Sherlock Holmes in my hunger either. Hell, I wasn't Sherlock Holmes fed, fat, and focused. What's this got to do with anything? I'll tell you: I didn't have to be Sherlock Holmes to understand who'd been reigning the chief in around here. Chief didn't kill Vinnie until Coons was good and far down that road. I also didn't have to be Sherlock Holmes to understand that Coons' men, beholden to Coons, kept the soldier apprised of anything untoward here in Hevans. And there was nobody more *untoward* here in Hevans than our tin pot tin star. Any of sarge's unit sticking around would be a problem for the chief, therefore.

From behind the counter no one could tell Barbara'd been trying to pass for soldier. If she were around the other side of that corner she'd be exposed and that'd be a different story. That was my story: the tale of a man sitting in the wide open in fatigue bottoms, his army-issue top sitting on the counter in front of him... I took the shirt and nudged Barbara in the direction of one stool over. I, real slight, twisted around the bend and sat where she'd been. I threw my shirt away along the space between the stools and counter. Barbara did the same.

Those dumb vigilantes couldn't tell a thing now, long as we were on this side of the—

"You two..." The chief was talking over his shoulder at us. "You folks mind moving over to where I can see you? Anywhere over there." He faced the bulk of the crowd once again. "Now calm yourselves..."

I squeezed the countertop. I was weak but getting better but really? Wishful thinking? Whatever I was, it wasn't enough to take these guys on. I took Barbara by the hand noticing she'd already taken mine in hers. We moved into the nearest acceptable booth as quick as we might in our wooz.

"Just calm down, damnit!" But a uniformed cop was rising out of his booth, hand on his holstered sidearm. "Now Charlie," chief said, catching him, "you sit back down. Sit until ya know well and good enough. Know it's for the greater good, Charlie." Chief started acting the orator again, speaking for us all. "Come on now folks. How many of you in the last couple days came across a devastation, a family torn to shreds because somebody... somebody weak... wouldn't do what had to be done? Loaded gun still in his hand? I know I sure have. How many a'you nearly died yourselves because of someone next to you wouldn't pull the trigger?" He pointed at Vince's men in handcuffs. "Their *not acting* is bad enough. Their not acting to put those ghouls down is enough to get our families killed. Now you're gonna abide these cowards making sure we can't act to save ourselves? You saw them. You saw them and Vince. They see us saving lives—your families' lives—and they call it 'blood simple'. Well, I say if it's my daughters getting it or one of them ghouls getting it, then it's the ghoul gonna get it. If it's me or you *been bit by them ghouls* gonna get it or your family gonna get it, it's us who've been bit gonna get it. But that's not good enough! If it's someone wanting to protect a ghoul over my girls, any of your families—just gonna let our families die to save a ghoul—then it's them protectors gonna get it too. What say you?" And Charlie sat himself down, both hands on the table. "Alright, now all you citizens are free to go. However, I want you to remember what you saw here today, what happens to anyone callous enough to sympathize with a ghoul... Like Vince's boys over here *and* you Charlie." Chief motioned to two more of his men. They headed for the officer.

"No!" Charlie shouted in protest. The men held him in his seat.

"You're either a constant force or a threat to us, Chuck. You may have relented, after a time, but if you acted that way to a stumbler, even someone bit by a stumbler, you—and maybe any one of us in this room—woulda been dead. Take him fellas." And they pulled Charlie up and out of the booth. They moved him to be with Vince's boys. "Well, folks," chief continued, "you're free to go. And seeing as you're all such good citizens, I expect to see you at town square this morning." We all nodded. "Well, head on out then."

And we rose—Barbara, me, Janie, the rest of the staff, a few more. We headed for the door.

"Wait chief, these two are in uniform."

Goddamnit he meant us! Some lackey'd gone and been perceptive. I'd throw these guys through a wall if I hadn't just been poisoned. Was it poison? How long was this going to las—

"Sorry you two, only civilians." And the chief gestured for us to head to where his men and the uniformed police were situated.

I put a finger up *wait one minute* style. Nothing came to my mind other than: get the hell out of this half-a-gulag.

"What?" asked the perceptive lackey, looking at my finger.

"W—We're not army," Barbara slurred. "They gave us these uniforms when they found us." Yes Barbara! Yes! Go on girl! "In that culvert. They found us hiding—soaked."

Good girl!

"Yeah," I mumbled. "Ever see a girl in the army?" I tried to point Barbara's way. It almost made me lose my balance. I stifled myself.

Chief eyed us up and down like maybe he was *juuuust* about to relent, to send us on our way. Well, go on, do it ya ignorant ass!

"I don't know," he said. "Might be a secretary to some bigwig or something..."

"I don't think so chief. They're drunk as hell. Look at 'em." And the lackey nudged me and I tipped. I'd have fallen all the way over if I hadn't done a little jig to right myself.

"So?" chief said.

"They were talking to the sarge for like ten minutes. He woulda put them in the brig for that."

"Might be faking..."

Goddamnit chief you officious mother-fu— That garlic was coming back up! I ralphed. It splashed at ol' Con's feet.

"Get them the hell out of here!" he barked, and his lackey nudged us on our way.

Phew! Free!

I shuffled. I turned to an equally shuffling Barbara. "Yes, let's get ourselves the hell outta here and never look ba—"

But one of the vigilantes was lifting Vince off the floor for what I could only assume was his disposal. The vigilante dragged him from under the armpits through a pool of blood ol' Vince had left behind. What a heavenly bouquet...

Why'd I think that? Barbara was digging her fingernails into my arm.

Vince's feet dragged much of that pool along with him, streaking like a tail... a coulis smear. Lot a' that blood still in him. Be a shame to waste it. I felt not a hunger anymore. The deeper I breathed, the more that hemoglobin tingled my insides. Barbara dug into me deeper. I licked my lips, could barely feel my light-headedness. No more poison. No more hunger. I felt only a thirst.

Something. Had. To. Give...

And we flew—or at least it felt like it. We were on the corpse in an instant. Barbara chopped at the vigilante holding Vince, stronger than mortal though barely. Vigilante still went down cold. She caught Vince's corpse as it fell and held him up. I helped from the other side. We fixed on each other a moment, our eyes golden.

We dug in.

She went for the carotid, myself, the jugular. I became clear-headed immediately, though the hunger-induced strength was gone in that instant too. I was still feeling the effects of that tuna salad, but all was otherwise glorious! Consider us square for that whole shooting me in the face thing, Vinny boy!

"They're not drunk!" the chief shouted. "They're a couple'a' them ghouls!"

And his vigilantes opened up on us! We were gettin' peppered.

We had the choice here of defending ourselves or of continuing the drink. We chose the path of the glutton and that meant, in our nourished though poisoned state, those bullets would eventually take us out of commission.

"In the head, boys!"
Bang! Bang!
And all was dark.

iii

We awoke to another pyre, tied to posts. We were slated to be burned alive: quite the surprise to a chief thinking he'd pulped us. We weren't in any town square either! Hevans didn't even have a town square. We were in the empty lot of a used car dealership. Probably for its massive array of lights. So whoever wished it could see the torment. And why an empty lot? Town fall on hard times or'd the chief commandeer this place and its wares too?

"Ben?" Barbara grumbled. I think she was trying to whisper. She was tied up behind me. We were smack at the top of the pile, looking down on everything. "How ya feeling?"

"Like a spinning top. You?"

"I had my tonsils out as a kid. They gave me ether. Was a cup of black coffee compared to this."

"So, better?"

"Quite a bit."

"Well don't get too excited, the sun's coming up."

And it was, the kind of wash of amber on the horizon so faint you'd only see it in your peripheral vision. Yet, there it was. If I could see that amber, then I could see the east side of the lot. Barbara, naturally, could see the west.

"At least they gave us a last meal…"

"Listen, I'm thinking we hit the sweet spot where this high's gone enough and the sun's still under that horizon, we might just get ourselves out of this."

"Feeling better already."

"Break out of your bonds *better*?"

She wriggled behind me.

"No."

"Oh god! Oh god!"

We had company by the way.

"Oh my god they're not dead!" It was Charlie. He was tied to a post of his own. "Not even destroying the brain'll work! Oh god! Oh god!"

"Relax, Charlie," I said. "We ain't one of them."

He was hyperventilating. "Wh—Wh—What are you?"

"Lottery winners, like you *two*."

One of Vince's guys was in front of me too. I could only infer the other of his crew was in front of Barbara. Even ol' Vinny himself was here, not tied upright to anything, just tossed at my feet. Wasn't fit for any sort of symbolic torching like the rest of us corpses?

The lot had a few people milling about it, though they were certainly no mob. The chief was in a rush. I assume it was because he had to get all this done before the sarge and his unit returned. Didn't have time to mail the invitations?

"Oh god..."

"Quiet, Charlie! Whining won't get us out of this. Trust me, follow Barbara's and my lead and we'll get out of this just fine."

"The *lead* of a couple'a' ghouls or god-knows-what?"

"Got any better suggestions?"

"Right. Follow your—"

"Shut it, Charlie!"

And he did. And Barbara and I went still, dead still.

"Those of you who've come out for the trials," the chief issued, "you're a tribute to the town of Hevans!" He had arrived, obviously, entourage and all. He and his vigilantes and the handful of people milling constituted the entire of the crowd—unless you count us lamb chops. "We're under siege," he said. "From out there, from within." I pulled against my bonds, careful to betray little movement. I could feel Barbara doing the same. We didn't make much headway. Didn't matter. We'd been torched before—by that same asshole down there! I could always pounce once the ropes burned away. Burning'll hurt like hell though... "If we're gonna survive this," the chief went on, "and we will, we need absolute consistency. Unwavering loyalty to the cause. You've heard my case. I won't belabor it any more than to say: you see your neighbor sympathizing with a ghoul, that's hesitation. That hesitation's the single second any ghoul needs to pounce. And where will the hesitant man's sympathies be then? Not in his dead ghoul-eaten brains, that's for certain. If you're depending on me to keep you and your family alive—if you're next to me in the fight—you know I'll never waver. Can you trust any other of your neighbors? Can he trust *you*? Next time you look into the eyes of your kids, pink-cheeked and giggling here in Hevans, you understand this is only so thanks to your loyalty, your neighbor's and mine. Unwavering." He turned to those of us on the pile. "Any last words?"

"Stick your head up your ass, Con!" This was Vince's guy's contribution.

"Yeah!" Vince's other guy added.

The chief just smirked.

"I—I would like to say something," Charlie said.

"You go right ahead there, Charlie."

"Thank you, Con. T—Thank you, good people of Hevans. I just want to say, you're in good hands with our chief a—and, although I strayed, I know I'll be in good hands too, right up to the end. You see, I realize now not just the importance of loyalty, but the importance of consistency, like the chief said. I broke that chain. I broke it I did. Despite that, that doesn't mean I can't help the cause one last time—"

"Get to the point, Chuck."

And he did. "T—Them ghouls you killed up above me ain't dead, chief! They ain't dead and they ain't ghouls. Look at them, their skin's like ivory. Where're the bullet holes? Look!"

Chief put on some spectacles. "My god Charlie, you're right. They're as pretty as dollies. Go check 'em out, boys." And a couple of the chief's men scrambled up the wood pile.

"Damnit Charlie!" I said.

"S—Sorry you too. T—The cause, you know."

"Well, lookie lookie," the chief said. "No point climbing any higher fellas. Those demons ain't playin' possum any longer." *Bang!* And he shot me! Shot me between my damn eyes! Things didn't go black this time which was nice, but those damn bonds still weren't breaking, but he shot me in the son-of-a-bitchin' head! I glared at him. "*Oooh*, that'll show me," he scoffed. He turned his focus back to the rat. "Why, thank you Charlie. That was all really helpful."

"R—Right, Con. A—And there's plenty more where that came from. You can count on me."

"Like a' said..." the chief tipped his hat, turned back to his men.

"So, um, so, you gonna cut me loose?"

Chief sighed, turned back. "Charlie boy I told you: *absolutely consistent in your loyalty*. No breaks in the chain. You broke that chain and there's no refastening it. You showed me I can't trust you once and that's enough." He pointed at me. "Hell, ya showed your ghoul friend he can't trust you either. That's two for two, Charlie."

"Please!" Charlie begged.

Chief shook his head. "Charlie, this is undignified of you, of me in entertaining it. But lookit, I'm not a man without feeling. I tell you what I'm gonna do. I'm gonna cut you a break and not let you burn alive."

"Oh, Con! You won't regret this! I'll make you proud Con! You'll see. First thing I'm gonna do—"

Bang!

And Charlie was dead. The chief got him right between the eyes. His MO.

"Hell!" he shouted at his men. "If Charlie boy doesn't want to burn alive, then Charlie boy's gonna burn a corpse." And the men started to shuffle a little. Most turned away or looked down to hide the tinge of disgust they were feeling. Chief caught this, put his gun back in his belt, got into that orator posture again. If he had suspenders he'd have one of them in each hand. "I feel I ought tell the couple of you eyeing me so sullen: don't think I don't see your judgment and don't think the more loyal of the men among you haven't seen it too. Don't think they haven't voiced these concerns in private either." The men looked around, curious yet furtive. All they saw were other men, none of them dissenting. Of course, those men weren't dissenting because all they were doing was looking around for other men dissenting. Since all any one man saw was a lack of protest, he took this to mean everyone else was in agreement with our dear chief. All of any one of those men went back to staring at the ground. "Now, rest easy boys. I won't be naming any names. But understand, you few facing me in such a state of conflict, your loyalty hangs like the sword of Damocles. What's that mean? Means it's still there, no breaks in the chain. Means it's hanging by a thread, though. So, don't none of you go giving any of the others a reason to come tattling to me anymore. We clear?" The men shuffled more. "We *clear*?" he shouted, and they nodded. It wasn't vigorous, though it was agreement of a kind. "Good! Now let's get this show on the road!"

He picked up a thinner slat of wood from the pile and pushed it firm into his thigh to brace it. He busted it lengthwise with a chop of his hand and threw one of the halves away. He waved a henchman over. The guy came with a tin bucket of something brown. Chief sloshed the narrow end of his half-slat around in the bucket a few seconds and lit it up.

The henchman threw the rest of the bucket onto the pyre.

"Well," the chief got to within torch length of the beginning of the kindling. "Burn."

"What, no last words for us?" Barbara said.

"Ha! A ghoul's already said its last words."

And he lowered the torch into the pile and *whoof!* The accelerant went right up despite the wood hesitating as though green. It didn't completely resist. That fire would climb, get to Vince's guys ahead of us. If they were lucky, it would be the smoke that killed them. They wailed.

"Well Ben," Barbara said. "I guess this *isn't* the end..."

"Har har." But I could see that defiant fool of Vince's tortured down there. "Hey Barbara, we got a problem."

"And what's that?" she asked amidst the smoke and the flame and her bonds.

"By the time we *uncook* from all this, that chief might be long gone to the next town and the next mob."

"So?"

"*So...* I'm hungry now." And I ripped myself free, shredding the ropes binding me! The sun was a peeking sliver though still a sliver. I had at least five minutes to suck that sucker dry. I leapt high into the air, my canines elongating as I climbed, creeping further and further down to dessert.

The chief stood straight a moment in petrified delay, then his back arched and his head pitched to better see the curse rising above him. All except torch was parabola. His terrified wet eyes—seemingly all pupil—were the primary driver of the carnal architecture he was contorting so perverted to see. I was through those eyes! I would taste the fear in them.

At my apogee, I corrected to have him in my trajectory. I opened wide. I could smell the stench off him I knew would be the zest, the bitters to his bouquet. I cupped my groping claws in preparation that he not fall out of my grip on arrival!

Now I smelled more than adrenaline: ammonia, his fears reified in piss! I fell, I fell, I fell! I gnashed!

And then the sun came up.

Damnit, I'd failed to account for those car lot lights. The sun wasn't any mere sliver. It was a wash of brightness. I hadn't five minutes, just one *now* gone.

I went limp. I couldn't even flail. I was falling like a wet shirt.

I landed square on the narrow end of the chief's torch burned to a point. It pierced my heart. All was going dark once more.

So, there *was* something it was like to be a stumbler...

And the fire crept on up: *you alive down there?* said one of Vince's guys, hopeful. *Get us the hell off this thing!*

But I only hung limp on that torch. Chief didn't even realize he was holding me upright—didn't even realize it was his adrenaline giving him the strength to do so.

"Chief?" said one of his men.

Chief startled alert. "W—What the hell is this thing?"

And Barbara had escaped her bonds as well! She tumbled down the pile, rolling over the growing flames. She stopped at the feet of the chief's entourage and smoldered a little. Why would you think she'd be any better in the sun?

And the fire crept on up: *Son of a bitch, the girl's out cold too! I think the soles of my shoes are starting to melt!*

"Chief?"

"Well, what are you waiting for?" the chief bellowed. He held up the slat with me on it. "Drive one of these through her."

"A ghoul?"

"The wood! The wood—"

I was alive and on the stumble now! Alive on the pike. I groaned and the chief screamed.

"*Eeyuhhhh! Eeyuhhhh! Eeyuhhhh!*" he kept screaming. He let one hand off his torch and grabbed his gun and started firing it into my forehead.

Meanwhile, they'd staked Barbara.

"*Rrrraaarrrrr!*" And I was back to cursed, baring my teeth at him, reaching. "I want to suck your—"

"*Eeyuhhhh!*" And he screamed and shuddered at me despite my having no real strength left out here in the sunshine. He kept shuddering and inadvertently gave that torch a twist and my heart, having healed around it, was cleaved once more!

And the fire crept on up: *If you save us now, it won't be so bad—kinda like reverse frostbite...*

Bang! Bang! And they shot Barbara on the stumble!

"*Grrrrooooaaaannn,*" and I was back on the stumble myself! And this time I had the chief by the forearm. I pushed against the torch and lowered myself to his plump fleshy flailer. That slat slid near all the way through me as I went—and boy did I go! I arrived. I chomped, tore dermis, muscle, fat. It wasn't glorious, like the feeding of an accursed, though it was something.

It was something that snapped the chief out of his pissy-pants fears.

Bang! Bang! And I was in syrup.

"Son of a bitch!" He let go of the slat and pushed me back and I fell.

His men had swarmed in on Barbara. They had their revolvers, rifles, and shotguns pointed at her and she was just a' writhing in the sun in that syrup too.

"Leave them!" the chief shouted, wrapping his gun belt around where I'd bit him. "They're weaker this way." He was searching around, frantic. "Where's a shovel?"

"Huh boss?"

"Shovel? A saw? Anything?" The chief started dragging me over to Barbara.

"Axe?" the henchman offered.

"Yeah! Oh yeah!" the chief said, satisfied. "Axe!" He lined Barbara and me up, toe-to-toe.

A henchman pulled the axe out of the stump used to split the kindling, hustled it over to the chief. He took it in his hand, ran his finger perpendicular the blade.

"*Dull*," he growled in lust. He angled the axe handle at Barbara. "Hold her!"

His men did as told.

And the fire crept on up: *what are we, chopped liver?*

"Let that ghoul head of hers poke out a little further, boys!" And they held Barbara down at the shoulders.

"I'm sorry, Barbara girl," I said into her ear. "I'm too damn tired..." She reached out and took my hand.

And the chief lifted that axe to chop... "Let's see how far you get in a twenty-piece bucket!" He brought the thing swinging down!

But something took it in a flash! Flew right by the vigilante, ripping that tool out from his hands! He spun around and around at a loss.

And the fire crept on up: *I don't know, can you even barbecue chopped liver?*

Chief held out his empty palms, turned them facing down then up. He flew into a rage. He knelt down and started strangling Barbara.

But the flash was back! It was Thumpy! He'd pounced onto the chief from behind. He somehow *sans* leverage pulled the tyrant off the girl. He pulled the tyrant up! Tyrant spun again, this time to throw his attacker away. Thumpy hung on though. He had ol' Con by the neck at first, strangling him less to choke, more to find his bearings, then the li'l torso took to working his way downward. He was letting his fingers do the walking when Con got a gory grip on him! Li'l guy managed to latch onto the chief's gun belt just before he was sent flying. He pulled that belt like a lawnmower recoil as he went.

Instinctively, the chief reached to the gash on his arm re-exposed, half trying to soothe it, half trying to hide it.

Thumpy was pointing frantically at the wound. The men already saw. They took their guns back in-hand—like by instinct.

"N—Now, fellas..." the chief insisted. "I—I know what this looks like. I got it... I got it..."

"Nick yourself witch hunting this morning?"

"Fellas..." But he stopped groveling. "You *need* me!" They just raised their guns. "Think of your families."

"We are."

And they moved in, apprehensive, as though they didn't want to do what they'd been told so often they had to. One of them took the lead. He put a hand up and held the remaining men back. He pulled the slide of his pistol and they got the picture.

He put the pistol barrel to the chief's forehead.

"P—Please!"

But the leader just shook his head. "Not a break in the chain." He pulled the trigger!

Click!

There was that ammonia smell again.

He got in the chief's blubbering face. "Didn't hesitate." Then he turned to the men. "Get Vinny's guys down."

Oh, thank the lord!

And three vigilantes started raking the burning timber away, working their way to Vince's boys who were mostly fine. They wouldn't be walking so well for a week or two, but they'd be fine.

Then the leader pointed to the chief curled up in his own excrement. "Couple a'ya, detain Connie here. Use gloves."

"Boss?" one of the vigilantes said.

"I ain't your boss," the leader rebuked.

"Jimmy?" said the vigilante, and leader Jimmy turned to listen. "What'a'ya want to do with those two? A—and a half?"

Jimmy crouched down to Barbara, Thumpy, and me. He lifted my lip, saw one of my canines. "They ain't ghouls..." he said. He snapped his fingers and a few of the vigilantes lifted us to our feet. "...But we can't just let them loose."

"Well, what are we going to do?"

"Gentlemen," said a Dutch accent. "Allow me to be of service, to tell you exactly what you are dealing with and what, maybe, you should do about it."

11

THE CONFRONTATION PART I

OCTOBER 8, 1968

Quassy showed concern. I would not be deterred.

"You must rest, master."

He was correct of course, though there would be none of that, not with that amulet calling.

"Bring it to me, Gilbert."

"It?"

"The eye."

And he did.

"Hold it close."

He held that warrior's amulet to my pursed lips.

They taunt me, my ward. They want me to see!

ii

Others had harnessed the power of the video too, so to speak, though not of tape or film: of my mind's eye.

The amulet to my lips was the key.

I can see my heart, dear Gilbert. Oh, how they taunt me!

"At HelCorp headquarters?"

No.

"You said—"

I said it would be there when we arrived. I closed my eyes to better see. *And it will. There are two with my essence, Gilbert. Ah, a pair after my own heart! Its keepers. Good boy.*

iii

They were aces again, *aces* being what this man Ben took to denote sound health. They had been put out of the sun, sat at a table at the rear of a mobile laboratory. They were hardly ameliorated by this fact and neither was I. The mobile lab had a HelCorp logo on its exterior.

"You know anything about these guys?" said the one named *Barbara*. She said it between coos directed at my heart.

"Knew a guy drove truck for them. Moved a lot of soil."

"Soil?"

"Yeah, dirt from all over the—"

The trailer's rear doors were opening. A man entered, tallish, blonde, prim, proper, dressed out all in grey save for his black leather driving gloves.

I was, for whatever reason, attuned to Ben's thoughts at this point. He noticed those gloves too. *Hey!* he thought, *Those things were more practical than you'd think... Take it from a trucker, a steering wheel's a garden hoe you drive enough hours. Need them gloves—*

I would leave myself to Ben as vicar from here. His window to all this was mine now, and it was more fruitful to play participant than spectator.

"Dear lady! Meneer!" shouted blondie. "So happy to have finally met you!" Clearly, this was the guy with the

Dutch accent. Guy was pleasant alright. Big white teeth, hadn't stopped smiling 'em at us—

But what was that thumping keeping me from enjoying all the cordiality?

Surprise surprise, it was Thumpy. He was trying to wedge himself under and behind Barbara as she sat. She patted him to soothe him. The thumping stopped.

"Now you two," the Dutchman continued. "You two've got yourselves into some garlic! I can see it in your eyes."

"Garlic? Look, my name's Ben and this is—"

"Introductions in due time! I must ingratiate first, dear meneer. Allow me to *wow* you!"

Wow me, Barbara mouthed in my direction. I smirked.

"Indeed!" he said, clapping his hands at us. "Let me guess, you're new to this so you don't know. You're hungry, you eat something, it burns. It's got a little garlic in it and you're on your *kont*."

"Hey, there's a lady present!"

"It means *rear end*. Though I am right?"

"Well yes, but—"

"Drink this." He handed us a couple of vials of something clear. We took them. We didn't drink them. "Ah, I haven't yet gained your trust. Fine. Do you want to know what you are?" We leaned in. He went on. "You two are the spawn of Dracula himself!"

Barbara turned to me to grin a slowly growing grin that didn't finish. I reciprocated. We turned back to blondie. "The Count's dead."

"Yes, at the hands of that nationalist in that car in Sarajevo... At the hands of the FBI in that theater in Chicago... We've all heard the stories." He raised an eyebrow. "At the hands of my dear departed uncle in that crypt at Carfax Abbey..."

Now we raised *our* eyebrows. "You're a—"

"Bram Van Helsing. But you can call me *Helsing*—" He appeared to catch himself in something. "Oh my! Where are my manners? What I mean is, the family now goes by *Helsing*. You can call me by my first name, *Bram*. Oh boy..." He was embarrassed at this though not enough to let a word in edgewise. "You've heard about that Venus probe causing all this unfortunateness?"

"Venus probe my ass!" And this made Barbara snicker so I smacked an admonishing hand in the air at her even though I was laughing inside too.

"It was all over the news. Non-stop..." he *probed*.

"We were indisposed during all that," Barbara said.

"Oh really? The two of you had absolutely no time to hole up somewhere and take a breather and have a TV or radio drone on in the background?"

"Yeah," I said. "But it was a moon-landing gone bad caused that radiation. Happy? Who they think they're fooling?"

But Helsing sure wanted to know more... "So you did hear? And you knew all along they were *fooling*?" He angled an ear in our direction.

"We were in mixed company," Barbara assured. "And you don't talk about the moon-landing in mixed company." I gestured in agreement.

"Don't I know it!" he beamed. He pointed at our vials. "Ready to drink that?"

"Not yet."

"Ha!" And he moved on. "What if I told you those stumblers are the spawn of Dracula too?"

"What!"

"That *that* crash in the sky was the lunar lander you mentioned, that Dracula was on board, and that radiation was really his diffused essence spread all over the eastern seaboard?"

We handed our vials back.

"Ha! Once more!" He didn't take them. "You have Dracula's blood in your hearts, those stumblers have it in their brains. Well, all us mortals have it in our brains now. We die, we stumble. That is our fate. Though not yours! You have it in your hearts!"

"Wait a minute. We got cursed only yesterday. Pretty sure we were nowhere near that blood sucker."

"Oh, but you were, the both of you. *Heart to heart*, so to speak." He pointed to our cowering little friend.

"What? Thumpy?"

"*Righty*," Barbara insisted.

"*Thumpy*," I corrected.

Thumpy began to shiver under Barbara. She took his hand in hers.

"The heart of the Count," Helsing said and he took out a little jackknife and he slashed his hand wide open.

"Whoa! Whoa! Whoa!"

He held his bloody palm out at us.

We started to feel that tingle.

"Hungry, no?" He waved it, brought it closer. A little of the blood splattered on the table... "*Thirsty*, better? You desire to tear open my neck and drink to ecstasy, though you'd prefer not to. Isn't it interesting how, until we face a dilemma such as this, we take for granted that *preference* and *desire* are the same thing? They are for Dracula. They aren't for you. Curious."

"Stop!"

"Drink that!" And he was pointing at our vials again. We took a second look. "It all goes away," he promised.

I nodded to Barbara. "I'll go first," I assured.

She nodded back.

I downed it.

Heaven!

"Ben?"

I gawked at her looking like Julie Andrews on the poster for *The Sound of Music.*

She downed hers.

"*Whoawaweeny!*"

"That," he said, "is the human blood you need to sustain you *minus* the human. Purely synthetic." Then he sprayed something onto the gash on his hand and that damn thing healed right up! "It gets better!"

"Huh?"

"In return for taking care of... Thumpy?"

"*Righty.*"

"*Thumpy.*"

"In return for taking care of the heart of the Count, you'll be the first we make right as rain."

"Right as rain?"

"The cure. Got it back at headquarters."

iv

Helsing had left. He wanted to give Barbara and me some time to consider his offer. Before he did, he explained of his company's history with the Count—its history with the cursed in general—of how they needed the Count whole to cure us, how that was the catch. It also meant they'd be taking Thumpy. Barbara protested of course, only for Helsing to assure her Thumpy's days were numbered should he not be reunited with the Count.

He went on, said the Van Helsing line had personally executed the Count a half-dozen of his known executions, that none had yet to take. He said the Count was the only of the accursed they ever impaled to come back and, I quote, *the vermin came back at least twenty-two times!*

Helsing said the plan now was to study that wily Count in captivity, find his vulnerability and end him once and for all. Barbara again protested in defence of Thumpy. Helsing allayed her: *death to the Count's heart not entailing death to the Count* only ensured no impaling. This meant Thumpy's survival which meant he and Barbara's reunion. The Count would die and Thumpy would live. And in this—that is, the true death of the Count—lay the cure Helsing offered. A saving grace for the accursed.

And then he left us to decide.

"I want it," Barbara said, not even a second thought to it. "I'm going to take it." I broke eye contact with her. She noticed the disagreement in that. "You want it too, don't you Ben?"

I didn't. "Now, let's not be hasty here."

"We're demons."

"We're immortal."

"We're unfeeling."

"We're *immortal.*"

"What good is that if we can't live by day? Can't live as human beings?"

"I can take better care of my family this way, even if only by night."

But Barbara really knew how to stick it in... "Who'd want to live with an aberration who slept all day?" ...Then push it all the way through. "An aberration who wouldn't hesitate to feed the second anyone got so much as a paper cut!" I lowered my head. "I'm sorry Ben—"

"Barbara, they don't want to live with me *any* way." And her expression softened. She softened as anyone would understanding the pain in another if not the meaning. I tried to explain. "They're up north because that's as far away from me as they could get: other side of the glaciers and the mountains."

"Why—"

"I didn't beat them and I didn't cheat."

"Then, why?"

"Sometimes it's easier to cut a person right the hell out of your life than have him only ever comin' and goin' but mostly only ever goin'—no matter the feeling."

"If you love someone, don't you take them in any measure?"

"It wasn't just love, Barbara. It was a marriage. The former can't sustain the latter if the latter's only cherished in half-measure—like all the sugar in the world won't bake the cake alone."

"I'm sorry Ben. I got no reference is all—"

"A broken marriage with no love lost can be more a heartbreak than the worst of betrayals." And with that, I was done being the sad-sack. Time for the upshot... "But I'd die for my kids and I'd die for my girl and now I can do that the rest of my life."

She nodded. Face didn't lift that last trip down though... "So, this is it for us?"

"No."

"No?"

"HelCorp is north of here. I'm heading north, no point turning down a free ride." And she smiled at this but I was lying. I wouldn't be making it to any HelCorp headquarters. Something told me, considering the company's penchant for killing any and all cursed over the years, they wouldn't take kindly to me telling them I'm gonna take my chances as the very demon they've built an institution on destroying.

Nah, I'd be slipping away at some point. Though a few more miles north, and a bit more time with my friends—ahem, *friend*—kept me on that train.

There was a knock at the trailer door. Barbara got up to answer and something about this upset Thumpy. He tugged at me. "Ya thirsty, boy?" Little guy was holding out one of those vials. I reached for it and—

"So!" Helsing said, re-joining us at the table. "Have we made our decision?" Then he took out a small ceramic trinket. It was red in the middle, grey at the edges, like an eye. He snapped it in tw—

v

So, the keepers of my heart intend to be instrumental in its cleaving? Even if unwittingly? That girl will be in for quite the surprise when that rat Helsing simply impales me at my other side and that is that. My heart can't hide its right hand forever.

"I will rest now, Gilbert. Please prepare for our flight as I do."

And he lowered the visor.

vi

HelCorp headquarters was a fortress. It beamed in the night, shining despite no sources of incandescence, fluorescence, or mercury vapor evident. The structure was made of the same material as the spaceships in that new hippie movie: *2001 A Space Odyssey*, I believe? It was no Looney Tunes short... What a conceited devil that structure was, a perfect candidate for categorization as—appropriately enough—*that which can be seen from space*.

The headquarters beamed without fear. It was protected at its back by a two-hundred-foot-high dune butting up against the lake and protected everywhere else by a thirty-foot-deep trench to the front of fifty-foot-high rampart barriers. The trenches were covered with fine-mesh ultra-field optical lasers at ground level. Each side of the barrier possessed two sentry towers atop it—that's eight in total—with any one tower featuring a mounted chain gun firing 30mm high-explosive rounds, though not for long...

Boom! Boom! Boom! Boom!

Boom! Boom! Boom! Boom!

And the Phantom's bullpups destroyed them all! Good work, dear Gilbert. We were out of missiles but then again we weren't. *Then why land...*

The headquarters' sirens were blaring and its siren beacons flaring by the time my beloved Phantom smashed into and through its main barrier gate.

Farewell, you alloy-boned beast.

Gilbert and I wafted past our horde marching over the horizon toward the complex. They were the largest I had ever commanded! A thousand strong! Our desire at present was to land behind the vanguard, to where Coons and his men would be waiting. The problem was, neither my ward nor I could fly a parachute. I could guide it, if not keep it sufficiently aloft. We landed just short of our tank company and in the middle of our rear-vanguard. However, Gilbert flew through the stumblers, me under-arm, and we reached Coons in no time.

"They will be at the trench in three," I assured.

"And you're sure they'll be dense enough our tank will get through that gate?" Coons asked.

"Their sacrifice will not be in vain."

"You better be right."

"*One* minute..."

vii

The wretched approached the trench. They didn't approach it with apprehension. They approached it as stumblers would. A thirty-foot drop and they would have toppled right off if Gilbert had wished it to be so. They would have seen themselves shredded in that laser light if Gilbert had wished it to be so. But that was not his wish. Nor was it mine.

"Halt them, Gilbert."

And he did. Those taking point stood teetering on the moat's edge.

I would address them a last time.

My dear friends, you have been compelled for far too long. My ward, at my behest, has brought you to the brink. However, neither he nor I will drive you past it. You have followed my heart from the moment of your birth and I have no doubt that you will continue to. However, from here on you will have to follow my heart by following your own. I hereby free you, in the best of faiths!

"Do it, Gilbert."

And he freed them.

They teetered more. All of the horde seemed to be waiting for whatever poor wretched bastard was in front of him to move before he did.

They teetered, then they spilled forward, pouring through that laser light and landing at the bottom of the trench in pieces. Soon those falling were landing on the fallen, the pile of them growing higher and higher, filling the moat.

Higher and higher.

In short order, certain of our friends were able to walk above the laser light. Some were able, not all. Should a stumbler's foot sink into a depression, that foot and any leg attached to it up to the laser line would be minced. The stumbler would then fall into the pile at some angle, possibly sinking below the laser light where landing, mincing more.

The mass compressed denser and denser as the walking, falling, and crawling stumblers moved. It was squeezed compact enough now that all were strolling over it and through the breach in the temple barrier.

"They are in!" I said to Sergeant Coons.

"Platoon, move out!"

And they were on their way.

Curious. "Gilbert, bring me that amulet once more..."

12

THE CONFRONTATION
PART II

OCTOBER 8, 1968

The sarge and his men had breached the compound. The bridge had held, allowing even the tank through. After the crew of four in that tank, Coons had a man driving the Jeep, another at the Jeep's fifty-caliber, a third feeding him ammo, and four troops dispersed amongst the horde. Within that horde, the tank and the Jeep would be the only elements of his platoon conspicuous.

The rest blended in just fine among the hundreds of stumblers moving across the two-acre compound.

A soldier came trudging up to Coons. "What ya think we'll find when we get there, sarge?"

"Get back in formation, private."

"Come on, what ya think we'll find?"

"What makes you think we'll even get in there, Smithie?"

"Ah, you kidding me? Look at us, sarge..." And Smithie took out a grenade and squished it to mush in his hand.

"Mind that ordnance, soldier!"

"Come on…"

Sarge grabbed Smithie by the lapel. He dragged him along while he conducted the reprimand. "You'll never know, no matter your advantage, when something like a single hand grenade may serve you. You think you won't need it? Well let me remind you of one thing: we're carrying out this mission to aid a ten-thousand-year-old immortal in getting his life back because he gone got himself quartered because, despite all his strength and cunning, he let someone get the drop on him. Think he wouldn't have wished for that hand grenade then? You get me?"

"Sir, yes—"

Boom!

The tank was gone! Track was blown and its turret jack-in-the-boxed. Fire escaped the hull.

"Where's it coming from?" shouted private Dickie.

And lights flooded the compound.

"Ultraviolet!"

"Stay in formation!" shouted sarge. "Can't touch a Quassy. But get those masks on. They'll use…"

Pffft! Pffft! Pffft!

Three plumes of a yellowish white fog spread among the horde, near-instantly blanketing a fifty-yard radius.

"…Garlic."

"They're using gak bombs!" shouted private Mox.

"No shit," said sarge in a hush.

Private Smithie didn't get his mask on in time and got a big dose through the eyes. He was choking and on his ass and gak drunk.

The rest of the troops managed to cover up before the dusting but now they had to contend with the source of that tank killer. Three Iroquois helicopters were rising above the complex.

Gunner in the Jeep opened up on the copter closest.

"Hickie, Mox, help him deal with those Hueys!"

"How?"

"Son of a bitch!" And sarge was pushing through the horde as fast as he could.

The targeted Huey returned fire. It blasted at the Jeep with the same chain guns as were housed in those sentry towers. Explosive rounds shredded the gunner, driver, and munitions tech. The destruction of their masks did the real damage however: the dose of gak they got will keep them in pieces the better part of the mission.

Sarge kept moving. He was heading for that tank. "Stay out of that gak, boys. Those rounds can't touch you if you ain't dosed."

Now all three of the Hueys were firing on the stumblers and it wasn't a question of *how will they get out of this?* but a question of *how long will it take those 30mm rounds to dust them all?* The answer: not long. There's still the hope those HelCorp gunships will run out of ammo? Yeah right! Not with *the man* financing them!

Sarge got to the M551 and hopped on, leaned in through the collar where the turret had popped. The crew was alive, of course they were, but they were dosed to hell. Of course they were...

"Stay in that hull!" And he reached in, grabbed a couple turret rounds, and got back to ground. He had a quick look around at the chaos. Dickie was gakked and in pieces. About two-thirds of the stumblers in the courtyard were gone. Nowhere near enough reinforcements were filtering in to replace them as cover.

"Hickie! Mox! Stop those gunners!"

"How?"

Four fifths of the stumblers were gone and counting...

"Goddamn it!" But sarge was moving with purpose, tank rounds in-hands. He got to that popped top turret lying upside down. He drove one of the rounds into its breech and turned it on its side. He angled it up at the gunship closest to him.

Boom!

The Huey with the rocket pod fired on the barrier. At the Phantom breach. The explosion left a pile of rubble high enough no more stumblers would get through.

Hickie and Mox ran up and crouched behind the M551 for cover.

"Whatcha doin', sarge?"

Sarge ignored this. He reared back. Clenched what was reared into a fist. "Talk about pissing into the wind..." And he drove that fist into the round's primer setting off the desired chain reaction driving that shell out the barrel. And the shell flew and it flew true! *Boom!* The Huey was bits.

"Yeah sarge!" shouted Mox, and sarge had had enough. He grabbed Mox by his belt and his neck.

The Huey with the rocket pod circled into firing position above them.

"W—Whert yeh dewring sirge?"

"I told you to deal with those choppers!" and he threw Mox right through the windshield of that circling gunship.

Mox quickly got to work driving the thing into the ground by not letting anyone drive it at all. He threw out the pilot then sat in the man's seat grinning at what HelCorp forces remained. They were him except their fatigues were gray and their faces not. "Bet you wish you could turn that thing on me," he said to the gunner still holding chain gun triggers. Naturally, the Huey went into a spin.

Sarge moved to the last grounded subordinate. "Your turn Hickie."

"No. No! Not me sarge—"

"C'mere."

And sarge threw Hickie all the same. The last of the stabilized Huey's dipped its main rotor and cut Hickie in two at the waist. Bile splashed on the windshield leaving the pilot flying blind for just long enough that he too went into a spin. Happened at the exact instant the other Huey hit the ground with a *Crunch!*

Crash!

Now the last copter bit the dust!

Coons had himself another survey. A few stumblers here and there were on their feet. Many more were in pieces. Many of those pieces were still moving, many more were not. The tank and Jeep crew were still gakked and chunked themselves. Hickie, Dickie, Smithie, and Mox were MIA. Place was a mess of smoking smoldering calm.

"Well, you got your sacrifice, Count." The entrance to the complex was less than a hundred yards away. Sarge drove his second round into the breech and picked up the massive decapitated turret like a buckler. "Now I'm gonna make sure it wasn't in vain." He moved forward.

"Whoo! Sarge!" shouted Hickie and Mox in unison. They were all better, evidently.

Sarge turned to them. "Behind me, men—" But a barrage of wooden spikes flew over his shoulder. He ducked behind his turret shield. One of those flying spikes hit Hickie in the chest, another hit Mox the same. There were more of them projectiles flying though two were enough. Hickie and Mox were dead and stumbling. "Try to get your heads smashed, men! I'll see you on the other side..." And sarge was charging that entrance!

Over the tippy-top of his army-issued buckler, he could see HelCorp security pouring down the entrance steps and forming a phalanx. The spikes they'd been sending were fired from what had to be modified MM1 launchers. More flew as we speak, splintering off of sarge's turret.

As the soldier beat on, something tickled at his peripherals—to his right. He veered in that direction, strafing.

He got to the rear of the Jeep with the fifty-cal. He crouched. He rolled his buckler up along the driver side to let it lay there. He took the gas can from its mount, popped its top and angled it against a wheel to empty. Gas poured onto the grass in *glugalug* sounds. Then he assessed the ordnance, lifting a couple ammo containers to check their weight. Satisfied, he picked up the empty gas can and drove the fingers of his flattened palm into its top, peeling the side away.

Phalanx was no more than thirty yards out when...

Sarge popped up from behind the Jeep. The thin sides of his gas can were molded around his left shoulder and the broad sides were hanging to cover his chest and back. Spikes splintered off the front chest plate as he moved to where he lay the turret. He grabbed hold. He didn't need that turret as buckler anymore, he needed that turret as turret. He drove his fist into the primer of his last round and sent it smashing into the complex entrance. The shell exploded throwing door and agents in pieces all over and sarge was already on that fifty blasting through whoever was nearest to get to whoever was furthest.

More of those spikes splintered off his armor.

Shell casings were a' flyin'.

He was a force.

The man didn't flinch.

ii

The smoke had cleared. The gak had cleared.

Sarge peered over the fifty's sights. Threshold should be easy enough to cross in all its slack-jawed vacancy. What would they have in store for him when he crossed it? No time like the present to find out—

But the ninjas were on him! Four! HelCorp warriors in form-fitting stealth gear. Ninjatō were out and each had a sharpened jutte fastened to her right forearm. They were circling the sarge in that Jeep. He put his hands up.

Was it all over?

No!

He flicked a zippo and let it fall to the ground. The gas from that gas can went up in an instant, engulfing three of the four warriors, the sarge too.

The fourth had managed to flip backward out of the fire's perimeter. She couldn't tell her comrades from the sarge. They were all similarly engulfed. She swiped her sword at the flamer closest, severing the aorta. Flamer fell dead. She jumped high into the air, twisting and spinning herself into position to land behind the next nearest flamer. *Schwip!* And that flamer went down dead too. *Whishhh!* And the human torch that was the sarge bolted out from behind the Jeep. He was flying for the tank hull! The warrior readied two shuriken in her right hand and pulled back for the throw, only... *Boom!* The gas tank on the Jeep blew! Blew her back on her ass!

She rose slowly, brain rattled though not enough to keep her from her mission. Just as she was about to conclude the last of the flamers snuffed and the sarge in retreat... *Whoosh!* He streaked by her still afire! She swiped her ninjatō. He was too fast. *Whoosh!* There he went again! *Whoosh!* And he was right behind!

She spun!

But it was only a stumbler sarge had lit up. In a blink, she drove her Jutte into its head and the flaming stumbler was dead but now it was Mox resurrected! He was grimacing, still alight, baring fangs like he fancied her a meal. She jammed the jutte into his chest!

Grrrrr... He was a stumbler again so she drove the jutte into his brain.

Arrrr! He was the accursed! She pierced his chest!

Grrrrr... She stabbed his brain!

Arrrr! Chest!

Grrrrr... Brain!

Arrrrr! Chest!

But she was done. She observed this anomaly of a flamer confusedly a second then settled on something. She readied her sword as though dismemberment was her only option, then *Snap!* A charred sarge had come up behind her and broke her neck. She toppled.

He quickly tore off his armor and removed the army-issue tatters underneath. He tried extinguishing Mox' flames with the dinky cloth but it was hopeless. He toppled the soldier to roll the flames out of him.

"Lay low on the stumble, private." At this Mox writhed and groaned and groped from the ground. Sarge pinned the soldier down at the chest and took a couple grenades off his duty belt. He clipped them to his singed own. "I'll be back to collect you and the rest of the troops once this mission's complete."

He stood. He turned to face the complex. Then...

"*You*," he said.

"*You*," Barbara said back. She was holding a spike launcher on him.

"You shouldn't be here."

"Neither should you."

"You really gonna use that?" He gestured at the weapon.

"Look man, I just want to get cured."

He was some kind of confused at this—little angry even. "Cured? Why?"

But she shook her head. "I can't keep having this conversation."

"Those men in there are not the good guys," he said, protest in his tone.

"And your boss is?"

"My *boss* never would have done that..." He gestured over the annihilated multitude.

"They wouldn't even be here if he hadn't sent them."

"*I* failed to anticipate those Hueys. Not his fault."

"You *turned* are all such sycophants."

"We've both got his blood in our veins, civilian."

"At least I can—"

"What?"

"I never—"

"And *I* have those same dispositions. Maybe it's because I believe in the mission?"

"I just wanna get cured."

"And again, I ask you why."

"You really think these powers *so* wonderful?"

"It doesn't matter what I think."

"The life's inhuman."

Coons gestured at her launcher again. "Didn't get that way until you hooked up with HelCorp. I don't want to kill you."

"If I ever get to something killable again, you'd've been destroyed trying to stop it."

"Fair enough. I don't want to *hurt* you either."

"I just—"

He approached. "Come on, give me the gun." He had his hand out.

"Don't!" she demanded, raising it to her shoulder.

"Come on." And he kept moving.

"I'm telling you, don't..." She put the bead on him. "I just want..." His left hand was on the weapon. She fired! Quick as a flash, he put his right palm to his chest. The spike drove itself four-fifths of its length out that palm as he moved it away, keeping the projectile from his heart. Barbara pulled the trigger again but sarge was already pivoting to behind her. He balled a fist around the spike in-hand and, mid-spin, sent it into her back.

She cried out. Her eyes tracked downward to the bloody barb driven out her chest. There was a weakening, a fading. Her legs gave out from under and Coons caught her.

She looked back for him. The angle wouldn't allow her to see his face.

"I'm listening," he said, holding on.

"Good. Don't doddle about it will you? It'll really hurt." She was dead.

He laid her down. He was gentle about it, though once she was at rest, he moved quick. He picked up her spike launcher and had its sights on her before he stood.

He watched her. He watched her and he calmed. He calmed because she was calm. She wasn't yet a stum—

Rrrrrrr!

No hesitation. He fired, drove four spikes into her. Two in her shoulders and two above the knees. She was pinned.

The bits of her not immobilized wriggled. He went to the dead HelCorp swordswoman, took her ninjatō.

Standing at Barbara's feet, he raised the blade. "I'm sorry. It *will* be quick."

But he was overtaken! The sword was jarred loose and he was driven into the dirt. His attacker was off him so fast the creature had to be cursed.

"Don't you touch her!" I said, standing between Coons and our Barbara-kept.

"Then take her away from here."

"What?" I wasn't expecting that.

"Take her away from here. Resurrect her where you flee. You don't care about this place."

"What makes you so sure?"

"You cared, you'd have been right here with her. You don't want any cure."

"Yeah..." I stepped back and across Barbara. I looked down at the girl once again on the stumble. She seemed more pained this time, and it wasn't for what had her pinned. Coons was right. I didn't care about this place. I wanted to get north. I didn't want any cure... "But she did."

And with that, I struck a fighter stance.

"And she was worried the curse made us inhuman..." And with *that*, Coons moved in.

I took a swing. Missed. He easily outmaneuvered me. I took another. Same result. I was moving flash quick of course, but the sarge moved quicker. All the strength and speed and intelligence in the world cancel out at the level where all are cursed. It's down to the one thing that doesn't come prepackaged: knowledge: pure honed technique. And I had none.

Crack! Coons hit me with a backhand. He let me shake it off. "Take her away from here civilian."

"When she's better!" *Crack!* He hammered me again, this time with a roundhouse. I spun.

"*Better?* How's mortality better? She's been given a gift!"

Crack! Crack! And he sent me on my ass.

"Ain't her Birthday!" And I lunged! Sarge pivoted, throwing me off and away.

I landed prone next to Barbara. Coons approached and I scrambled to get into a propped position. I lay there a second, revealing what I had taken off his duty belt. He stopped. The pin was already pulled.

He shook his head as though disappointed. "You're only delaying the inevitable. That won't stop me."

I grinned. "It's not meant for you." I flipped away the spoon and turned to Barbara. Coons made a move. I was quicker. You'll thank me for this girl. Now open wide. And I stuffed the grenade into her snappin' maw.

"No!"

Boom! And Coons went flying!

When the dust settled it was me and Barbara, shoulder to shoulder, ready to rock.

Coons readied himself too and moved into the fracas.

Superior technique, indeed, is all that matters when both combatants are cursed. That's *both*. It doesn't work the same when it's two against one. Maybe a single mortal could take on two others of his disposition. He could stun one to isolate the other, say. Stunning would be about the only means or else his opponents would simply strike at once. Can't stun an accursed though. You can knock us down. You can knock us back. You can't knock us out.

Coons would go after me and Barbara would pounce. He'd go after Barbara and I'd do the same.

We fought in circles. I scooped up the ninjatō and Barbara the spike launcher. Coons would disarm Barbara and I'd have his arms off with the sword. Coons would take the sword and Barbara'd have him hobbled with spikes in his knees. He couldn't stun us. He couldn't stop us.

I slashed his legs off from under him and Barbara spun him going down.

He landed on his back and she drove four of those spikes into him in reciprocity. He was pinned, though not yet the stumbler. She put the sights over his heart. He stared up at her, indifferent.

"You'll be cured too," she promised.

"What makes you think it's a dis—"

She fired. Coons was dead.

iii

Barbara gave me a big hug and I back. Then she smacked me a good one across the chops!

"I hate Irish goodbyes, Ben. Hate 'em. My family was all about that and I couldn't stand it and we ain't even Irish!"

"It wasn't *you*, girl."

"Sure it wasn't. People jump out of airplanes at me all the time and it's because they love me to pieces!"

"*Pieces*," I chuckled.

"Shut up! What an idiot I was. You in that bathroom so long and I'm wracking my brain. *Maybe you ate too much dairy?* Like we can even get constip—"

"It wasn't you. I had to slip away from *them*."

"Them?"

"Come on, Barbara. They're real sweet with the cured and all, but when it comes to people like me, I'm *the most dangerous game*."

"Then take the cure, Ben."

"Barbara listen to yourself. It's like you know they'd'a' done it to me."

"They just want us safe—"

"From what? *With* what? This?" I gestured around at all the carnage.

"They were attacked!"

"And they pulled gunships and rocket launchers and ninjas out of their asses at the sight? That's a war chest. They're the aggressors, Barbara."

"Not all cursed are as chaste as you."

"He was." And I tilted in Coons' direction. "Ask yourself Barbara, they were feeding us that synthetic plasma from the second they caught up with us. Plenty more where that came from, they said. If they're so righteous, why not seek coexistence? Why not give the cursed the stuff and keep the thirst at bay?"

"It wouldn't work—"

"They never even tried!"

"Enough! What's the upshot here, Ben? *It's either you or them*?"

"No ultimatums, Barbara girl. A deal. I'll help you get the Count, help you get your cure, then you're helping me get my hands on the recipe for that juice. Then we leave HelCorp to whatever it is HelCorp does."

"What good will the plasma do you? My cure is your cure."

"Not necessarily. I got that covered."

"How?"

"I'll tell ya sometime."

"And after you re-*turn* yourself?"

"Come see me some night."

And she latched onto me again. Guess we had that deal...

Then things got real hot. "You feel that?" Then things got real bright. "He's near." we said in unison. "To the east." But we were shining brighter still! "He's moving." Like he knew we had him. Something caught my attention other than our gleaming. It was a different flicker, coming from Coons' pocket—burning out of it! It was a red ellipse. Looked like blondie's little trinket. "It's that!" I tried moving for it but we were hopelessly entwined, becoming one.

We *were* one!

We were the wolf!

The smell of the Count couldn't be stronger. He *was* on the move!

We loped over to that glowing red eye. We took it in our jaws, chomped it to dust—

❧ 13 ❧
THE CONFRONTATION
PART III

OCTOBER 8, 1968

They were coming for me!

Gilbert flew, but against the form of the canis, we were no match. They would be on us in moments if all we had was our speed and not tactics.

"To the hills, Gilbert!"

ii

We came up over the bank, the west of the valley walls. If we could only escape into a stream or forest below we would be well hidden—

It was all floodlight! What was this monstrosity? Another HelCorp? It was concrete, artificial. There would be no hiding in this place.

"Gilbert, what is—"

But of course the bloodhound was on us! Then one became two and the woman spoke.

"No point runnin' anymore, Count." Oh, she was a wily one!

"We'd smell ya a day away." And he, more so!

The game afoot, of foot, no more.

"And who might you be?" Ben asked my ward.

Gilbert only grinned at first. "What's that, master?" And my dear, he held me closer as though listening. Now he would address the hounds. "Master says you spoiled his plans."

"Yeah, well," Barbara said, "he spoiled a lot of people's plans. Tell him we know damn well he can talk."

"What now, my children?" I asked.

"We ain't your—"

"The very keepers of my heart, unaware of their bloodline?"

"*Keepers?* Thumpy?"

"Where is that little devil anyway?"

"Safe."

"Undoubtedly. You are adequate as far as servants of mine go." They stirred as though to protest, again. I would not give them that. "Now! What will be done in the immediate?"

"*Now?* We're all just gonna wait for the cavalry to arrive."

"Seems like you have us restless natives under complete control there sheriff..."

"Our ride then."

And there was a silence.

They stood, assessing, as though they did not already know the score.

Relax, my servants. You have us. We are all out of moves.

"Hold me higher," I said to Quassy and he did. "What is that monstrosity?" I was once again assessing that massive flood-lit concrete pad down in the valley.

"Would have been a shopping mall," Ben answered. "Came by it on my way over."

"Ugh! Whatever happened to Main Street USA? Anything for the insatiable, eh? They need climate control for their buying buying buying? Eating eating eating!"

"Your lineage goes back to a literal castle," Ben said, "Show some respect."

He was a wily one indeed, and defiant! Gilbert got noticeably agitated at the defiant one's imperative. He was squeezing and compressing the fabric of my vessel. Bah! Of no concern. I studied Ben of a strange curiosity, the kind provoked by a familiarity not granted in mere acquaintance.

"Yeah, I know a' you, Count," he said. He turned to that massive complex. Talked to it really and not to me. "You were living in fancy penthouses and lavish hotels before you lammed it, before they tore you down in Chicago. You really ask for a guillotine after the FBI found out what they got?" He didn't let me answer. "What was it: maid services, in-suite laundry, theater, radio, private elevator, central heating, gourmet food and drink—not that you ate... All for you, a man smaller then than in that hat."

"Are you going to let him talk to you this way, master?"

Unfortunately, Gilbert, there is something about these two. The first to keep my heart, yes, though selected while predisposed to the wretchedness. For that, they've come to possess a force impenetrable when it comes to my powers—of my deduction AND my will.

"Well, I don't have any such impediments..." And he dropped me, launched himself at the defiant one.

"No, Gilbert!" And Barbara stepped closer to Ben. There was a gleaming. She intercepted Gilbert, redirecting him in mid-air. Sent him up and flying down the hill. My, these two, neither one alone would be a match for my ward and yet together they *is* god. Should I have informed my Quassy of this before his flight? He will be fine. I must focus on this Ben while I have the chance.

I glanced up at my interlocutor from where Gilbert had dropped me. "Strike a little too close to home, trucker?"

"Could say that..."

"Parents clock-punching little piggies? Lumbering down to the trough?" I'd point to the mall but I had nothing to point with. I'd use Gilbert, but he was still climbing.

"You know..." Ben shook his head. "People like you, you scoff, you resent. Worst case scenario for the folk use these places is three loaves a bread a week instead of two."

"Three loaves are more than they need."

"And what is necessary for quality of life? What is *necessity*, Count?"

"You wish for me to get philosophical? Even with my blood flowing through your veins, your mind couldn't take it. As for the former question, they don't need three loaves when one will sustain them—"

"I said for quality of life, not mere metabolism."

"And what do *you* think they need for that Ben? Barney Fife on the TV? A little ham from a tin once in a while to liven up their Wonderbread? Then why the stockpile? The gluttony? An arena that size, full to the brim, would have moved two hundred thousand dollars in goods in a day."

"Man, you can't see the narrowing slices for the growing pie."

"Pie! One more thing these piglets get too much of."

"Goddamn it I can't stand people like you."

"Like I said, a little too close to home? You should be so lucky as to be in the company of people like *me*."

"I know your kind."

"Prove it."

"A woman, a poet. A poet all her life. Never sold a damn thing. Never had to. Her daddy was rich, invented some sort of compass they use in missiles now. She'd luxuriate. She'd pretend to read her Proust and her Balzac and her Dos Passos. She'd pretend to read her Shakespeare and scoff at Rod Serling on the TV, oblivious to the contradiction. What'd she think, if she lived in Shakey's time she wouldn't be turning her nose up just because he wrote what the people wanted? *Lurid, trite, pedestrian,* she'd say *then* like she says *now*. And make no mistake, she scoffed for no other reason than the people didn't. *The people* being anyone beneath her and *anyone beneath her* being anyone not of her daddy's standing. She despised whoever she believed to be down there and she especially despised whoever she believed to be about halfway down there. See, they were too low to be redeemed but could afford her trash purple prose doggerels and didn't want 'em, any of 'em. Her daddy's ilk didn't want 'em either, see, but it's funny how the people at the top always beg down never across... The middle definitely didn't want 'em and to the poet it was a *how dare you lick at my feet and not anoint them* kinda situation. It consumed her. Nothing but venom in her by forty. I knew that catastrophe of a poet well."

"Let me guess, your *mama* cleaned the poet's house? Took you with her when you were on summer vacation?"

"Knew another guy, made Hollywood movies. Made what was, by his estimation, rubbish. Was what the people wanted though. Made him millions. Then he makes what is, by another of his estimations, the great American novel on celluloid. Didn't earn him a dime. Like the poet, he blames the masses for their lack of taste and not the fact that his 'most honest of meditations on the human condition' was more fantasy than his *men in the rubber monster suits* movies. I know your kind alright."

"I'm curious, how would a person of your stature come to know people as sophisticated as you describe? Who were they? I must know. Oblige me, my dear." But he only turned away to face that valley again. "At least tell me their names."

"*Mom* and *dad*."

I sniffed, grinned enough my left canine emerged. "You are not lying. You are an interesting one."

"And you're testing me."

iii

Helsing had shown up along with his men. He wanted to be at the site of my apprehension. This would be the first serious development for the company while under his leadership. His first success. His men held their spike launchers on Gilbert at present, as Helsing assessed the situation. He wore tinted glasses despite the night.

"Where is he?" he asked. "In there?" He meant in my vessel though only inferred. Gilbert had quite thoughtfully lowered my visor. Helsing moved to us, lifted the gold, did so unmoved by my ward's protective demeanor. "Ah, beautiful!" he said. "So you are the little head that's started this war? We haven't yet met. You and my uncle have." He waited. I would not speak yet. "What? Bat got your tongue?" He was laughing before he even finished the line... "Ha! You must excuse me, I couldn't resist."

"He has no interest in you," Gilbert assured.

"Oh dear," Helsing feigned. "But he has a real interest in you, I see? His most trusted of confidants? Well, allow me to show you just how much he cares." And he snapped a finger.

One of the agents put his spike launcher onto Gilbert's chest. Another reached for me. Gilbert resisted, held onto me fast.

Let them have me, my ward. All need not be lost despite this one defeat.

"Master?"

Do it.

And the agent with my vessel in-grasp ripped me away. The other pulled his launcher off Gilbert while keeping him in his sights.

"Hold the Count on us," Helsing ordered. "I want him to bear witness." He returned to Gilbert. "Your master didn't tell you did he? Of your role in this?"

"I am Quassy, servant to his majesty. Apprentice to Count Dracul."

"A mere apprentice?" Helsing chuckled.

"I am to be fully turned."

"Turned? You think you're going to be turned. That's nice. The boy's an optimist. You actually believe he is going to *complete* you?"

"When worthy.

"Oh, you're worthy."

"Don't listen to him, Gilbert!"

"Ah, he speaks!" Helsing fired at me. "Too late..."

"Do not listen, Quassy."

"Yes, master."

But Quassy faltered. I failed this test myself when my time came...

"He was never going to turn you," Helsing said. "He was only ever going to kill you."

"Master?"

"Don't, Gilbert."

"I—"

"Yeah," Helsing said. "He needs you dead to get that body of his back. Part of the whole reformation rite... *And so we shall grind to seasoning, that which is born of the father, in the commingling of the father*, so says the liturgy of the *sárx mía*."

A tear fell from Gilbert's eye. "Is this true?"

I could not lie. "Yes, my ward. What I begat, will be sacrificed in my rebirth."

"And that's you, little buddy."

"How could you, master? After all..." But he could not reminisce. He only examined himself, gesturing across his form, ashamed. "A mere accident, so of no worth? Or, no accident because your discarding of me *is* my only worth?" He sank.

I looked away from him. I couldn't bear to do otherwise. My averting left me fixed on this Helsing, however. I could smell his revelry. I nevertheless chose the image of disgust not of grief. I would address my Quassy a last time, though I would face my enemy in so doing.

"Gilbert, are you ready for your final test? Do you believe yourself worthy?" He was kneeling in the grass. More tears fell. He shook his head. "Don't think, because I am no longer worthy of you, dear Quassy, that the inverse must apply. Hate me if you must, in how you carry yourself from here, only, do not throw all you've achieved away. Complete your *doctrina*. Show so many more than me, that you truly are worthy."

And with that, I had him! A last time...

"Yes, master." He rose.

"Gilbert?"

"Yes, master?"

"Show him the dagger."

Gilbert reached into his coat.

Helsing's men readied their weapons. The boss waved them off.

My ward slid the artifact out of the sheath at his ribs.

"Show him the inscription."

He held the steel hilt out to Helsing. He twisted it, slowly. What came into view was:

Азъ ни хощу и самъ искушати исправити сие.
Подписахъ: Гералдъ Сїмонъ Їамесонъ.

"Is that of significance to you, Van Helsing?" And just as I suspected, the ancestor only surveyed in silence, embarrassment even. "Your great great uncle would certainly understand the meaning."

He grew uneasy. I noticed, Gilbert noticed, so too did Ben and Barbara. And believe you me, Helsing noticed their noticing. He took his gloves off.

"Give me that!" He wrenched the dagger from my Quassy.

He twisted it and twisted it again. I could tell by his whispers he was reading the Slavonic as Romanian Cyrillic. It was senseless. I couldn't let him embarrass himself any further.

"*I, Vlad Voivod, son of Dracul, by the mercy of God, of the land of Wallachia!*"

"Impossible!" Helsing insisted.

"I assure you, no." I looked to my ward. "I assume now, dear Gilbert, you will excuse me my insisting on our little excursion?"

"Yes, master."

"Well what the hell does all that mean?" Barbara asked.

"It means, my dear, that dagger is of my creation. I rolled that steel. I forged it in my own crucible. I *begat* that artifact perfectly fit for my *commingling*." Gilbert grinned at this, not a dignified expression in my opinion, not a negation of his readiness either. "You are worthy," I said to my ward. "You are turned."

His eyes went from the familiar silver to gold.

And Helsing shook his head, inspected that inscription a last time. He no longer smelled of embar— "Whelp!" he said, flipping the dagger to angle its hilt outward. "Congratulations on your turn little buddy. But since we have this now..." He held the weapon out to Gilbert as though an offering. "We don't need you." And a wooded projectile shot out of the sleeve of Helsing's blazer. It struck my ward in the chest.

"No!"

Ben and Barbara lunged like of instinct. The agents admonished them yet didn't threaten. The admonishment stifled the pair regardless, if only due their confusion.

"Master," Gilbert said, reaching for me as he fell.

He was kneeling once more, making a cradling gesture below his wound as if begging me to remove the piercing. He gasped. It came across as a shrieking wail, though it was a gasp, his death throe—*our* death throe.

There will be no pain, dear friend.

"Yes, master."

And he collapsed, gone.

iv

He was dead. He was not like me: a heart to the right. He was not like them: able to turn to stumbler once pierced then back again. He was pure. He was gone.

"Well, he's gone," Helsing said.

"You have no idea what you have wrought," I warned.

"Get him out of that thing."

And they pulled me out of my vessel. They tossed it onto Gilbert's corpse. They had a second container waiting. Another of those ornate oddities—the kind with the cross of the hasps.

"You could have cured him," Barbara said.

"No," Helsing assured, "Not one who's a direct descendant. He had to die."

Not true, I insisted as they lowered me into that box. *What of Mina?*

"Yeah!" Barbara said.

"What?" Helsing asked.

"I mean…" Barbara gathered. "That's not true. Your uncle, he saved Mina. She was a direct—"

"*The keepers of his essence—the dual—will have him in proximity,*" Helsing recited. "You led us to him. You've served your only purpose. Don't make me rethink my offer."

"You said—" Ben reached out to Barbara, squeezed her arm. She quieted… For about a second! "You said it was in gratitude."

"My dear, I say a lot of things."

They spun the hasps for the lock into place. The cross would make me ache though not alter my will. The lock clicked shut and Helsing reached for me.

His uncle must be spinning in his grave.

"What about your uncle? His vision? Do you not want to honor him—"

"Alright!" And a burst of ultraviolet covered Ben and Barbara! They were brought to their knees. Helsing's *modus operandi* it seems. "Let me tell you something about that doddering old fool and his legacy," he teased, losing his accent in the process. "We need the name, the brand! That's it. But all the name-brand recognition in the world won't protect us from breach of contract, not after this fiasco!" He sat me on the ground in front of the pair. He put a foot on my casket. "Just when I thought we'd vanquished this disease for good..." He gave me a little boot. "Clot sucker goes and burns a curse across the sky! All *brought to you by* HelCorp®!"

"It's more than a brand," Ben labored. "Your lineage. You're a Van..."

Helsing stepped over me and closer to my keepers. Another spring-loaded pike shot out from the sleeve of his coat, only this time it landed in his hand. He lowered himself to the wily one. "My! Name!" he said punctuating each syllable with a stab to Ben's heart. "Is! B! Z! Har! Row!" And Ben was dead. "BZ Harrow!" he reiterated. "Feels good to dispense with all pretenses."

"The cure..." Barbara tried.

"Ha!" He recommenced with pattern. "You! Want! The! Cure!" he stabbed. "Take! The! Cure!" And Barbara was dead. Harrow stood, took out a handkerchief and wiped the spike clean. He released the cloth, daintily, and it fluttered down onto Barbara's face. "Burn them."

But he wouldn't see this culmination. He moved for the HelCorp van with me once again in-grip—his sole fixation, his treasure. He intended to begin his experimentation immediately. He got into the vehicle, shut the door, and it sped away.

The agents left-behind were reaching for their flash-lights when they heard a rustling. They clicked them on simultaneously, shone them downward.

Ben and Barbara had returned as stumblers.

"Whoa, I didn't know they did that," said the agent holding his flashlight to a launcher.

Bang! Bang!

"Well, now you do," said the other holding his flashlight to a smoking pistol.

Ben and Barbara were back to accursed. Ben had started to move but Barbara took his hand in hers, squeezed. They went still.

"Alright, let's light 'em up."

❧ 14 ❧

THE PAST, REVIVED

OCTOBER 9, 1968

Another day, another pyre. We burned. And burned... And it was really the only truly painful thing an accursed ever had to endure. Barbara would disagree. She felt dismemberment had a horror to it all its own. I told her she'd never been dismembered so what would she know? She told *me* Thumpy told *her*. With what? Sign language? I only yammer because, like I told *you*, we burned.

And burned...

"I think they're gone," she said, smoldering.

"You have a look?"

"Couldn't not. My eyelids burned off."

"Ew."

"Last thing I saw were taillights... Before my eyeballs exploded."

"*Gyechh!* Gross, girl!"

"You're not burnt the same?"

"Nah. Must be your mascara."

We rolled off the pyre. Truth be told, all that made up

the mound beneath us was Gilbert. Poor bastard. We rolled a bit more in the grass, putting ourselves out.

We were already healing in the moonlight.

ii

So the two of us lay there on that hill, waiting for integrity. Fires were out. Stars were out. Could be worse. We'd be naked again when we fully reformed. Not the greatest inconvenience this night. Not an inconvenience at all in a world lacking prudishness. That was certainly Barbara's and my world now, considering how the curse filled us with such undue pride! The mortal world *was* a world of prudes, however—prudes *and* stumblers *but* prudes. We'd have to get some clothes where we'd be going.

"So, what now?" She asked.

"Get dressed."

"I meant after that."

"You want the cure. I want the recipe. Nothing's changed."

"We just storm the castle?"

"Why not?" I asked.

"They'd hit us with their ultraviolet the second we set foot. That'd be that."

"Well then, we'll have to come up with a plan a little better than *just walk through the front door.* Good news is, you skulked around inside and I skulked around outside. You know the castle. I know the kingdom. Let's pool that knowledge and get to work."

"I barely got through the door and the Count's forces attacked. I saw those lights, launchers, and ninjas. I saw some helicopters they *used* to have. What did you see on the outside?

"Trees."

"Yikes."

"I guess that's our knowledge pooled. Time to get to work."

"Where do we start?"

"How about that mall?"

"What are we gonna do there?"

"Some shopping."

iii

The National Civil Defence Council today urged the public to remain vigilant despite no sightings of infected outside of the northern midwest. The infected, though continuing to grow in number—amassing in populations comparable to small cities at times—all seem to be moving toward a single location in the Great Lakes region. 'This is no reason to let down your guard,' said the head of the council, 'as the radiation is still present in the atmosphere and will infect all who become deceased...

"I guess we're where the action is," I said to Barbara.

"Pretty desolate."

"Well, you know, the 'news'..." And I shrugged.

Communities on the east shore of Lake Michigan are at greatest risk of encountering stumblers...

"...Blown up by 30mm artillery..."

"Gimme a hand, will ya?"

And she did, and we latched onto the back of a steamroller sitting next to the mall's foundation. I pulled and Barbara followed my lead. Between the two of us, we made short work of inertia. The machine was moving fine.

If you should see a stumbler, the first action you should take is—

And the am radio I thought was sitting on the access

step went under the drum. It must have toppled in our jerking the roller into motion.

"Nothing we don't already know," Barbara said.

"Hold it! I think we're good."

I moved to the front of the drum, scratched at the gravel. Didn't stop until my fingers hit tin. I took the handle of a buried lunch box and pulled it out of the grit.

"What's that?" Barbara said, moving closer. She near tripped on the oversized coveralls she was wearing.

What'a'ya want! Only articles of clothing we could find. Not a bad find for an abandoned construction site either.

"Goddamnit!" she said.

"What?"

"Not exactly functional." She was tugging at the loose fabric. "Worse than those fatigues…"

"You're looking at me like it's my fault." She kept looking at me like it was my fault. "Hey, don't blame me for the fact it's the men of the world doing all the fighting and the building. We get everything back to normal, far as I'm concerned, you gals can have at it."

"Us gals 'have at it', there'll be no fighting."

"HelCorp agent! Behind you!"

She spun a one-eighty, fists cocked, ready to rock. I laughed.

"You scoff," she said, turning back. "But I didn't start this. They drew first blood."

"Fair enough. C'mere." She did. I held the box out to her, flipped the top open. "Took as much as I could from that mobile lab of theirs."

"Beautiful," she said, real pleased.

"We'll still have to ration it. For now…" I picked up a couple vials, handed her one. "Bottoms up."

Beeheeeyewteeful!

Now that we were fed and clothed, it was time to get down to brass tacks.

"What's the plan?" she asked, like she knew what I was thinking.

I raised an eyebrow. "Who on this earth knows more about the Count—"

"The Count."

"Let me finish. Who on this earth knows more about the Count *and* HelCorp combined?"

"Combined? Can we combine *knowers* too?"

"No."

"Haven't the foggiest."

"Who on this earth has more reason than anyone—than us even—to want to force a reckoning onto the Count and Company®?"

"I thought you said *on this earth*."

"Oh, he's *on* this earth." I took something else out of the lunch box. Showed her the crimson vial.

"That what I think it is?"

"Your thumpy little friend was real insistent I have this." I grinned. "Just a drop'll do ya."

"*Righty*." And she grinned right back. "Just a drop'll do ya." Then she set her sights on that complex, in its direction anyway, over these hills and across these plains. She was wistful about it and I knew why.

"Barbara?"

"Yeah?"

"Take my hand." And she did. "You feel him?" She squeezed. "Day we do this and either we don't feel this, or you're cured, we stop. Until then..."

And she had that grateful gleam she gets that made you glad you were keepin' on.

"We should get going," she said. "It's a long way—" She stifled. "You're not ready to leave."

"There's one more thing."

"I know."

I picked up a large concrete block and a length of rebar —held the rebar like a pen. "He was a great man in life, Barbara."

iii

Etched into the concrete was:

Here lies

Lieutenant Gilbert Mandrake, USAF

May 31, 1930 — October 2, 1968

First Man on the Moon

That block would have to do as headstone. His EVA helmet would have to do in lieu of flowers.

"Do you have anything you'd like to say?" I asked Barbara.

She thought a second, then, *"Vita mutatur, non tollitur."*

I gave a solemn bow. I put a hand on Gilbert's helmet. "Rest in peace lieutenant." Barbara took my other hand. I backed away from the grave, the vestiges of my gesture lingering in reach. She set out walking only to stop. I held her firm, anchored, letting go of her once she understood the inertia. "G—give me a minute," I said. "I'll catch up." She smiled faintly at this. She kept on.

I considered that headstone a moment more, the mound of earth and rocks, that helmet. He didn't ask for this. If we ever got out of all of this, if Barbara got her cure, if we could ever learn to deal with those stumblers, I'd be sure to let the right people know what happened to this man, of who he was before experiencing the misfortune of crossing paths with that bastard Count.

iv

Listen, don't let anyone ever tell you I'm lacking in patriotism, alright. The 4th of July is more than hot dogs and fireworks to me, always has been. But goddamn it if I'll ever hear the expression *on American soil* ever again and not feel an itch all the way up and down my spine, up the crack of my a—

I digress...

Back home, the constraint that an accursed had to sleep in the soil of his homeland meant we could still lie on some sort of mattress at least. We need only be in a basement or somewhere similarly sunk.

On an ocean liner to the Netherlands, that dirt *was* the mattress! For six days!

v

We stood at the rim of the volcano, the summit of *De Berg*, at the entrance to the mausoleum.

"I can still feel it all the way up my—"

"Stop whining," she said, "I slept in the same dirt."

"We're flying home is all I'm saying..."

"Where's the door?"

I assessed the stone tomb, not to find what Barbara was searching for. I assessed to confirm what I had studied. Indeed, the vestige consisted of a single wall. The remainder was built into the volcano's edge.

"There isn't one."

"Then how do we—"

"We knock." I cocked my fist.

Boom!

The stone facade crumbled. We entered.

"And the sarcophagus?" she asked.

"Further in."

The entrance was built at the opening of a pyroduct, a long-dormant passage that carried—and was formed by— molten lava. The doctor would be at its end.

"How do you know so much about all this?" Barbara asked as we worked our way down the stippled tubule of walls perfectly ironical: of a demonic meringue of tortured proboscis somehow agape, screaming in warning. Damn this night-sight of mine—

"Ben."

"Yeah?"

"How do you know all this?"

I chuckled. I appreciated her interests, and for more than the usual human—ha, *human*—for more than the usual reasons. I appreciated the distraction because if these walls were to ever give in on us... I mean, any mere mortal could at least look forward to a quick death. Even an eventual death would be preferable because a couple of accursed like us would be buried alive in here for all etern—

"Ben!"

"*Ahem!* We all have our attunements Barbara. You to the li'l demon, us together to the big demon, and me... to *something*. I felt it strongest when we were in that lab of HelCorp's. It wasn't talking to me. It was informing me, like an education. I feel like I have a map to this place behind my eye."

"Well, how much further?"

"Seven-hundred and thirty-two paces."

"Your map's got a weird scale."

"About a half a mile."

"So, a ways?"

"We could take bigger steps—" And that was a bad joke, but that wasn't why I stifled myself. "You hear that?"

"No."

"I hate to do this to you Barbara, but ease your stride. These ducts are quite fragile."

"You mean, walk even slower?"

I shrugged an apology as I rounded the corner and into... the crypt?

"This shouldn't be here."

"Maybe whoever, or *whatever* sent that map screwed up?"

"You mean I got a bum attunement?"

"Who cares, we're here."

"Easy for you to say. Worst case scenario for you, you spend immortality in stimulating companionship with that torso—"

"Let's get the lid off this thing." And she gripped the stone cover of what turned out to be a humble little sarcophagus. She was raring to go. I wasn't. Something felt off and it wasn't for any attunement or crumbling conduit. "Come on, Ben. Help me out here."

"Barbara, would you go back if you could?"

She put her hands flat on the top of the coffin, leaned closer like she was entertaining me though with a short fuse. "To what?"

"To what we both agreed was not nothing?"

"Oh Ben, if that bum attunement stuff's got you rethinking the whole immortality thing, we can talk about it after—"

"Not me."

"Then who?"

"Him." I pointed downward. "You ever feel deprived of it?"

"I wasn't dead long enough to get accustomed."

"Maybe he was... *is*."

"He *was* as ascetic as they come," she said. "He devoted every minute of his life to fighting the accursed. If anything, death deprived him of that.

"He was an ascetic in life. That didn't mean he'd give up peace in death. For all we know, that was the reward."

"Then he'll reclaim it once the Count's dead."

"That's *if* the Count's death breaks the curse."

"It will."

"We need to be prepared for the possibility it won't—"

"It worked on Mina. He killed the Count, the curse was broken."

"That only brings up another concern."

"Oh my god Ben!"

"You said it yourself: he devoted his life to fighting the accursed. Now we're gonna turn him into the very evil he spent his whole life fighting?"

"Any other ethical dilemmas? *If you had a time machine would you go back and kill baby Dracula?*

"You gotta take this seriously!"

"It's academic at this point! He's not even back yet."

"And we're one drop away from turning thought experimentation into human experimentation."

"No, we're not, because I'm *suuuuure* you've got a million more things to hash out before—"

"Oh, get on with it you two!" And he flung the lid off the coffin.

"It's empty," Barbara said. And it was. It was empty because the man before us, our impatient adjudicator, was...

"Abraham Van Helsing, pleased to make your acquaintance." He extended his hand. "Gentleman and gentlelady." We both marveled at the guy. He noticed. "Permit me." And he lowered his cowl. "Yes... Yes... How long have I had these little marks?" They were at the main artery to his left throat, two little wounds, white with red centers. Looked familiar... "And the answer: sixty-eight years. The century turned and so did I."

"W—Who got the drop on you? You of all people... I—I'm sorry, that was rude."

"Oh, it is fine," he assured. "And there was no *dropping*, if I have your euphemism. You were right about me being an ascetic. You were wrong about me fighting the accursed. I fight evil. Certain of the accursed are evil, and I am one of few who can vanquish the accursed. It was only natural, then, that it be my privilege. In truth, the very notion of *fighting the accursed* evokes a cruelty: they're cursed, they've already fought a battle and lost. You were right about my asceticism, however."

"Not all accursed are evil?"

"No. Take for instance the generous soul I commissioned to turn *me*."

"Who?"

"Of no relevance."

"You commissioned it? To what end?"

"Ah, an antinomy of equivocation is what you desire? Because that is what the two of you will get: evil has not the reward of eternal sleep, why should I? To *what end*? To *no end*: to live to fight another day so long as that day is the sequel to any ever christened a tomorrow."

"But you can't fight from this hell."

"No. Though perhaps I am not yet needed in the fight? Even if I was always so disposed?"

"Like, you're on call? I don't see any phone around here."

"I have remained in this conduit living off my concoction for nearly three generations." He pulled a wooden crate from a recess in the channel wall behind him, set it in the coffin. He took an empty vial from it and showed us. Barbara and I exchanged a quick glance as he recommenced his account. "I told myself, if any ever made the pilgrimage, that's how I'd know I must return to the world. Not before then." He fixed his gaze on me. "You were prepared to take those additional steps. For that, you are no mere pilgrim."

"So you—"

"Yes."

"So you know, because we're here—"

"That a formidable evil awakes, the scheme already afoot."

"You can't know the whole of it—"

"I have my attunements as well, my boy. I have my intuitions in addition. I have always had my intuitions. In fact, all I had were those intuitions the day—"

"You killed my master!" And Gilbert leapt out of the shadows at the doctor!

Van Helsing merely pivoted, throwing his attacker over the coffin. "He crossed a line."

A rumble emanated from the channel wall where Gilbert had landed.

"The structure—"

"You'll do it again!" Gilbert insisted, pulling himself up by the inside of the sarcophagus.

"He crossed that line *again*," Van Helsing reminded. "Or, what else explains you?"

Gilbert's rage only grew. He pulled closer that wooden crate. He smashed it to pieces and from them selected a sizable enough splinter. He took it in-grip but Van Helsing moved faster than perception. He leapt over the coffin and had Gilbert's spike, holding it to the disciple's throat.

"You are well fed," Van Helsing said. "I ran out of my concoction a quarter-century ago. I'm more an ascetic than you'll ever know. For that, I am not a trifle." Though he eased up with the weapon. "That said, we have more pressing concerns than your master and his myriad of iniquities." He shoved Gilbert away and into the wall again.

More rumbles.

"This conduit won't take much more—"

"You brought him back?" Barbara said to me, pointing at a Gilbert contemplating his next move.

"He was duped, manipulated," I said. "He also has a direct link to the Count. That's a fifth column. Gets us closer to your c—" I turned to Gilbert. "To Harrow." Even more rumbles. "We've got bigger problems than—"

"You buried me alive!" Gilbert shouted.

"You weren't alive yet."

"You buried me alive *eventually*!"

"Only up to your lips... We needed a head start ya goddamn bloodhound! But we really need to focus on the conduit—"

"Lookit, Barbara said. "We're all cursed around here, right? We've got that much in common? And we can all admit HelCorp's gotta be stopped?" We all sorta nodded at the floor as the integrity of everything around us continued to lessen. "Well good!" she said. "Put the Count and cures and the semantics of live burials out of your heads for now, until those are bridges we have no choice but to cross. In the immediate, we work together to shove that HelCorp temple up BZ Harrow's misappropriating imposter asshole so far it'll flush the whole turd toilet into Lake Michigan. Kay?"

We gestured at each other as though to suggest the proposal reasonable—oddly phrased, but reasonable.

"Who's BZ Harrow?" Gilbert ask—

"We are in agreement then?" the doc said. "Good! We are leaving!" And he launched the lid of his sarcophagus into the ceiling causing a cave-in.

"Why the fu—"

"I must remain *dead*." And he pushed Barbara and me together and we burst with light once more. "Fly from here!" he said, and we were already transforming. He grabbed onto Gilbert and this yielded the same luminescence! "Fly, servant!"

The conduit began swallowing itself. The demon stipple was collapsing from bowel to gullet. There would be no reversing it.

❦ 15 ❧

THE RESEARCH PART I

OCTOBER 15, 1968

Mutatis mutandis.

Thank god all was left to the movement of the fates.

The dagger worked the charm. Exactly what was needed to assuage the reluctance of my heart: a fact of being in separation for as long as we had.

The remaining steps of the rite were carried off without a hitch—as these things left to forces outside of human control tend to be. If only all that was required of any would-be puppet master was the laying out of his ingredients and the saying of some magic words, perhaps then we'd have been saved from his primordial tangle of strings: his good intentions.

I was whole. I would not have been if it weren't for those wonderful movements beyond physical mechanism and man's volition.

Oh these mortals, they can take it apart, they certainly can't put it back together.

Speaking of such analyses...

ii

"Well then, let's just focus on your life *post* turning."

She sat in her chair with her pad and her pen and a host of other materials suited to her role. She sat outside my cell: a lattice of empty crosses.

I stood within this lattice. *How could I bear it?* you wonder. Understand, the mesh did not pain me as, altogether, crosses at these angles make diamonds. Now, should I attempt to smash through these walls, the disintegration *would* make crosses once more, and that would not be pleasant.

They had thought of so many of such means of containing me. Some I knew of. Some I did not. It was truly an embarrassment of inflictions. So many I couldn't help attending to them a good proportion of her dissection. A *truly embarrassing* distraction in addition. I must try to keep my focus...

"I did not say I was turned."

"So you weren't?" she asked.

"I did not say that either."

"There have never been any known cases of the emergence of an accursed *sui generis*. No spontaneous conversions, no births from the non-accursed."

"Nobody has ever borne witness to the emergence of matter from vacuum..."

"Are you saying you're eternal?"

"I am neither natural nor artificial."

"So, eternal?"

"There is more to creation than matter, energy, and

mind. It need not have always *been* simply because neither your theories nor your will explain it."

She tried to redirect me. "At the point of your turning or, perhaps, subsequent to your first awareness of your being accursed, what were your attitudes in regard to things lost, what may have been lost—your inner states, feelings, pleasures, things external to you, your relationships? What changed? Do you miss any of it?"

"Ah, my dear, what a mouthful. And to what end? The exploiting of such patent semantic trickery: *let us avoid talk of the past, let us talk of what the historian espouses at present...*

"And you won't be fooled?"

"Maybe in a past life..."

"Your withholding of facts about yourself, as well as your opaqueness of language in sharing what little you share, as a tactic, is telling in itself. You betray motives, hence character, in your attempts at hiding these very motives. Now, I don't tell you this to suggest having one-upped you, only to help you. To help you understand that your transparency would be a far less taxing means of informing me of what I'll inevitably infer."

"My *attempts* at caging my past could always be play-acting, to entertain you."

"I'd know."

"Not even I can suss out an intent to deceive, in even the most ardent of dullards whose heads I find myself in."

"You don't have my training."

"Well, don't keep it all to yourself. Enlighten me."

"Absolutely. It's textbook. When psychopaths lie, they tend to—"

"Psychopath! You think something like a whimsy of indifference drives me to do what I do? Or better, is the lubricant of my will in my subsistence? Let me enlighten you my dear. You have those of your ranks hopelessly dependent: mind and body crippled until they feed. Those who, unlike me, can divest themselves of their thirst by sustained will and fortitude—but who never do. Imagine any of your opium addicts thirsting for blood like they do the poppy. Would they be half as chaste as I? Scale this lust by a factor of centuries and you have an idea of my restraint though it is only the *thought* never the *sentiment* attesting to the power of the thirst. You are impoverished in this regard. You couldn't possibly feel the tensions within me to truly understand those tensions. Pray you never do."

"I—I'm sorry. Not only was my revealing such judgements unprofessional, so too are the prejudices underlying them."

"Ha! Now *you* deceive. Provocation is your only window."

"Not when the patient is aware of such a tactic."

"You had no awareness of *my* awareness until this instant."

"True." And then she redirected once more. "What would you ultimately like to get out of these sessions of ours?"

"To ensure things remain purely masturbatory."

"Would you like me scared?"

"No."

"Then why do you sit in the shadows? It is not day."

"Why does *he* sit in the shadows?" I meant that skunk Harrow, sitting barely beyond the analyst though outside the glow of her reading lamp. "To be merely the observer and not participant preserves authenticity in our subjects. Though, unlike him, I do provoke a fear—and a far greater one when in the dark. That is enough to taint my subjects."

"And yet you risk doing that now? In your dark?"

"Depending on the subject, this is not always unwelcome…"

"Do you wish for him to be scared?"

"No my dear, I wish for him to be *even more* scared."

And I lunged! And immediately I was hit with a blast of ultraviolet. I could see him, behind the scrambling psychiatrist trying to lift herself off the floor. I was right. About everything.

But I collapsed. Despite the light being sufficient for my impotence, they'd cured my clothes in essence of wolf's bane besides. They had gone out of their way to overdetermine my helplessness. I was useless butfor my verbiage. Though I would certainly not hesitate to wield that…

"Those glasses you wear," I said to Harrow. "They are not for this glare, are they?" I focused on the psychiatrist gathering her things, hastily, seeking to flee. "You're not rushing to put anything similar on her after all, and not for a lack of chivalry." He didn't flinch, though he stank. "Take them off. Look into my eyes. Test your will."

And he slithered away, not even holding the door for the poor girl still blind and scrambling.

iii

"You hate me, and yet you wish for more of me."

"If something impure is needed to preserve that which is pure, then so be it."

"Will you make the same sacrifice?"

But he once again withdrew, receded into the darkness.

They had sat me under a halo of those lights, under a robe of wolf's bane, under cloak of garlic, in a chair amidst a host of medical apparatuses. A tube exited my left arm, another entered my right. An agent sat next to me, similarly disposed, the two of us in our chairs in perfect symmetry.

They drew blood. A pouch hanging above me filled, as did another above the agent. Once of a desired volume, the drawn blood in the pouches took to emptying, only out of a secondary tube. My bile entered the agent's vein, and his hemoglobin entered mine.

There was no stench, not that I could rely on my senses in this state. I could, however, see the representations of the agent's vitals on the machinery next to him. Pulse at seventy-one, blood pressure never climbing above one-fifteen over seventy-five.

"You are a brave one," I said. He didn't flinch. "How I do wish you'd gaze upon me that I might know you are fortified in addition... and not merely stupid." Again, he didn't flinch. "You know, erectile dysfunction is a side-effect of the curse..." Nothing. "Ah, fortified."

The technicians began withdrawing our tubes. I guess the experiment was complete.

"Get up, agent!" Harrow shouted this as he marched over. The agent stood at attention. "How do you feel?"

"Honestly sir, the same."

"Your hand."

And he extended it to Harrow and Harrow cut into his palm with a scalpel. He set the scalpel down and lifted the agent's hand, palm up and open, cradled in his own. He observed it intently.

The agent bled and little else.

I laughed. It caught Harrow's attention.

"What?"

"It won't work with me weakened."

"Nice try," he said, spraying his healing spray over the agent's wound.

"Yes, *nice*, though a successful attempt too. You will see. You will relent soon enough.

iv

And they did.
They even brought in some of my earth for me to lie.

v

I was seated once more. Under only incandescence this time. Why not the moonlight beyond if they wish to be so accommodating? Well...

As for matter other than light: another lattice of crosses was suspended above me, ready to drop to disintegration the second I moved. The lattice spanned the whole of the massive room we occupied. Other than Harrow, his test subject, the requisite technicians, and myself, there stood a good fifty HelCorp agents, all in a circle surrounding us, all holding one of those launchers.

"Would you like to put the needle in?" I asked Harrow. There was only more recession despite no darkness to hide him. I glanced over to the test subject. "You again." He did not respond. I liked that.

The second procedure began identical to the first—an exact recreation up to my blood mixing with the agent's. And in this instant of variance something within him began to stir. And you might think me one to reminisce in these moments? The man turned would be the successor of my dear Gilbert after all. You might think this so, as the agent was certainly of superior stock indeed, where now, with my blood in his veins, he was supreme! However, he was not of my will. He was the product of another's: Harrow's. Should the devil wrench from your chest the rib to mold your destroyer, would you love and cherish what it was this devil would kiln? My little devil's agent would be no destroyer, make no mistake, but he would be no child of mine either. No child but a theft. Thief too, as he abetted Harrow. Loot and looter. Plunder and plunderer in one. A blasphemy.

Though, let us never forget, with my blood in his veins, he was certainly supreme...

"Get up, agent!" And Harrow had that scalpel again. He sliced. The wound healed near-instantly.

"It worked, sir."

"We'll see. Are you ready Agent Ranson?"

The cursed agent stood straight, hands behind his back, abdominal muscles flexing. "Yes, sir," he said.

Harrow snapped a finger. Another agent came running, armed with a bowie knife. "Agent Hacken, you ready?"

Agent with the knife readied the weapon. "Yes, sir."

"Get to it."

The armed agent approached the accursed. He pulled the knife back like on a pendulum. He plunged it into Ranson's gut. Then he withdrew and jabbed it in several times more, deep and quick as bile spilled.

"Enough! Ranson, lift up your shirt."

And he did and the wounds were already closed.

No way! was heard from somewhere along the circle of agents.

"Quiet!" Harrow shouted. He held out his hand. "Your sidearm." And Hacken put his pistol in his boss' hand. Harrow inched the slide back inspecting the chamber. He held the weapon in both hands and *Bang! Bang! Bang! Bang! Bang!* Five shots were distributed around Ranson's trunk. Ranson didn't flinch.

You see that!

Harrow gave the circle an admonishing glare.

"You've hit all except one of the vital organs," I said. "Neglecting the most vital in particular."

Harrow shook his head, smirked. He raised the pistol again. I waved my hand ever so slightly. *Bang!* He hit Ranson square in the forehead. Ranson collapsed. A stench of desperation on Harrow now. Glorious.

"Hardy har Ranson. Get up!"

Nothing.

Harrow commanded of him once more as he rushed over. His mumbled command came out weaker than usual for his scurrying.

As he neared, he saw that Ranson's wound had not healed. He pulled a cross from inside his blazer as he knelt and I recoiled! Oh, how these icons do awaken the bad humors in me! Ranson stayed still. Harrow lowered the cross to his forehead and Ranson still did not flinch.

Brave, indeed.

"He's dead," Harrow said at a frantic loss.

Yeah, you killed him.

He stood spinning to catch that rebuke. None had the courage to take credit. They were probably wondering what he intended to do with that gun now...

"What the hell happened?" he asked no one in particular.

"You think I lack control over my wards?" I said, gracious enough to allay him. "What do you think made Mina revert to mortal despite my never perishing?"

"N—No, or you'd have taken it away from those two we used to catch you."

I sighed. It's always a gesture of some exasperation or other as I do not breathe, yet something told me this buffoon, in all his helplessness, could hardly know that.

"Ben and Barbara," I reminded. "The two you burned along with my Gilbert." He did not start at this and not of ignorance. He knew damn well what he had done and to whom he had done it and yet he stood stone at the arousal: his last chance. "Now!" I shouted, and at this he did startled. "Why, oh why is it I'm forever having provoked in me this fleeting delusion, this *déjà vu* that you really are a Van Helsing? The only convincing thing about your ruse was the accent... Nevertheless, I do relapse only to be quickly reminded by the same mechanisms of provocation that you are not of my nemesis' stock, that you pale in comparison... that you need be told things directly and in very small words: nearness is key, my boy."

He flushed. "You were standing right next to them."

"Ah, perhaps you are not so dim. But then again, maybe you are. I was not standing, fool."

He came at me with that gun, held it to my forehead. He must have been raving mad now. His men came closer with those launchers too. "How'd ya do it?"

"Perhaps it is an act of the heart, not the intellect?"

"Yeah, well, play dumb, worm." And he took a pike from the magazine nearest him, tapped the point at my left chest. "Whatever it takes," he said, "we're gonna crack your code."

"Have at it, my dear."

vi

And he did *have at it*. And he succeeded! The scoundrel!

He stood outside my cell. In his hand was a syringe massive in size and possessing a needle as deadly as any wooded thorn! I stared at it only in curiosity as it wasn't the tool that was cause for concern, it was the look on its bearer's face: like a grade-schooler who stayed up all night studying and knew he was going to get a C and couldn't be prouder.

One thing I'll credit him with: he knew he had me.

"You know I got to thinking..." he said. "...Yeah, you're probably drumming up some snide response to that right now, about me *thinking*. I'm not such a poor investigator though, because I got to thinking about those foils of yours —the keepers of your heart—a conversation we had about their turning. You never had to feed off them to turn them did you? There's something about the concentration of blood in the heart of an accursed."

"I still hold the power. I may revoke the curse any time they're near."

"Yeah, I got to thinking about that too. Thought, maybe that power skips a generation." He snapped his fingers and two of his ninjas entered. They were not alone. "You remember your grandson?"

It was Coons. Brought in wearing a wreath of garlic. He was woozy. Would he even recognize me in my current state? "Serg—"

"Yeah!" Harrow interrupted. "Maybe Gilbert has that power over soldier-boy and yet somehow I doubt it. See, Gil's dead and the sarge is still cursed. Something tells me you're the only one with the power of revocation, that it may only be revoked from direct descendants unless it's in death, and that all we need is the blood of the heart!" And he plunged that needle into Coons' chest! He pulled back on the plunger. "I about break your code?" Then he stabbed the needle into his own chest! "Yes!" he said through grit teeth as he forced the essence into his heart. "I can feel it!" And *I* could feel it. And my heart was burning alight and all could see *that*, damn him. There was no hiding it. And he pulled one of the warrior's ninjatō from its sheath and promptly cut off one of his arms. It grew back. "Go ahead, Count! Steal it back! Revoke it!" But I couldn't and he knew it. He only smirked, standing there with that syringe hanging out of his chest, the little weasel. Only smirked and said, "How's that for sacrifice?"

❧ 16 ❧

THE RESEARCH PART II

OCTOBER 15, 1968

And boy did we fly.

We took the red eye back from Saba, sure did, as the doc said he was good for it. But I mean before that we *really* flew! Barbara and I did that beaming fusing thing to take the form of a winged beastie: a flying fox, a fruit eater not a blood-sucker if you can believe that! Then Van Helsing and Gilbert did the same and then we flew right out of that cave commencing to trying to swallow us!

Then we flew Pan Am.

Van Helsing sat between Barbara and me. Even with the separation, we couldn't help feeling the growing presence of the Count the further north we travelled. It was heartening to know the object of our mission still sat somewhere in that complex—if only because Barbara was not yet cured. However, a certain preoccupation kept us from any true meditation.

The whole of the flight we'd wanted to hear Van Helsing's record of things. All things: of the Count, of his legacy, of our powers. Sure, we were acting the gluttons around the doc but our horrors had been plentiful, our answers scant. Weren't we entitled? Despite our patent just deserts, Van Helsing demurred. He said it would be better to *show* us all there was to be learned and not *tell*. I guess he's got a Resusci Anne in his pocket, one for staking not reviving...

It turned out most of the ride home involved Barbara and me indulging Van Helsing. We served him. We served a man more deserving of the objects of his preoccupations than we were of ours if you really think about it—especially when you consider the guy's mileage. And he wanted what we wanted anyhow, at least in the abstract. We spent the hours bringing him up to speed on notable events of the twentieth century—both foreign and domestic—about what happened the last seventy years.

I told him about World War One, World War Two, Korea, Vietnam, Hitler, Stalin, Mao, Hiroshima, Nagasaki, the Cuban missile crisis, the great depression, McKinley, Kennedy, Spanish flu, Asian flu, Hong Kong flu... And more...

When I finished he had this to say: *And you only came knocking yesterday?*

Fair enough. To cheer him up, I told him about our civil rights movement,

At this, he asked: *so, all coercive authorities no longer hold power and protections and expressions of basic human rights are maximal?*

To which I replied: *No.*

But, I added. *Women can vote.*

Do they vote for people who just suit themselves at their expense, like how the men vote?

To which I replied: *Yes.*

How's that saying go? 'Better to be merely thought a

pushover, than to go to the ballot box and remove all doubt'? Are you trying to indict women along with the men? Surely they don't deserve such disparagement?

At least there's equality... I offered.

Which is not a good in and of itself, he reminded, *nor does it determine the thing equalized to be a good by default. Should men have taken to bashing their brains in with baseball bats every few years, the last few years, where women were not allowed to do so, would you cheer on their being granted entry into this franchise? Cheer on the bashing of heads with baseball bats? Your world sounds horrible,* he concluded.

But, I pointed out, *actually, by any metric, we've only seen progress the last twenty-five years.*

How is that even possible? he asked.

I thought about this a good few seconds, just a few—I was well-fed after all—then attempted an explanation.

I think, I said, *the trick is to get the right measure of bureaucrats around to make sure all politicians above them feel consequential but aren't and all police and adjudicators below them are ignoring any given law the right proportion of the time—in the right proportion AT that time—where you need these bureaucrats to otherwise function according to such convoluted processes they can't get anything else done, thereby eliminating any possible authority in function, if not in form, so that this 'form' persists to hoodwink those weirdos of society insisting on someone telling everyone what to do all the time, thereby pacifying these weirdos with the commands—if not consequences—of strangers all while the stifling convolution works to clear a path for the rest of us to just get on with our lives and be as productive as any one of us will be.*

He napped after that. I didn't know we did that...

ii

We'd landed, wayfared, and were back on the farm.

We figured it would be a safe enough place for us to lay low and mobilize. The stumblers that had amassed here were gone. In their pursuit of Thumpy, they'd managed to chase the little demon all the way to HelCorp. The acre-and-a-half of still-smoldering crematorium would scare off any looters or squatters in addition.

We walked through those mounds of ash and bone on our way to the house. Smoke wafted gently from them now and they'd shrunk by half in the couple weeks since we'd been here.

"Pardon the barbarism," I said to the others. "It's what will help ensure our seclusion."

Then I got an itch.

I stopped.

"What's up?" Barbara asked.

"Attunement," Van Helsing observed over his shoulder.

I was already moving into that horseshoe pile of corpses I knew so well. Didn't care about the doc's diagnosis in the least. Though I probably should've.

Barbara followed me. "You two head to the house," she said to Gilbert and Van Helsing. "We'll be there in a minute." And the two continued on in their direction, and we continued on in ours. "You're going to use more of that blood," she said in slight admonishment.

"I'm just gonna have a look..." But I wasn't. I was going to use that blood. Just a drop.

"You can't save them all with so little," she said.

"Just a drop."

And there he was, his protector still at his side.

The shepherd growled a murmured growl. I showed him

the vial and his growl turned to a desperate urging whimper. He licked at his ward's face in quick bursts punctuating his imploring.

The kid appeared calcified. It was the ash sticking to his dried cured form. He was emaciated, though otherwise well preserved. "Help me out," I said to Barbara. I put one hand on the kid's chest and the other on his lower back. She did the same from his other side. We rocked him over, careful and reverent. He was quickly supine. I took out the vial. "Just a drop—"

"Freeze!" shouted voices from behind.

We turned. Four soldiers were bearing down on us with M16s.

"What ya doing to that corpse ya perverts?"

"Oh, please!" Barbara said.

"Shut it!"

I asked the four, genuinely curious, "Why you pointing those guns like that, they ain't gonna do anything."

"Do what guns do..." they said.

"Then let 'em toil!" And I started marching toward. The shepherd joined me.

The soldiers stumbled back a little. "Come on man, quit it!" And they flipped their rifles in their hands to hold like clubs. They moved back in on us like they were at the plate. Thing about this bravado was, all but one'd get smacked by some other should they swing clustered up like that. I relaxed, watched them. Who were these guys—

"Hickie, Dickie, Smithie, Mox! At ease!"

And they spun. "Gilbert?"

"You know these guys—"

Where am I?

The kid had awakened.

iii

The four jokers had it in their heads there was some sort of claim on this homestead and they'd staked it. Nonsense! We stood at the virtual front door of the place, shouting over each other. Not even shouting in any way meant to persuade the other to let the other have the house, only to persuade the other to let the other persuade the other... if that made any sense. We were trying to yell our way to yelling our way through the front door.

Call it an emotional impasse if you want to be charitable, the screaming was getting us nowhere. Only one not barking was the damn dog! Perhaps rationalism was what was required? May cooler heads prevail...

"Hey assholes," I shouted. "Barbara and I died here!"

"So did we!" said the four.

"We were reborn here!" Barbara added.

"So were we!"

"Well, shit!" And I was all out of ideas. "What about you two?" I shrugged at Gilbert and the doctor. "Any sentimental attachment to the place?"

I was only being sarcastic... "I turned these men, right where we stand," Gilbert said.

"Jesus Christ!" I cried.

"Oh yeah!" said Hickie, Dickie, Smithie, and Mox. "Hiya pops!"

Gilbert brushed this off as he waved the shepherd over. The dog came and he gave him a friendly pat.

"Next you're gonna tell me you turned the mutt!"

"Well—"

"So, the doc's the only interloper around here?" Barbara interjected.

"Not exactly," doc said and we all stopped everything to

hear this one. "I *was* instrumental in choosing this as the location to hide the Count's heart."

"What possible reason could there be for designating this place, of all places, the place to put Thumpy?"

"*Thumpy*?" Van Helsing said, confused.

"*Righty*."

"*Righty*?"

"What's the significance?" I demanded.

"Think about it," Van Helsing said.

"All the alfalfa you can eat?"

"Think harder."

"Can't think of a single thing that would make this place worthy of the Count's essence."

"There's your answer."

Yeah. Pretty obvious when you think about it...

"You knew the Carters?" the kid asked. He was fully reformed now and wearing one of the jokers' trousers and blouses—

"Hey y'all," Hickie interrupted. "Since we're focusing on the new guy—"

"I was born and raised here," the kid said.

"No offense... No offense..." Hickie relented. "It's just, why'd I have to give up both my pants *and* my shirt to the kid?" And he had. He was standing in his undershirt and boxer shorts. "Surely another of ya coulda given up a shirt at least..."

"Oh yer already in yer damn underpants," Mox said. "You'd only come across the weirdo in a shirt n' just yer gitchies!"

"I'd come across half-dressed instead of not-dressed is how I'd come across!"

"You'd come across half-stupid is how. Man in his underwear looks like he mighta lost a suitcase. Man in a shirt n' no pants looks like he don't know how to *use* a suitcase!"

"I know how to use a suitcase!"

"Only cuz yer not inna shirt."

"Gimme yours!"

"I won't be party to you embarrassing yourself. You'll look stupid."

"Whatever happened to *half-stupid*?"

"Oh you'll look half-stupid: two halves!"

"Well let's find out!"

"Lookin' stupid's your default, what difference is a shirt gonna make? Point proven!"

"Oh you didn't prove a goddamn—"

"Men! Shut it!" Gilbert ordered.

They shut it.

"Who are the Carters, son?" Van Helsing asked.

"The people who owned this place," the kid said. "They lit out the day before the trouble started."

"I'm sorry, I'm not familiar with them."

"But you said you chose this place for something..."

"The location. It was long past my time that anyone would have been selected as caretaker. If I have any connection to the Carters, it's through our both bearing some relationship to that damnable HelCorp, which is no real connection at all."

"What's HelCorp?"

"You don't want to know, kid..." Gilbert said.

"HelCorp is immaterial," Van Helsing assured. "Though I'm sure the Carters were selected for their legitimate interest in working this farm, nothing more. People acting in earnest to keep up the homestead, who know nothing of the company's doings, nor care, would be the company's best cover."

"They were good people."

"I'm sure they were."

"*They were*. This place is special?" the kid followed up.

"Yes."

"How?"

"As of late? It has served as a confluence for a great many parties who will be instrumental in resolving... *this*." Doc gestured all around the yard. He stopped as soon as he faced the north, moving his hands at the sky like he was molding something. "All of this... We are here for a reason."

"And why were we here last week?" I asked, a bit of playful chiding in my tone.

Van Helsing didn't smile or anything, though he understood the levity. "How was I to predict HelCorp would commission NASA to explode the head of an ancient Count in outer space turning millions of Americans into some braindead form of the accursed pursuing the essence of that Count motivated by a mystical connection all descendants bear to said essence only to cross paths with and subsequently drive the lot of you perfect strangers right into the tomb of the chamber of the embodiment of that very essence in the pursuit?"

"Think about it," I said. Then I turned, clucking my teeth in Barbara's direction. This caught her attention so I angled my head away from the group. She followed me that way.

"What is it?" she asked.

"I'm not liking how quickly the pro-Count camp is expanding. With Gilbert and those chuckleheads, that makes five against three in the Count's favor. Four if we get the kid on our side. Those five against us have military training."

"*Guard reserve* training. I'm more worried about Coons. If those jokers managed to get out of there, he sure did."

"Yeah. Any other of our adversaries left unaccounted for—"

And there was a smashing at the door of the house! Another!

Hickie, Dickie, Smithie, and Mox readied their weapons swing-away style. Gilbert moved between them and the porch, motioning that they should cut it out.

Barbara and I moved closer.

Another thump! A crash! And then out he stumbled, my dental records all over his arm, that popped bandoleer hanging off him like a calling card.

"Son of a bitch!" I shouted.

"You know this guy?" The jokers asked.

"Speaking of turning... He's mine!" And I pounded on toward that bastard chief now stumbling across the small deck after the front door. I got to him quick, took him by the scruff of his neck. "No! No! No!" I dragged him around to the side of the house. "Nobody has time for your shit anymore. Not in life. Not in death." And I booted him on his ass and started him stumbling north.

Away he went.

I spun, commanded. "Hickie, Dickie, Smithie, and Mox!" They hopped to it, gave me their attention. "Barbara, doc, Gilbert, and I swore an oath to send HelCorp to the bottom of Lake Michigan where, after that and only after that, would we commence to settling any of our many many personal differences. You want in on this oath or are we gonna start settling those differences right now?

Gilbert nodded at them. They all started nodding at each other... At the general ambiance? "Y—Yeah sure... Why not... S—Sure."

"Well!" Gilbert demanded.

"Sir, yes, sir! We're in on it, sir!"

"And what about you kid?" I asked.

"Huh?"

"You in this?"

"No," he said matter-of-fact. "I don't know you. I appreciate what you did for me and all, but I'm not gonna throw in with you just because you're whooped and whooping everybody into a frenzy. I don't know you or any HelCorp. I'm staying here." And he put his hand on the dog. "*We're* staying and we're gonna take care of the Carters' place until they get back. Sorry."

"No need to be sorry. What's your name kid?"

"Glen."

"Glen, mind if we stay with you maybe a couple days?"

THE RESEARCH PART III

OCTOBER 15, 1968

Let's talk solace...

At least with Harrow now an accursed—and I mean an accursed of my descent—my death would mean his. Only in a manner of speaking, yes, but the feckless-turned, you must understand, ought sooner wish to be dead than mortal. Consider, if offered resurrection from the cold cold grave, would you want only your previous self at one one-thousandth of life? Ought a king at the peak of his virility and magnetism wish to return, forever, to toddling in diapers? You see it now. Should that gutless Harrow pierce me at the right and simply be done with it, it would be as though taking himself from sage to stumbler.

My death might have meant his. Unfortunately, my torture did not. He could no longer keep me subdued in the manner he had been. The light, the crosses, the wolf's bane were his vulnerabilities now too. Of course, he found other ways. A buffoon he was, and I stand by this, but when it came to the tormenting of the undead, he was an idiot savant!

A few of the mere mortals of his agency—of a *very few*, as he had been turning agents faster than he could draw blood from Coons' heart—were tasked with fitting me out in some sort of jumpsuit inspired by the iron maiden herself. It was made flexible so I would feel their fists and their cudgels. Its interior was lined with barbs—hollow so that a form of garlic extract could take to my flesh in whatever measure they desired. It had to have been a synthetic extract—that, or they discovered some antidote—as they were able to increase or decrease the potency of its effect at will, to strike some desired balance between docility and receptivity to their torments. They could even eliminate the effects in an instant. Once I was removed from the suit—for further of their head shrinking, say—I was back to aces. Always in an instant.

Now, don't think me in esteem of these technologies, or their technologists—nor should you think me indifferent to the horrors all above have imposed upon me. Though I speak of all but Harrow in cold facts, withholding judgement, such judgements *are* forthcoming. With plenty more reserved for that rat imposter, make no mistake!

You've heard my assessment of their tools, now hear my account of their methods.

The very second I was suited the torture would begin. I'd be made some degree of senseless and put in that vast space, the same where I sat for those forced turnings. Harrow and the accursed of his lot would test various of their hand-to-hand maneuvers on me, their weaponry— blunt, bladed, near, far—their chemistry and their methods of dissection even. Harrow always attacked from a distance, the coward, though he was growing more and more adept with that spike launcher: fast and able to thread the needle, maybe the fastest I'd ever seen. And you might believe me the type to hope this is true and to hope I find myself in his sights so that his swift disarmament at my hands be not just the relieving of him of his power to kill and compel in the immediate—of his fleeting potency—but of any last confidence in the existence of something, anything, he might be or become that would grant him advantage over even the excrement upon which twists the worm: those forever under my boot. You may believe me the type, though I have never *hoped* for what was a foregone conclusion. I cannot honestly say I have ever been the type to hope. He's as good as stated.

One last note: I said I was made senseless, yes? I meant that in the ordinary use of thoughtlessness and ineffectuality. Don't think, those of you accursed who've experimented with aromatics as though occult recreational toxicologists, that there was ever the saving grace of absolute desensitization: what sometimes occurs given the right measure of this weed: what you've undoubtedly experienced yourselves, though purely by accident, some long dark day of the void. Be assured, though the garlic numbed me to a degree, I was never given enough to be the analgesiac.

I was in a constant unremitting pain, and those men were loving it.

It got to the point where my only comfort was in their returning me to that cage, where I might languish under the hunger of the wolf's bane and the fatigue of the ultraviolet.

That was my only comfort, if not my only pleasure.

These agents, even the warrior princesses, would be no match for me, I promise you, should I have possessed even a tenth of my faculties. Some of them were so clumsy they were no match for me now.

I managed, you see, every once in a while, to nip into the

neck of some useless flailer who'd gone and gotten too close —to get a decent gulp of his bile. *What good would that do me?* you wonder. Us cursed may subsist off such dilutions, to no definition of adequacy, though I hungered for nothing. *Of course* my captors ensured me well fed. My starvation only meant my strength after all. I'd take in their bile nevertheless, if for nothing else, to elicit a decent stock of their screams.

The ones I bit would forever keep their distance, happy to penetrate me from twenty yards away, never again coming close enough I'd see their smirking false bravado in this. It was their defeat in paradox. The simpering was meant to establish their long-distance piercings a revenge. Their piercings, for the very fact of their distance, would not allow for any discernment of simpering. Though I had an inkling... "More," I'd taunt, and the scent of their smugness would fade.

These were my only indulgences throughout the course of events. Everything else was that unremitting pain—something I was not made for. Something I would allow to continue for just long enough that when I finally pulled the rug out, when I finally deprived them of their tortures, the degree of lament in them would be maximal. For their deprivations, they would suffer.

Small solace, as even as I speak I have an unreasonable number of their projectiles in me. They concentrate them— in their sadism—on the regions of my body most vulnerable, most private, most remote.

Small solace indeed. Now might be the time to pull that rug...

ii

The last two of Harrow's mortals hit me with those lights and I hit them back.

"Oh no!" they screamed. They were truly horrified.

The bile had pooled on the floor next to me, dripping from my torso. The thorn I had managed to smuggle out of that torture chamber, now in my right chest, ensured of that.

What were these agents thinking? That that skunk Harrow would have their heads? Let them suffer this. Though they really ought be thinking of the collective failure of all at HelCorp to ensure it was *their* thorn resting so solid in my elusive heart and not *my own*. I had beaten them to the punch! I had won!

They ran to me, observed me in my stillness. All would become darkness soon.

But not so soon. I flinched slightly as though this was my death throe. It was a paltry and weak expression. If this was all I could muster in the moments before my demise, take me early!

The agents reacted accordingly.

"Damn it, don't let him die." And I writhed.

The more prudent of the two hovered over me, shielding me. "Christ, the lights! Get 'em off!" And the other rushed from my cage to the control panel.

He flicked the switch and my cell went dark. Then screams! He turned the lights back on and it was just his partner lying in the pool of the bile I had been pilfering. The mortal's blood mixed with it now, slow.

Before the corpse's partner could even figure, I was through him. He would only live long enough to see my hand thrusting from out his chest, holding his heart to him in offering.

He died and I withdrew.

I tore off the blunt thorn I'd harnessed to my chest. *Why not put a true pike in there near enough the heart?* you ask. An impaling an inch to the right would have ensured I not see myself through, yes. However, it would have only expelled itself in my healing, possibly at the instant the mortals discovered me feigning. Everything had to be convincing.

Now everything had to be *de rigueur.* And these clothes, these tatters they insisted on putting me in, they were hardly better than the iron maiden.

iii

Their archives were a monument to me! Sure, they had killed others of the undead, but never of my stature and never had those slain persisted so heartily so as to allow the accrual of more and more of their wares for posterity. I perused. So many of my treasures. Admittedly scant compared to my store at the Bârgău estate, though a nice gesture.

And there it was! I rushed to the ensemble, took the medallion in grip first off, ran my thumb along the serpentine emblem at its center. It had been so long.

But any further reminiscing would have to wait. Surely they would be discovering my empty cage soon, if they hadn't yet. I would dress then seek my freedom!

iv

I stepped out into the hall leading to my torture chamber. Ha, *chamber!* It was an open-span fortress within the fortress. You could house the Titanic in there. I had no choice in this passage, however. If my instincts were correct, I would need progress through it to get to the exit corridor.

So I moved swift, and in this swiftness I felt something I hadn't felt in generations. My cloak was flowing in my stride, my tailcoat caressing my svelte form. I was feeling my purpose! Finally I was whole! Of body *and* mind *and* persona.

Which of my sorely neglected powers would I enjoy first? Perhaps I'd use telekinesis.

And, ah ha, no time like the present...

I had rounded the corner and there he was: Harrow, with a half dozen of his agents, conferring about something or other of no importance. I eased my step, stood solemn. He hadn't noticed me yet so had no idea what was coming.

"Harrow!" I shouted, and he looked up from some document. "Come to me!" And of course the coward turned tail.

"Stop him!" he shouted as he fled through a stairwell door.

"You may try," I offered. And an agent smashed through the glass of a cabinet next to him. He pulled out two spike launchers, one in each hand. He distributed them and grabbed himself a third.

I believe I *will* use my telekinesis on them...

They fired and their thorns veered in all the directions I sent them. Some I captured to ensure a swift return. I gave them back and in so doing impaled all but one of the agents. And that agent flew fast as any accursed to be at my feet. He arrived and I went back to solemn. He took to confusion at this. I handed over one of my undelivered pikes. He accepted it, wary.

"My heart won't cleave itself," I scolded, and he pulled his arm back to thrust just as he was overtaken by his stumbling colleagues.

I recommenced moving toward that chamber as my friends at my back tore the agent to pieces. They were pristine stock, these stumblers having turned from the perfect accursed. The agent wouldn't overpower them so long as they remained under my control. He was dismembered only to reform, dismembered only to reform...

I stopped at the sally port to the chamber. "Say the word and I'll have them rend you," I promised.

"Never, you vermin!"

"Come now, how lowly could I be in all my grace?" I waved my hand and one of the stumblers removed the thorn from his own chest and drove it into the agent's.

v.

The ninjas dressed out the chamber like the most threadbare of sashes. There were three of them stretched across its width, equidistant each other. State-of-the-art weapons were everywhere as this was my torture chamber after all, though the warriors seemed content with only their ninjatō and shuriken.

"You must be his best," I said. "You deserve me at mine."

It was only fair...

I became the wolf.

They threw their shuriken to start, though were helpless to penetrate my hide. I had chosen the correct of my powers it seemed. I leapt and they circled, reaching for their blades. They readied as I found my first target, landing square on her chest and taking her left arm in-jaw. I gave it a rattle and it tore off at the shoulder. Before the others could overtake me and reformation could steal away that appendage, I spun, flipped that sausage in the air and caught it again at the forearm. I felt the jutte hidden in-sleeve and so flung my head. I drove it into the chest of my quarry.

But I was out of practice. That assault took more time than I intended and so the remaining two were on me, slashing. They sliced away with abandon and the clock ticked: the one I dispatched with would be stumbling shortly and the others would merely cleave her brain to revive her.

They were on me to be sure, relentless, and I was thankful. The very confidence driving their flurry would mean my escape. They thought they were slicing into any old anthropic accursed and not a beast of my leather. There was little puncture, little hurt, so I spun. One toppled as the other hopped up and flipped over the whip of my tail. I pounced onto the toppled and commenced to gnawing. I nipped and tore and dug, quick as could be, right down to her lifeless heart. I took that pump in-jaw and pulled, wrenched it clean.

And the other's jutte was in my side, at the chest.

Another saving grace!

My heart was not at the right in this form. She thought correctly of *me*, though wrong of the canis, and I had already pulled free. She recalculated. She wouldn't miss a second time. She readied her two jutte in her hands, angling them at me. I flung my head and opened my mouth to send the heart in it flying. Instinctively the warrior defended. She caught the organ in the tip of her left pike. Before she could reckon with what she'd done, her hollowed partner was dead. Now she, the last, was angrily wiping the heart of that fallen comrade off one jutte with her other.

I backed away and she followed, believing I was scheming. And I *was* scheming. I was inching into a rack holding wooden spears. And what a scheme it was! I couldn't wield a spear in my state! Though I could get her on my side of the chamber while I sent her stumbling peers to the other. I could also get my bearings for a good lunge...

And I had. And I did! I flew, gnashing at her.

But she caught me, right in the left chest! She had me with that spiked jutte clean. She didn't smile however. She didn't gloat. She had pierced right where my heart sat as wolf and yet she didn't revel—though it would be perfectly in keeping with her character to do so.

She didn't revel because she was frightened. She was frightened because I had returned! She had me, though only in my anthropic form and only in my left chest where nothing so vital sat. I had her wrist in my grip, fast. She struggled. I grabbed her at the throat in addition. There would be no taunting for this one, no giggling in any ears as tortured victims grope blindly. I lifted her and arced her onto the rack. All spear tips found a home in her, the nearest to me, through her heart.

As I stepped into the latter port of the chamber I couldn't help but feel remiss—a neglect. I sent Harrow's lattice of crosses tumbling to the floor. It was by the mere press of a button they had so carelessly left within my grasp. Why deprive myself?

Those crosses rained a cleansing rain on all objects of the chamber, of organic artifice and not.

Try making a simple task of reviving those ninjas now, I dare you.

vi

I could see the moonlight at the other end of the corridor. I was there. I could hear them mobilizing behind me but I was flying, once again the wolf and I was as good as there. I plunged on, a mere fifty paces and I would be—

The alarms were raised and a titanium door was sliding closed ahead. I picked up speed. I loped and I bounded in what I'm sad to say was some desperation. But I was—

Closing...

I was going to—

Closing...

I was going to make it—

No!

I screeched to a halt, near slamming into that metal barrier.

"Got him! Shouted the agents giving pursuit.

I assessed. I was *me* again. I moved to the titanium. I reached through one of the portholes so tiny it was hardly able to deliver my wrist. Freedom was on the other side but, even at my strength, this metal would not be moved.

And the agents were on me. I recognized many of them. I had only moments ago killed them. Someone was thoughtful enough to destroy their brains?

I put my hands up. I couldn't help but smile.

"What's so amusing?"

"Whoever designed these doors," I chuckled. "Didn't have me in mind."

And I transformed once more, into the fox who soars! I merely fluttered out one of the portholes and was gone.

vii

I burst out the front passage, reveling in my freedom. All I wanted at present was the touch of a little moonlight and I had it. I am a man of simple pleasures, not greedy. And now, for the simplest of pleasures...

I re-entered the stronghold.

viii

Harrow had fled to the basement: a space near as large as his torture chamber. He sat in the center of the room, in a solid iron cell. The cell sat amidst a halo of ultraviolet. Outside of that halo was more darkness. I waved a hand just past its edge and touched the contrived sunshine.

"I can smell your stench," I said.

"I've nothing to be afraid of in here."

"It's of a *desire*. A desire to be on the outside of that cage. To have me hopeless and in your clutches. It's all the same odor. Come out why don't you?"

"You'll be overtaken soon enough," he promised. "I'll be on the outside soon enough."

"No."

"You're filthy!"

"Then make the world a mite cleaner," I said.

"Step on into the light."

"*Soon enough.* Sun's coming up."

Even from behind that iron, I could hear his scoffing cluck. "You may escape these walls, Count, but you'll never escape my reach. I'll never stop looking. I will find you."

"No."

"Such arrogance."

"I have the luxury," I assured him. "You see, you are simply in error of premise. There will be no escape. I cannot take what is yours—all you've built—if I am to simply walk away from it. And I *will* take what is yours: your life, your castle. I will destroy you and all that you leave behind will be my dividend. Consider this my domain already.

"*But!* I will not take you as you are—in such a state. You

must be taken at the height of your powers. The fall must be greatest.

"I will lull you. I will give you a swath wide and long so that you might plan and organize, come to believe your technicians the masters of the tools and the techniques required of my ultimate suppression. You will see me help-less—and I will be truly helpless—and you will become complacent and sure of your domain—and that domain will surely be great—and your mind will find a peace.

"And *that's* when I will strike!

And I touched at my heart. "But you are already mine," I said. "Though you do not yet know what it is to be had.

"Now, if you need me, I will be in my cell."

❦ 18 ❦

THE RESEARCH PART IV

OCTOBER 17, 1968

HelCorp CEO, Bram Helsing, had this to say: Well, first of all, it was a team effort. Yes, HelCorp's beacon was instrumental in mobilizing those infected and onboarding them to our treatment facility—an initiative, in itself, keeping our children and elderly safe, as well as others who are vulnerable. And yes, our subsequent quarantine program has all but eradicated the disease. Though, I feel I need stress: none of this would have happened without the help of the public in following the directives of those tireless servants of the National Civil Defence Council.

A brief moment to myself, of respite, and here I am watching television. A brief moment of respite, and I'm watching a television broadcast featuring one of the worst of my murderers taking credit for murdering millions, getting credit for saving millions, all while I should be mobilizing to stop him from murdering millions more!

I clicked the thing off.

"What is that?" Van Helsing said from the bedroom door. "Some sort of fortified crystal ball?"

"Ha! No. You'd be lucky if this thing could tell you what happened last week!"

I flipped it on again for him. I changed the channel. It was that episode of Andy Griffith where Barney learns karate to take on a bully only he isn't very good so his karate instructor steps in and—

I watch too much TV... But the doc's seeing it for the first time apparently.

"Before I sequestered myself," he said, "we had moving images. They were displayed on screens ten feet wide, and of much cruder quality."

"Oh we still got those, though bigger and clearer."

"Bigger?"

"Yeah, like forty-foot wide screens."

"Forty feet!" he said, astonished. "And they simultaneously made screens bigger and screens smaller?" He was pointing at the television.

"Not really. That tube's a relatively new thing. Kinda put a serious dent in movie theater profits since people prefer to watch TV at home now."

"And this is a *television*, a *TV*?" He put his hand on the device. "And film screens are in *theaters*?"

"You got it."

"So the trend is the making of screens smaller and smaller now?"

"Not really. TVs have doubled in size compared to this one."

"So this one is an older version?"

"Nah, new... *ish*."

"So they make these things of all feasible sizes to accommodate all possible preference?"

"That's about it."

"And nobody goes anymore to—what must be massive —buildings to watch films on forty-foot screens?"

"Not quite. People go if you make it worth their while."

"So films must be really really good?"

"Noooo... More like they'd have to be something you hated yourself for missing. *You can't afford to miss the cultural event of the year! Be the first on line for the movie event of the summer! A motion picture everyone must see!* That kinda stuff.

"So, they use guilt and fear?"

"Exactly!"

"What do you foresee, considering these trends?"

"Never really thought about it."

"*Well*, think about it then. Think about television for a second, and that will bring us back to film. There are four and only four options when it comes to this television trend: televisions do not get sufficiently large or sufficiently—"

"*Sufficient* for what?"

But the doctor put a quieting finger into the air and continued. "

- Neither sufficiently large nor sufficiently small, *or*
- sufficiently large but not small, *or*
- sufficiently small but not large, *or lastly*
- both large and small.

Those are the only options and the chances of television screens not getting *so* big or *so* small are only one of four. Not good, especially considering these devices are already shrinking and growing at once."

"Soooo... what?"

"The *what* of it is: If televisions become sufficiently large, they will be like theater screens in the home and even a television of moderate size..." He put his hand on the tube again. "...Like this one, will be portable by comparison. Most people will have a second one on hand so that they may watch in the kitchen, the dining room, the bedroom, even on the toilet. Conversely, if television screens get too small, portability will be maximized, with there existing televisions smaller than can be imagined."

"Still not getting the point here—"

"The former scenario will hasten the latter, and the latter scenario will simply mean the latter scenario. If Televisions get too large, there will inevitably be multiple televisions in the same house, for portability, and because a big screen will always be an option in houses like these, there will be no portable television too small—save for, maybe, something that destroys your eyes. And even then, if you can't see the small screen, watch whatever you're watching on the big one. It is always an option. Televisions are only going to get smaller and smaller as a result of televisions getting bigger and bigger, to the point, I predict, they will fit in one's hand.

"No way. Screens are solid glass. A portable's too heavy for the hand. A big bastard's too heavy for the living room floor."

"There are other materials."

"Maybe—"

"And entertainment will be forever dramatically changed. A handheld television will allow people to watch not just at home, but on the bus, in a break room during a coffee break, at a red light even. This will entail that certain television programs be no longer than a bus ride, a coffee break, or a red light, therefore. These programs will get shorter and shorter and shorter and this will lead to a disharmony. Not everyone will want to watch episodes so brief. Programmers will start offering multiple channels: those with shows for sitting at a red light and those with shows for doing the laundry."

"Yeah, those short shows don't sound so fun. They sound like commercials—"

"And the laundry watchers will be red light watchers too in some proportion and there will be a conditioning effect. People will get used to the quick self-contained episodes— even come to prefer them for their being satisfying while requiring very little time and commitment. Programmers who move exclusively to television episodes lasting no longer than a red light will see a boom in popularity. Other programmers will quickly follow suit."

"So, no more TV?"

"Not quite. Consider what your theaters are doing already. As you said, people attend films they are otherwise indifferent to on the grounds that this serves some social function. That is, they can proudly say they were party to the cultural phenomenon that attending said film determined or, at the very least, they'll have ensured they not alienate themselves from those demanding all be party to such phenomena. People selling television shows will simply treat watching TV as serving the same social function."

"So, we'll still have TV shows?"

"No, you'll have television *events*, much like you have film *events*. Worse, you'll have the exact same television event all day long, every channel. People will quickly realize they can meet their pro-social quotas by turning on the big screen 'event' while they sit and enjoy their small screen entertainment in-hand. *I watched! I watched!* they'll say and it'll be smaller screens in front of bigger screens in every living room. Television programmers will notice everyone tuning in and not watching and understand that as long as something, anything, is flickering and popping in front of "viewers"'s faces—and is something they *can't afford to miss* —they'll tune in. TV content will become standardized because less variety is just as desirable as more, and less variety means less spending. TV quality, already low as people aren't watching for entertainment anyway, will hit rock bottom..."

"I'm not sure I like the sound of—"

"And commercials will get really really loud."

"Good god!"

"Then theater owners will see all the money to be made following the *they'll sit in front of anything they think makes them a better person knowing they can watch something else anyway* trend and want in on it. However, because sitting in a dark theater with a bright screen beaming out of your palm is the peak of obnoxiousness, and because theater owners will underestimate the number of people more than willing to do this, owners will initially offer something like a *meta-screening section*: a part of the theater where patrons can sit with a smaller screen in front of a bigger screen— maybe in the last few rows or something like that. *Screening or non?* they'll ask. Then they'll notice that their screening sections are always at capacity. Screening sections will get bigger and bigger until the whole theater, any given night, is blindingly alight with smaller screens in front of bigger screens."

"No!"

"It will be smaller screens in front of bigger screens everywhere, in short order, in perpetuity, and that will be the end of every form of audio-visual entertainment as we know it.

"But those lights, in all our hands all the time, will also mean an end to the dark. *Our* dark.

"OUR DARK?"

"We spend near half our lives in the earth's darkness. To think this feature had no hand in shaping a good proportion of what we are would be a blasphemy of our histories. Merely consider the vestiges of the dark's effect. Consider the trust maintained by the multitudes sitting in those darkened theaters—not able to see each other's faces, movements, motives. This is no different than our earliest of ancestors huddling together within the niche of a cliff's face, lucky even to have the moon over their heads, putting complete faith in not just any other's willingness to defend the multitude from elements without, but to not turn on anyone within. To not take even the slightest of advantages despite the ease with which anyone might in that dark. We've spent thousands of generations taming it, learning to live in it, happily, joyously even, in our diversions. And in so doing, it's tamed us. We're far more trusting for it, cooperative, civil. And now we're on the verge of vanquishing that dark forever, with our small screens in front of bigger.

"And an end to our dark will simply mean…"

The End

"Doesn't that terrify you?"

"No."

"No?"

"I live in a cave as an immortal." I looked at him bemused. He looked at me like he wasn't done. "But you don't live like me. Your kids don't. Nor should you, they, anyone. Hold on to your dark my boy." And then he walked off.

I think he went into the kitchen...

ii

He did go into the kitchen. He was working away at something. Took the kid with him.

All of the rest of us were in the living room. The jokers were relating their last moments at the complex.

"And ol' sarge, I came upon him just smashing his head into the ground, smashing at his brains until he came back to life."

"What?"

"Yeah. I can't explain it cept'n' to say, if ya couldn't keep sarge down in life, what makes ya think ya could keep him down in undeath?"

"That's some discipline," Barbara admitted.

"Yeah yeah," Mox said. "And then sarge said to me, *Moxy*—"

"He never ever called ya *Moxy* ya fool!"

"Fine! Then sarge said, *Private! Shoot the rest of the men in the head and tell them to fall back to rally point!* Then he barreled on into that complex. Wouldn't let me help. Never went it alone like that before."

"Ah, gimme a break!"

"Huh?"

"With guys like us backing him up, he only ever went it alone!"

"You callin' me chopped liver?"

"Nah. Some people actually like chopped liver."

"You callin' me ineffectual?"

"Is that bad?"

"Yeah."

"Then I'm callin' all of us ineffectual. But especially you."

"You son of a—"

"Enough!" Gilbert shouted.

"Ah, hell! He's right. We're just a bunch of duded-up weekend warriors..."

"Yup!" Gilbert said to Mox as he yanked one of those vials out of his hand. "Take it easy with that concoction, private."

"No need!" Van Helsing said, entering the living room. The kid followed carrying a sloshing soup pot.

"One sec, doc," I said. "So what happened to the sarge?"

"He ran into that complex and I haven't seen him since."

"Just barged in there?"

"It was the mission..."

"Ah..." I turned to the soup. "What were you saying, doc?"

"I'm saying, drink up boys! Gentlelady!" And he lifted the lid off the pot. We tingled! "There's plenty of concoction to go around—and plenty more where that came from."

"No way!" and the jokers dug in.

"How'd you pull this off?" Barbara asked.

"Easy. It's a single ingredient."

"And what's that?" I asked, taking a sip from one of the ladles. *Heaven...*

"Distilled wolf's bane."

I spit. "Wolf's bane! That'll put us on our ass!"

"Ever consider why?"

"The same reason garlic does?"

"No. How do you all feel when a mortal bleeds before you? Especially when your thirst is maximal?"

Like I'm gonna die if I don't get that sip...

Wanna explode...

There's a churning in the guts...

Can't do anything until the fix...

"And how do you feel next to Wolf's Bane?"

We all just stared blankly.

"That can't be..." the doc said, confused. "Anyone?" He offered this to the room.

We all shook our heads.

"What's Wolf's bane?" Smithie asked.

"I assure you," doc recommenced. "The sensations are the same, only differing by intensity."

"So that means..." Barbara said.

"Yes. Wolf's bane affects you because—and this isn't chemistry, it's ethereal—what it is in that weed that is poisonous to mere mortals is functionally no different than the purest of blood, in the richest of veins, to the most ravenous of accursed. That's why it stops you in your tracks."

Gilbert once again reached out to stop Mox from overdoing it. Took the ladle out of his hand. "It's quite the batch, doctor, but it'll still go fast with these boys if we don't ration it."

"I said there was plenty more where that came from."

"Surely you used the last of your store with this cook?"

"I did. And yet, there's plenty more."

"Where?"

"Everywhere!"

"Well, that's convenient," I said

"By my contrivance it is. Why do you think I chose this location for his essence? Surely as you walked through those woods you noticed it flourishing? Ah, of course you didn't! What am I thinking? You would have been naturally famished. However, merely walk in those woods now and you won't help but sense it." And he stared at us a moment.

We nodded, no reason to disagree. Then he kept on. "Walk in those woods *now*! We will need as much as we can get for our mission."

And we left to go flower picking.

iii

We'd harvested the resources necessary to sustain life, now it was time to harvest the inverse.

The jokers had a transport truck parked around the back of the house. Dickie was about to show us his wares.

"Went back to the diner," he said, walking around to the tailgate. "Place was deserted. All of Hevans was trashed. Grabbed what we could—"

"What do you mean trashed?" Barbara asked, barely hiding her insistence.

"Like the stumblers rolled right over it: that horde the sarge and us guys were suppressing when we turned. The biggest!" Barbara put her hand to her chest as though she needed it there to breathe. Good thing Dickie was such a talker... "Thank god we got those folks out in time."

"Out?"

"Oh yeah. Place was basically a vigilante stronghold by the time we left... Hell, look who I'm talking to, you musta saw it from that pyre ya told us about."

"Yeah," I said, bumping Barbara's shoulder. "Come to think of it, that was a pretty paltry mob."

"Yeah yeah," Dickie concurred.

Barbara smiled at me. Then she put a hand on the truck box. "So, what we got?"

The soldier lowered the tailgate and pinned back a flap of canvas. "Whatever was left." He pulled out ordnance crates and ammo boxes.

"Couldn't have been much if you gotta use your rifles like baseball bats..."

"Oh we got plenty of ammo. Why waste it on a couple civilians? No offense you two."

"None taken."

Gilbert and the doc came over to observe.

"What we got?" Gilbert asked.

"Was just sayin' pops, little bit of everything."

"Don't call me that."

"Right, the nepotism... *Little bit of everything, sir!*"

"Don't exaggerate soldier."

"No, seriously, we spent the better part of last week scavenging all up and down the state, taking anything we could carry, starting with where we fled." He opened an ordnance container. Inside were a number of shuriken, ninjatō, jutte, a couple spike launchers.

"Good work private."

"Gilbert," Van Helsing broached. "Can you train Ben and Barbara to handle these weapons?"

"In one night?"

"He's right, doc," I said. "We're low on time."

"You have heightened ability in any regard you've bothered to consider," the doc reminded.

"We've never had *any* ability to use this stuff..."

"You do possess the ability to acquire and hone new skills don't you? If everything you know how to do you do better, then, since *learning* is one of those things, you'll do that better too, no?"

"Worth considering..." Barbara relented.

"Alright then," Gilbert said. "Choose a weapon. Only one. No thought. Let your intuitions be your guide. This will determine your specialty." Barbara grabbed a Winchester Model 70 .30-06 sniper rifle with an Unertl 8x scope. "Beautiful," Gilbert praised. I grabbed dual ninjatō. "Excellent! Now let's begin."

iv

I'd gotten pretty good with the blades if I do say so myself, and Barbara with the rifle, and in short order! Doc was right again.

Schwing!

And Gilbert cut my arm off.

"What the hell?"

"You've got another. Fight!"

And we squared off. He wasn't any dummy this Gilbert. Besting him even with both arms available to me, *ad libitum,* would be no easy trial. By this very fact—

Schwip!

He cut off the other one!

"Don't look for vulnerabilities like I'm some scarecrow!" He turned to Barbara. "Alright, while we wait for his arms to grow back, let's see how you do with a target that's actually accursed." And he burst high into the air. At the point where gravity caught up with him he struck a pose as though prepared to tear Barbara to pieces.

She raised the rifle and fired and missed by a mile. Gilbert landed on her, cutting her head off with that meat cleaver chop of his. Then he sat her up in the grass and propped her severed head on her shoulders. She looked disappointed in herself but wasn't shaking her head or anything...

I waited for him to turn back from this task. My arms were back and I was raring for a second chance.

There was something behind Barbara that had caught Gilbert's attention. He was reaching for it. It was elusive. He kept reaching and my own interests became piqued. I moved to see over his shoulder, just in time for—

He pulled a sword from behind there and slashed! My left-hand blade parried in the nick of time.

I backed up, both ninjatō raised.

Slash, parry—thrust, parry—and I was doing great!

"You just gonna let me beat up on your sword?"

So I swung! And he took off another arm! Again!

"You chose those blades for a reason. Pay attention to your attunements!"

"Well how the hell do I—" But he went for my other arm and I parried again.

"It doesn't involve any thinking."

So I shut my brain off just as he tried a slash from above. I cut his throat out. "Holy shit!"

"Gerd," he said holding his bile-dripping wound. Then he leapt up into the air again, spinning, reaching out for Barbara with those Ginsu choppers.

Bang! Bang! And she shot both his hands off.

"Good," he said, landing.

"Good! Good!" Van Helsing agreed, clapping. "Great work, Gilbert!"

"Gilbert?"

"Oh you both deserve credit too!" Then he addressed our sensei once more. "Gilbert, might I have a moment with these two?"

"Sure." And sensei was gone.

Now was the time for that *showing* not *telling* the doc had promised us. All we had on were the military fatigues available in surplus thanks to the jokers' scavenging. Maybe we should be wearing something more athletic? This wasn't going to be your average run-of-the-mill training session after all—no mere slashing and shooting.

I pulled at my fatigue top.

"You are dressed just fine," the doc assured. He began. "The long and short of your powers, you two, is this: you can do everything the Count can and more. The only catch is, you must do it as one. Take for example your coveting of that vial of essence—*just a drop* and all that—why worry about its quantity? You may resurrect any you please any time you please, to no end."

Now *this* was an interesting proposition. But—

"How?" Barbara asked.

"As one," he said, embracing us. He eased us into closer proximity. There was the brightness. "You've become the winged. What else?" Before either of us could answer, "Ah, the canis. I see." He pressed us closer and the gleaming between us grew. "How was this determined so? I'll tell you: when your hearts became one you set off a certain reaction, though the results were not always the same. What was the missing ingredient? It's so simple, as everything has been. You desired to fly and you became that which flew. You desired to hunt and you became that which hunted. Now you desire to revive and you become..." And he let us go.

Everything grew to a crescendo: our commingling, the light. It all left in a swoosh. We were *one* alright. Though we weren't anything discernible—no bat, no wolf. We were humanity in amber. An amber of no hue, saturation, or lightness. We stood, though we had no real feature. We possessed a measure of definition sufficient to elicit in any who gazed upon us: *it's someone, isn't it?* We were a faceless personae.

Van Helsing beamed. "My, you're beautiful you two! Allow me?" He held up a large syringe.

We bowed in assent.

He plunged it into our heart. He withdrew several cubic centimeters then withdrew the needle itself.

"Now, to prove my hypothesis..." But he said this kinda coy. "I think it's time for an upgrade." And he drove the needle directly into his heart. He put his thumb on the plunger. He didn't yet depress it. We reached out to him. *Don't!* He only smiled and said, *"Don't?* Don't you worry, you two. I am but a mere accursed. If I am impaled, I die. There is no coming back and my charge is lost. If I am necessary for achieving the end of this charge, then it cannot be fulfilled." But, we thought, if only an accursed he may yet have peace in death. "Concerning yourselves with my mortality again I see. Very kind of you. And you have my full permission to take on this burden if you wish, though it is not for me." What was he saying? "Does the shepherd throw himself to the wolves, that they not devour the very flock he dreams will fatten him? I think not, for who would mind them so that later he may devour them, if, in this very minding, the meal is lost?" Eternity is no mere fodder. "No reward, no matter how precious, comes without the sacrifices of some proportion of its seekers. If I am of that proportion, then it is no true sacrifice to act with the end of this reward in mind, especially where the sacrifice may very well be *in* the forgoing of the end itself. It is my duty to deny myself." But he livened at this. "And, who knows what the fates really have in store for me, sacrifices or none... for you two... for any? After all, there are more things in heaven and earth..." With this, he flooded his essence. His heart was ours.

"Did it work?" Barbara and I said in unison. We'd separated, though *hearts as one* were hardly necessary for such communion.

"You tell me." he said, once again coy. What's he up to—

He drove a pike into his chest!

He collapsed.

"Did it work?"

v

We stood on the porch Barbara and I, looking out to the south.

"One man did this." I spoke in the direction of the crematorium though the object of my lament was far broader in its intension.

"He didn't light the fires," Barbara assured.

"If someone had done proper what we're about to, it never would have come to that."

She moved to between me and the devastation. I could no longer see. "I never did thank you," she said.

"For what?" I chuckled, unsure.

"For coming with me."

"It's a mutually beneficial arrangement."

"Oh bullshit."

"*Huh?*"

"You have your recipe," she reminded. "There's nothing in it for you anymore."

"And the peace of mind that comes with helping a friend, there's no benefit in that?" Alright, listen you all, there was an irony in what I just said, sure, but only for the fact that *peace of mind* wasn't my only motivation. There was no disingenuousness in my utterance. I meant everything and I'm hiding nothing. I want you all to understand this, because... "We made a pact," I reminded her. I took her hand. "*Either we don't feel this, or you're cured...*"

And she hugged on in that way that makes life worth living.

Then Van Helsing came out to join us. I guess he really did prove his hypothesis...

"Big night tomorrow you two. Best you get some rest."

"Not yet," I said.

Barbara bowed in agreement. "One last thing before we storm the castle."

"And what's that?" the doc asked.

I pointed out to that field of ash and bone. "They deserve a proper eulogy. A final gesture of reverence."

Barbara took my hand once more.

❦ 19 ❦
THE CURE

OCTOBER 18, 1968

And boy did they find a way to turn me truly helpless...

They left me in that iron maiden at full potency without end.

I was made to only lie in my cell, in my suit, in their dark, never to be let out—not even to face their barbarisms. This goes all the way back to that day I found my freedom.

And in this helplessness that idiot savant had discerned the one true torture, what could provoke any real measure of despair in me.

Understand, it wasn't the helplessness *per se*. I spent the last three decades *sans* body, you recall. Take my body and I'm helpless to bound, but who cares? I have my will to bound and I do will it because what a loss it would be for such a machinery to lie sedentary. Take my body and I nevertheless will that I bound and a servant—Gilbert, perhaps—comes along and moves me. I bound in effect therefore. You cannot deny my will, not for long, so there is no deprivation there. But, to take from me what motivates my will, my soul, my drive to not deprive the world of my effect—and that is what that weed took from me—take this, and I truly despair.

That was the torture: a complete and utter lack of consequence to my existence. I was of no consequence to them, sure, but in my constant state of intoxication I was of no consequence to me! The horror: To force me to lay in-stupor and therefore, in horrendous contentment at imposing no movement on this world whatsoever.

So I lay worthless.

Though I didn't lie in ignorance.

I held that amulet to my lips.

ii

My heart was alight.

There were stumblers.

They were roving to me, to my essence.

If I lay still enough—where my condition left me very little choice in this—I could almost feel the rumble of the horde approaching. What would Harrow be thinking at this moment? His great purge he called *quarantine*—that he called *eradication*—neither eliminated them nor, therefore, did it drive my essence from their minds. The fixed nature of the latter is the very reason he couldn't eradicate them. *They need only die to stumble* had been the slogan. They would never truly be gone and evidence of this absolute was rumbling toward. They need only die to stumble and in numbers like those approaching, they had to have died in holocaust.

At mind's eye I saw they had already breached the outer barrier. They were pouring across the courtyard.

Now came a separate rumble: HelCorp guards were firing those 30mm rounds of theirs at the wretched.

More quarantine, Harrow?

It was gray matter death for these poor souls in the company meat grinder. The artillery rounds left everything pierced and concussed so, *a fortiori*, they left all those stumbler brains the same. The battle would be short though there would be more like this. The mortals need only die. More will come to me.

Only a few stragglers remained... Fewer... And then there were none.

Now would come the clean-up. These procedures always seemed freakish to those of us with even a hint of sympathy, though they had taken on an air of the routine for the company. A dozen or so assessors stormed out the open end of the exit corridor, ready to get up close and personal: to shoot the brains out of any stumbler still wiggling.

There couldn't be, I thought, not with such overkill. But then! An undulation! A small mound of them was pulsing at the middle of the devastation. Two assessors ran to it. One hunkered and began sifting and lifting the destroyed wretched to get to what was moving underneath. The second he pulled the last lifeless stumbler off he was pierced! A jutte shot right through his chest! *Schwip!* Then a ninjatō took the torso from the legs of the assessor standing beside. Before his halves could recombine, our warrior possum's jutte took the heart of that torso-fallen. The up-to-now standing legs toppled.

Ben rose from that pile and *Swish! Swish! Swish!* Gak shuriken left his gloved fingers bringing the remaining assessors to stupor. Now our warrior could pierce them with maximal ease. He took to the task, lightning quick. He leapt from assessor to assessor helpless to defend as, even if they weren't gakked, all they had were nine-millimeter automatic pistols. Their job was destroying the brains of beings already half-decomposed-then-blown-up-in-addition—of all insults to injury. How were these milquetoast bureaucrats to handle a warrior trained by—by all observation—the gods' champion himself?

A hundred of them, sober as statues, would be no match. But maybe those gunners would?

One of the sentries had caught on to the warrior's ruse. The instant he did he opened fire—did so as the warrior was cleaving a fourth of the ten remaining assessors. All other gunners followed the first's lead. The warrior moved swift, made sure the explosive rounds stayed away from the brains of the now stumbling assessors. One wouldn't want them revived, if for no other reason, their re-cleaving would mean the slightest of inconveniences...

Swish! Swish! Swish! went more of the warrior's shuriken and all hit home, leaving the gunners too drunk to find those triggers. Must have been a heavy dose.

Too drunk for triggers, not too drunk to fall on the switch initializing the complex' mast system... Some one of them juicers managed to tip it either by accident or by the miracle of last-gasp drunkwork. Now multiple enormous arrays of mercury-vapor lamps were rising up from the earth. Their shields were opening like camera apertures not in acceptance of the light but to flood it upon our warrior: to flood him with ultraviolet! He faltered under it of course, though only for a second as... *Boom! Boom! Boom! Boom!* and those giant arrays exploded! A guardian angel watching over him?

Now came the HelCorp ninjas out that corridor! All of them! A good two dozen! And there were still those six drunken assessors besides. Oh no!

But the warrior was ready. His ninjatō were windmilling and not simply deflecting the shuriken thrown by the ninjas but slicing those stars in two. He moved closer to his attackers now. He was still the blender. They began to circle him, wary of his whirling tantos. Spiked jutte were hidden in the sleeves of their form-fitting uwagi but they'd never get the chance to pull them as our food-processor-personified had already commenced to slicing and dicing. Appendages of both ninja and assessor flew like the tossing of an accursed salad. The warrior's careful control of his ninjatō—too—meant finding vulnerabilities in the blades of the princesses while sustaining the integrity of his. He separated blade from hilt as frequently as he separated head from HelCorp staffer. They were all torso in short order though the reformation was coming. He leapt and spun to the staffers regaining form fastest and took his jutte to them. He skipped and twirled and relieved each and every one of those stumpy trunks of their tendency to not stumble. And all but one lonely ninja was kept from reforming. And the warrior just grabbed the jutte off a fresh stumbler and sent it her way flying. That was all she wrote.

Now came the rest of HelCorp! All of them save for that skunk Harrow!

Thorns were launched and flying in a rain that Ben was helpless to evade. He was impaled immediately and on the stumble. Now the bullets flew! He was shot in the head and back the accursed, already slicing and dicing. He got through a good ten of the agents before he was pierced again and stumbling. But...

Bang!

He was back in attack mode! Limbs a' flyin'!

Schwip!

He was pierced and peaked!

Bang!

Accursed and set to frappé!

Schwip!

Stumbler and set to stumble.

Bang!

Accursed n' killin'!

Schwip!

Stumbler n' stumblin'!

Bang!

Schwip!

Bang!

Schwip!

Bang!

Schwip!

Until...

"Cut it out!" yelled one of the more astute agents. "Stumbler accursed's just gonna keep on or do you idiots not even know yourselves?" And two agents grabbed stumbler Ben under his arms. "Get him in a cell. We'll figure out what to do with him after that."

They led him to the entry corridor while the remaining agents took to dealing with the slaughter in the courtyard.

Those massive titanium doors began to slide open for stumbler Ben and his escorts. Gates had been newly reinforced to protect against, among other things, turret fire from without and my escape from within.

And just as Ben was crossing the corridor threshold his head exploded! Then came the crack of the rifle that had to have taken the shot...

Ben impaled the two agents holding him and flew into the complex.

Barbara pulled back the bolt on her .30-06 and drove

another shell into the chamber. She did this a good kilometer away, lying up on a hill.

Now! Shouted Van Helsing and all those dead stumblers from down on the farm that turned out to be *revived* accursed rose up. They were pretend gooey and bloody for the ruse though otherwise pristine stock. The good twelve hundred of them surrounded the paltry ten-dozen or so agents who knew a lost battle of attrition when they saw it.

Van Helsing and company began detaining the agents the only way they knew how: by turning them to stumblers and corralling them.

Hold up...

Van Helsing, eh?

I must say, this is quite pleasing to me. Now when I take everything from HelCorp, I will take even more.

iii

Ben moved into that complex like air.

Hell, Ben danced into that complex.

The only two left in the place were Harrow and myself after all.

The warrior came through the east sally port into my torture chamber.

Entering the chamber, there was me, feckless in my iron maiden and laid across one of those transfusion chairs. Then there was Harrow standing at a terminal next to me. His hands were manipulating some controls to something or other.

The warrior approached us.

"Two birds, one stone," he said, pointing in our direction with his chin.

"Thought we lost you," Harrow offered.

"Never had me."

"Have the girl. If only by way of metaphor, like how we're the birds and you're the stone. She wants that cure and that makes her *ours*. But, and this is interesting, you're *hers*..."

"Went through a lot together."

"Well, if she has you, and we have her, I guess that means we have you too?"

"Buddy, you played all your cards the day you said the cure lay in staking him." He was pointing at me!

"Maybe I was lying?"

"Your namesake wasn't."

"HelCorp killed that old bastard seventy years ago."

"Killed this guy too..." And Ben meant me again! "Quite the track record. Maybe I'll inform your shareholders? Or, I could always take those staffers you've been turning and ram 'em up the Governor's ass. Wanna see what happens to your grant money then?"

"That's not funny."

"Think that's not funny? Wait'll he finds out the undead don't pay taxes. Now, if you'll excuse me," and he readied his jutte, "I owe Barbara this." And he marched forward.

"Us two birds on a platter you mean?" And Harrow was being extra casual about it all. Snake! "Well, you know what they say, *a bird in the hand*..." And he flicked a switch on his terminal.

Ben stopped.

It was a rumbling. Not of the stumblers. Louder and of artifice. I labored to lift my head and I saw. It was a large mechanical suit, pounding its way to between Harrow and our warrior. Ben peered into the cockpit of the massive beast. The man at the helm looked familiar alright. He looked somehow asleep but with eyes open and discerning.

There were plates in his head of similar circuitry as his suit.

"I believe you've already met Sergeant Coons?" Harrow said. "As you can see, he's been to the tailors." Harrow pushed a lever forward and Coons readied the suit for combat: fist drawn back, body twisted to avoid impact. "Get him, my ward!"

And with that, the machine began to bound fluid and swift.

Ben immediately broke his blades on the titanium exoskeleton. Before he could reckon what to do from here he was taken in Coons' grip. The metal beast tore him in two at the waist and threw both halves away. Torso and legs landed with a splat at opposite sides of the chamber.

Metal man marched over to the top half of a Ben reaching out, futilely, to the wall behind. He was slipping on his own bile trying to lift himself on legs that weren't there. The mech arrived and placed a foot to Ben pinning him against the wall, still. The concrete behind cracked and depressed under the force.

Harrow flipped a plastic cover off of a switch on his pedestal. This would be a culmination. Coons held steady, holding the warrior, waiting.

The skunk flipped the switch and—

Barbara fired Colt pistols through the hydraulics of Coons' crushing left leg as Gilbert leapt onto the sergeant's back ramming a ninjatō into the circuitry there! One of Coons' arms went completely limp and the pressure on his leg eased.

Harrow began tapping away at his terminal trying to correct the failure. *The Cur!*

Did I mention Ben's savior was Gilbert? My dear Gilbert! Alive!

And he and Barbara were not alone.

Van Helsing smashed Harrow away from the terminal and across the chamber. *I'm starting to like this Van Helsing guy...* The Dutchman then attempted to work the terminal though it would not register his inputs. *Unauthorized user*, it said.

Barbara had rushed to Ben's aid as Coons was spinning trying to shake my ward off his shoulders. Gilbert held fast to the blade in Coons' hardware so Coons took hold of the suit's immobilized arm and ripped it right off. He used it like a flyswatter to smash Gilbert flat to his back. Now the mech spun once more and my ward was tossed and the machine burst into the air on jets to chase him! It landed on my dear using its good arm to pin him: metal fingers acting like prison bars. Then the machine went mad with autopilot, squeezing Gilbert to mush.

"No!" Barbara screamed, Ben in her arms.

"Your hearts!" Van Helsing shouted holding Harrow by the scruff of his neck. "What you desire most of the present moment!"

And Barbara held Ben closer and there was a brightness.

Coons had rendered Gilbert an amorphous soup. Only his head was discernible in that bile. His visage was stoic as his usual though it wouldn't even be *that* much longer. Coons raised his fist for one final smash, brought it down swinging when...

Ben and Barbara caught that swinging arm in gorilla grip! They had taken the form of a silverback! A literal accursed silverback gorilla! And that accursed beast wrenched on that mechanical arm and took Coons into a spin—faster and faster. Then they let go and Coons flew. He flew but he didn't land. The silverback was on him in midair, tearing and thumping and ripping that mech suit to shreds before touchdown so there was no discernible suit left to land only cockpit!

That cockpit did land and when it did the gorilla reached right into it and tore the sergeant out holding him in-grip. The soldier was anodyne, limp. They reached out to his head encased in that circuitry, took the silicon in pinched gorilla fingers and peeled it right away.

"Thank you," sarge said weakly.

They laid him down.

And now it was time for the team to deal with Harrow! Van Helsing was the first to confront him as Gilbert was reforming and Ben and Barbara were coming back to two.

Doc tossed Harrow across the floor anew and stomped toward. "This is a travesty," he said of the complex.

"Worried about your legacy?" Harrow scoffed, rising.

"There are goods to be sought in this world far greater than the amelioration of any ego, my boy."

"Gonna give me that *greater good* crap?"

"*The greater good* is a conceit drummed up by the worst of our vain. What does the expression even mean?"

"Hell if I know. So, what kinda end we talking, old man?"

"Equilibrium."

And the two leapt from their level footing, catching each other in mid-air. The doc had the leverage and spun, throwing Harrow to the base of that control terminal with a smash.

The skunk rose to persist but Ben, Barbara, and Gilbert were approaching from his front with Van Helsing at his back. Harrow was caught and he simply grinned at all this and hammered a button on the control panel and fell through the floor into another of those damnable iron cages! But it was iron with aspirations! It was rising! It rose and I saw that it was launching. It smashed out of the complex like a rocket-propelled missile.

"That son of a bitch!" Ben shouted.

"Well this thing is useless," the doc said, pounding at the terminal.

"So what the hell now?"

"Only I have his scent…" I offered in a whisper.

And the four gave me their full attention. Gilbert ran to be at my side.

"Oh, isn't this just the biggest trick in *The Big Book of Bipedal Bats!*" Barbara said.

Gilbert reached for one of the clasps on my suit.

"Don't!" Ben shouted.

But Van Helsing simply freed me of the iron maiden, no hesitation.

"What the hell, doc?" Barbara chided. "You don't believe him do you?"

"Any better ideas?"

Ben caught me by the shoulders. I froze. "He ain't got any scent of that sleaze!" he said.

"Maybe not," Van Helsing said, "but you have his."

And Ben got an expression of consult. It was intended for Barbara and she caught it.

She stepped toward me, not looking me in the eye. "Is he still alive in there?" She poked to the right of my medallion. Smart girl.

And I decided to entertain her as there was no distance Harrow might run that I couldn't retrieve him. "As much as I wish to allay one so clearly after my own heart, my dear, the answer is no. He is not alive. The reformation rites destroyed what sentience there was."

Now she leveled her gaze. Did she hate me for taking her

companion? For my will to be one? Maybe. Though maybe she hated Harrow more? "Let him go," she said to Ben.

And he released his grip that wouldn't have held me much longer anyway.

With this, I was the wolf again and bounding.

iv

I was at the end of the corridor in no time, loping into the convalescence of the moonlight. Bounding after the bastard imposter lighting up the sky with that monstrosity of his: that monstrosity now at its apex.

Bounding. Moving through all of the accursed in the courtyard. To the thousands, every one of you keepers of my heart, I bless you! I bless even the four gawking joking national guardsmen!

Whoa! You guys see that dog?

On I ran, basking, whole.

Harrow went over the horizon but his scent was all mine!

There was the crash.

He would be in my bite sooner than he could step from that cage!

v

Harrow had crash-landed at the construction site of that shopping mall, little piggy.

He poked his head out from that smoking cell in-crater. Enjoy the silent stillness cur! It won't last long! And he did enjoy it. He adjusted his tie like a fop and readied himself to jump from the cell. Down he went and true to my word I had his calf in my jaws before he even settled his foot and had commenced to giving him a good death rattle.

I didn't want to tear the leg right off or anything so I tossed him away after a good concussion or two.

He tried finding his bearings. He failed. Even the accursed are no match for my wolf's tremor. I had had enough of the canis and became myself again.

I loomed over him, my cloak flowing. He tried propping himself up in his daze.

"Oh from what heights we do fall." I kicked him back to ground. I smirked in all due righteousness, my foot held to his chest. "I told you you were mine to be had."

"He must repair the damage he's done, Count, not be made to suffer under his own lingering devastations."

Ah ha, Van Helsing had arrived.

"You are not much fun," I said to the doctor, my foot still pinning Harrow. "You always did take yourself too seriously. Maybe your time in the air, as the fox, brought you a little joy at least? Or else how did you stay at my heels? Come on now, we all have those drivers in us, ensuring we attend to our pleasures sooner or later..."

"Could be it's making you wonder about such things, Count, that's what scratches that itch? Let him up."

"So that we may both have our fun? Absolutely!" And I removed my boot.

And now was the time for us to carefully quantify our next actions. We stared at each other intently a moment, none of us moving. And then I had a thought. "Only I may die," I said. "I was never one of those wretched stumblers. There is no coming back for me. You could so easily combine your forces to end me. And yet, only you hesitate Van Helsing."

"I will not align with any man who forsakes the charge."

"He is of no use to you and yet he lives..."

"Nor will I kill a helpless buffoon. And this man is both traitor and buffoon in one." He was pointing at Harrow—of course he was!—and this sentiment made me laugh. But he continued. "And, should I act alone in attacking you, Count, he would only dispatch with me the second I turned to take you in my sights."

"No. There is more to your reluctance," I assured. "Seeing as you refuse to attack either of us, and he simply *cannot* overtake anyone in a fair fight, what say you of *my* hesitation?"

"Same dilemma. You go for me, he attacks you. You go for him, I do the same."

"Ha! No," I insisted. "There is more to it once again."

"So what the hell, now?" Harrow asked. The impetuous sleaze!

"The three of you will settle this like men." And Gilbert was there, holding a launcher for each of us. "One gun, one spike. Make them count. Live or die, either way, it will be with honor." Then he turned to Harrow who I couldn't imagine was convinced. "The highest of honors..." And Harrow grinned at this.

We held out our hands.

He gave over those launchers and we split apart in angles ensuring no pair of us was any nearer or any further than the others. Our care for equidistance determined an expanding rotating equilateral triangle.

We spun across the breadth of the mall's concrete foundation, under the moon eaten by floodlight. If there could ever be such a fantastical thing as an accord among us—a trio of oil, water, and excrement—it would inform us of one fact: none would fire until the reaching of the edge of this stone.

I observed my opponents as we went. Harrow held his launcher at a forty-five-degree angle across his front left thigh, as he tended to in that chamber. I'd almost be fearful of such a familiar sight, so evocative of my tortures, if I weren't at the same time overjoyed at the prospect of outshooting him at his best. Van Helsing was no trifle either. He'd never held a weapon such as this and yet, the way it hung to his right, neither casual nor rigid, it made me think another accord in effect: a mystical connection between he and his shooter. As for me, I like to keep them guessing though not in a way that provokes a fear. I would die if a formidable air—something I struggle so much to keep bridled—ever did an ounce of the work I intended of my deftness alone. My weapon simply hung loose at my right lower abdomen.

And on we spun...

And more...

And it would be me who made it to that edge first. I stopped at the barrier. The others followed suit.

Now, who would be the first to fire? Would it be the pragmatist Van Helsing, who only ever felt honor a fetish distracting from the task at hand? The coward Harrow, who would discard glory at the first rumblings of a fear his pride could never best? Or li'l old me?

And why not me? My glory was all but guaranteed the millennia ago I turned, and there would be no historian so foolish as to attempt to deprive me of it. Why seek more? Why be greedy?

I readied my—

But Harrow drew! Then Van Helsing! He fired at Harrow damn quick but nothing flew! The doctor's gun wasn't loaded. Thank you, dear ward!

Oh but I was loaded for bear. I'd fired at Harrow but

he'd been quicker! My chest was once again pierced but now so was his!

My aim was true and he was hopelessly on the stumble. But the skunk's aim was true as well, hitting me squarely where the heart rests...

...Had I been him!

I pulled the thorn from out my left chest. "They'll never learn," I said, shaking my head.

I tossed the toothpick aside.

Happy accidents.

🦋 20 🦋

THE COMPROMISE

OCTOBER 18, 1968

We caught up with them just as Harrow had taken to stumbling.

"He'll never learn," the Count said as he approached his ward. "Ah, dear dear Gilbert! From Quassy, to whole, to keeper of my essence. Few of us cursed have enjoyed such privileged forms. Come here!"

And they embraced.

But Gilbert, though pleased to see his master, was not attending to the reunion with the same joy.

"My boy, you are not happy to—"

He pushed the Count aside and grabbed onto Barbara's thrusting wrist, squeezing loose the jutte in her hand and twisting her into my path. And the spike I held at the ready, intended for the Count's heart should she have missed, only pierced *her*. She became the stumbler near instantly. I withdrew my weapon from her chest and drove it into her temple. She revived but Gilbert had her at the shoulder now as well as the wrist. He launched her through a stack of girders thirty feet away. I corrected and pounced and Gilbert merely pivoted. I tripped past him as he took hold of me and threw me too. Thanks to the damned momentum of my staggering I flew further off than Barbara.

In all this the Count merely observed. Not observing like a man watching his mightiest champion, desperate to keep him alive and fighting off all comers, but more like a man watching a television playing the national anthem.

And where was Van Helsing? He had moved to the side of the stone opposite where Barbara and I landed. Machinery was there and he was reaching into the raised bucket of a front-end loader. He took hold of something and what he took hold of had weight. He removed a claymore. It had gems all along its fuller. The hilt had the same engraving as Gilbert's dagger. He took it in hand and turned to face—

But all lighting in the compound flickered then dimmed. A beaming came across the expanse.

"No..." Van Helsing whispered.

Barbara and I emerged from the steel, the human in amber: the faceless personae. We moved swift to the Count. We moved in stride though drifting—flowing really—for all anyone could discern of our nebulous form.

Gilbert made a move and we merely held out an appendage, halting him by force acting at a distance. He was still.

We were on the Count in a blink. We held in another of our appendages a splinter: small though substantial enough to impale. We raised it to deal the demon his final torment.

"No!" And Van Helsing brought the sword down cleaving the faceless personae in two, driving Barbara and I away from each other at opposite angles.

"Are you in league with him?" Barbara said, flying for the doctor.

And the Count just chuckled and Van Helsing spun away from our rushing Barbara to hold the tip of the claymore to the Count's throat. His other hand went up to her, stopping her, though not of anything mystical.

Gilbert and I watched, confounded at the imagery of it all.

"Why?" Barbara asked, ready to recommence with her attack.

"You can't kill him," Van Helsing insisted.

"I've come too far—"

"Too far to die a stumbler."

"All mortals die stumbling."

"You'll never be mortal." And this quieted her. "Kill him," the doctor continued, "and you may lose the curse, but you'll only revert to what you were before you were turned."

"No."

"Yes Barbara. You were turned deceased. You'll revert to deceased." She was listening but she wouldn't hear it. But she was listening. "That isn't all. You kill the Count, Ben reverts too—

"He has the vial—"

"The Count will be dead. The link will be broken and that blood useless. All who you've turned as deceased will simply return to wretched decay. Is that what you want for them? For you?"

"I wanted a life—"

"With the people you love—I know—who you're so certain will not love you cursed. Will they love you like this..." And he gestured at the dismembered Harrow. "I'm sorry Barbara, but you have to know this is not your cure."

She collapsed. He dropped the sword and went to her. Her words would be the skeptic's, her voice would betray the plea. She said, "What if you're—"

"Oh, he's not wrong," the Count assured. "In fact, he's jogged my memory." And Barbara was no longer in heartbreak but fearful. As was I. What was the Count's intimation? He grinned at us and said, "Mina."

And Van Helsing's head sunk. "Please don't."

"Ha!" the Count scoffed.

"Mina?" I asked, "What about Mina?"

"He was never slain," Van Helsing said. "Mina's curse was broken nonetheless. He may destroy the link any time he pleases, break the curse at will..."

"Like now." And he raised his right hand, angled it at me and Barbara.

"No!" she demanded.

The Count scoffed, "So now you don't wish to be cured?" And Barbara moved to in front of me, held out her arms. "It's not a bullet my dear. You won't save him that way."

"Master, please don't."

"Gilbert? I expected more from you."

And with that, he commenced with the ritual. The tips of his fingers twitched and fluttered at first. A glimmer emerged at those tips. Soon that glimmer was emanating from more than digit. His whole body was aglow and a streaking flashing gash was ribboning across his neck and slicing down his chest. He actually appeared pained by the process. The ribbon angled and continued its dissection from below his naval toward his right hip. He pulled back the hand that started the whole goddamn rite, still glistening like the sun, and leveled it at a Barbara now bracing herself. She closed her eyes. I closed mine. I held her tight. Then...

Nuffin!

We opened our eyes at once, to the Count flicking his fingers at us to no effect but his own confusion. The streaking flashing gashes at his trunk had left a familiar outline. The Count's right hand was no longer in his control. It was waving at us. At Barbara?

"Righty!" And she ran to take his waving hand in hers.

"Oh dear," the Count said, looking down to his disembodied little friend. "In that unbound state you had to go and find, of all things, love." And Barbara nuzzled Thumpy's palm. "I will never be whole again…" She kissed him gently at the dorsum and Thumpy stroked her cheek. "Please stop."

"Just count your lucky stars your lower half didn't go and *find* anything…"

"Oh god…"

"Looks like the only way to break the curse now," doc said, "is for you to die. I guess we're stuck with each other."

The Count looked up and away from all displays of affection. He sighed that dead sigh of his. "Will my going softly into this good fortune of yours, Van Helsing, be the first step of my long journey to redemption?"

"First of so many," Van Helsing said. "And I'm not so sure the discrete unit that is *a step* applies. Your redeeming movements must be continuous. You would need devote the entire of what remains of your life to acting only in the interests of others, and that's *if* you want to come a mere infinitesimal closer to meeting just a single of the plethora of conditions necessary for a redemption such as yours."

"You ask what's next to impossible," the Count protested, Barbara hanging off his hip.

"*Next* to?" the doc laughed. "But that's what you're up against."

The Count dropped all irony. "Van Helsing, why do you

not scoff at talk of my redemption? Why do you not disbelieve my earnestness?"

"Because, we do not entertain a man's redemption for the sake of just that man, but our own. I would be no better than the worst of us should I not grant the possibility of another's saving. If I scoff I am lost, for how can I believe any man's redemption possible if I don't even believe he has it in him to make the attempt? This is a faith that makes us human."

"And all may seek it?"

"All. Though that doesn't mean it will be easy for *all*. There's a reason your life, in the main, would be reduced to pure asceticism. You are truly one of our worst."

"Ha! I know! I know! Though I may still be attempting a ruse."

"Then prove your good faith right here and now. Take a true first step."

"I must admit, I am curious. What would you have me do?"

"Let me turn you."

"Ha!" But the doc didn't flinch. "You are not fooling," the Count realized.

"Your essence will be trapped in the brain of the stumbler inside you. The link can never be broken. Not even in death. You will save them."

"To be turned by anyone..." he pondered. "By Abraham Van Helsing of all of anyone! Would I fail my test if I asked for a moment to think it over?"

"I'll be generous. Though a moment is already up. I will give you a minute more."

"You have my grat—"

There was a beeping coming from Harrow.

"What the hell is that now!" I demanded.

The sound coincided with a red intermittent flash beneath the skin of the brow of Harrow's severed head. It was equidistant his eyes.

"What is it? A bomb or something?" Barbara asked.

It was a beacon, as strong a signal as the Count's own heart. How'd I figure that out? I didn't. I had a front row seat and what a geek show it was. Stumblers had begun writhing out from anywhere earthen enough to preserve but not bind them.

As their faces emerged from that earth I saw they had the same chips in their foreheads as the sarge. All hands emerging from that sod had wooded pikes fastened to them too.

Barbara came to me, we tried controlling them. It didn't work. The Count was struggling the same. His expression was dire.

The stumblers were attuned to that beacon and nothing else.

"There's gotta be thousands of them on those valley walls alone," Gilbert said. "We're not stopping them all."

"We're not stopping a single one of them," Van Helsing warned. "If any are accursed in disguise, we'll only be turning them to something much more difficult to defeat."

The buried stumblers were shaking the earth from their faces.

"Smash the beacon?" Barbara suggested.

"That won't work either. That bastard, he's a stumbler and he's still torturing us. Try to get to that beacon and you destroy his brain. You'll bring him right back as cursed and whatever hole you've dug will heal. You might impale him anew, but then you're back to where you started. Bastard thought of everything. Wanted the world overrun with stumblers the very instant he died.

"Why?"

"His legacy," Van Helsing said. "*The only man who ever kept them at bay.*"

"Who'll ever believe that?"

"All but the wretched. The desperate, tuning into emergency broadcasts looking for a way to stop the hordes, only ever finding the council blathering on about the past not the future, about their one-time success, about HelCorp's success by extension. Council won't go into that good night without massaging their image a last time, giving that bastard what he wants. The bastard Harrow! Outsmarted us all, even on the stumble—"

"Kill me," the Count said.

"What?" Gilbert demanded, apprehension in his voice.

"Kill me and I break the curse. For those wretched beasts too. All will fall like dominoes."

"No!" And Gilbert was pleading.

"It is the only way, dear ward. We won't survive them and let no one molest our friends any longer. Leave them to their rest."

The servant fell to his knees.

The buried stumblers were observing their surroundings, their heads free of the earth.

"What about Barbara? Ben?" was the doc's concern.

But Barbara and I knew our charge. A tear fell of her, and it was that tear that hastened what needed to be hastened. "But it comes, Ben," she said. "Just not like it used to."

"Real easy now though." And I was sure she could see the agreement in me. "Of all times, eh Barbara girl?"

"It's the only way," we said to Van Helsing. Barbara turned to the Count. "Don't worry," she promised. "It's not nothing." And the Count just grinned—enough the tip of a canine emerged.

And the buried stumblers were thrashing, trying to get that weighty loam off their chests.

"Hurry!" the Count said to Van Helsing.

And Van Helsing picked up Barbara's splinter and moved to the task. His eyes set upon the martyr's ashen visage in all its imploring and he was hit by a second's awareness of the absurdity of it all: his lamenting the death of this man. But he was indeed stricken and it was, nevertheless, an absurdity. He raised the pike, not heavy by matter though it wasn't light. Barbara and I braced ourselves. Gilbert buried his face in his hands. Van Helsing was indeed stricken...

"Poetic, isn't it?" the Count assured.

And The Dutchman pounced! And the spike fell to his feet. It fell to his feet unused as he'd taken the Count by the neck and buried himself feeding. His canines must have lengthened a good two inches before penetration. Count appeared to be in some sort of elation. Gilbert as well...

In all this, the stumblers had sat up and were thrashing the earth from off their legs.

Doc pulled back now, held out his wrist to the Count. "You wanted redemption, who am I to deny you?"

"You mean I didn't just earn it?"

"No! Drink!"

And the Count did and the doc looked to Barbara and I. "You're going to turn them all," he said.

"All?"

"A final gesture of reverence. They didn't ask for this."

"The sheer number of them—"

"The faceless personae. All you need desire of this force is an endless font." And Barbara and I felt the swell of realization. We bowed in assent. "But we cannot merely turn the stumblers," Van Helsing continued. "Once accursed, they'll ravage the mortals to food scraps."

"Are you saying it has to be *all* all?"

"All or nothing. It will be anyway, in time. If the mortals die as fodder they'll take to stumbling and we'll take to turning them. Getting preemptive at least preserves them of that torture."

"The people should have a choice."

"Then give them that choice. Only be sure to inform them of their—"

"Pops!" shouted the jokers nearly rolling toward us from down the hill—shouting at Gilbert, evidently, considering their use of *pops*. Gilbert just shook his head at them as those talkers kept talkin' "Stumblers are everywhere! Sproutin' like weeds."

"Men! Regroup!" And Coons came barreling on down after the jokers and past the stumblers rolling out of their shallow graves. He stopped at our feet, addressed the lot of us. "Any orders?"

And everyone looked to Barbara and me. And we just looked to each other.

The stumblers were on their feet now and... stumbling.

"There are more things in heaven and earth."

I took her hand in mine.

Our brightness came. We were alight. We were certain.

And so, we flowed out over these hills and across these plains. Across these wretched. These second chances. A font of just desert.

ii

The dead are coming back to life! I repeat, the dead are coming back to life! The dead who came back to life last week are coming back to LIFE life, able to think and speak and use moisturizer!

———

We're back on the farm. The kid and his protector move off the porch of the farmhouse to greet the Carter family having returned home.

———

Real-life war hero Barney Coons' stars in the movie event of the summer! You can't afford to miss his latest heart stopper: To Holland Michigan and Back!

———

We're on the street outside a convenience store. A store patron grabs a cola out of a vending machine on the sidewalk. Another patron grabs a bottle of carbonated wolf's bane from the machine next to it.

———

Two members of Hevans law enforcement and an area man are in custody tonight after a shootout at a local diner left none dead but one not-so-happy waitress completely out of Salisbury steak.

———

We're at the Cleveland Museum of Art, center of the atrium. Alister, out of his armor, is onboarding his latest staffer, Gilbert. Alister is yammering on about something or other when Gilbert gets an expression of concern. He puts a shushing finger to the curator's lips. He looks up.

———

Authorities say they apprehended four accursed-Americans and one stumbler in the break-in. Sources close to the investigation say the apprehended stumbler has direct ties to the Oval Office...

———

We're at the beach. The jokers are kicking back with some beers. Yeah, the accursed can get blotto. Especially these accursed... Hickie's wearing a shirt with his trunks though. Comes across as just plain weird.

———

Medical authorities are urging pregnant women to avoid turning in their third trimester.

———

We're in an office complex. One of the workers suffers a paper cut opening an envelope. Another particularly pallid staffer gets a look of overwhelm and turns to sip some wolf's bane.

———

Meet the San Francisco wiz kids who've harnessed the power of the microchip. An innovation that some worry may lead to unethical applications such as stumbler mind control, mechs, convincing alarmists that a computer program really good at telling people what they want to hear is an intelligence capable of taking over the world, and Leisure Suit Larry.

———

We're on the streets of London. A bunch of prudes burn copies of various VHS tapes. They wave signs that say things like: *Beware the power of the video! It will warp your kids' minds.* Many of the burning tapes have the word 'Dead' in their titles.

———

Could more stumbler radiation be the solution to the hole in our ozone layer?

———

We're in Germany. The Berlin wall falls and countless straddle the now symbolic border in celebration of freedom from people who believe utopia is the kinda place you ought be killed for leaving. Many decide right then and there to never let stumblers make socio-economic decisions ever again...

———

With special guests Regis Philbin and Howard Stern! And also, stupid stumbler tricks!

———

We're in a living room decked out in doilies and rock candy. Barbara's aunt is condemning Barbara's brother, Johnny, to hell. Again.

———

Meet the Seattle barista who's ditched the curse and gone back to stumbling. 'I was stumbling before it was cool. Grrrrrrr.'

———

We're on the Earth. The world is plunged into a global financial crisis after congress tells a bunch of banks to buy a bunch of houses to sell to people who can't afford those houses, promising to reimburse the banks—with money taxed from the people who can't afford those houses—for any unmovable inventory should the people who can't afford those houses not be able to afford those houses. Many decide right then and there to never let stumblers make socio-economic decisions ever again...

———

The FDA has issued a recall for 'Ben and Barbara's Naughty Clotty' flavored cursing kits...

———

We're at The University of Saba, Dutch Caribbean. Van Helsing teaches a graduate class in media studies. The title of his PowerPoint reads, *Self-Loathing in the Age of Small Screens in Front of Big Screens: Why You Literally Can't Afford to*

Miss the Movie Event of the Summer. Most of the students are on their iPhones...

———

Appearing at San Diego Comic Con, direct from Evans City Cemetery where it all began, 'Bill the First Ever Stumbler'! Come watch Bill just lumber around smashing things with rocks. Q&A with Bill to follow [Bill's reviving].

———

We're in that same office complex. People aren't happy to be there. *Really, really* unhappy to be there. A few of the staffers wear masks, believing themselves protected against the latest variant of stumbler radiation.

———

Keep my wife's neck out your mother-fucking mouth!

———

We're in America. The market crashes for the second time in six months after the president threatens to take more money away from American businesses so that American businesses will thrive. Many decide right then and there to never let stumblers make socio-economic decisions ever again...

———

Are you afraid of the dark? Maybe you shouldn't be. Research suggests our constant state of illumination may be responsible for the erosion of social cohesion we once took for granted. But with the recent resurgence of celluloid, are we finally turning a corner? Have we finally seen [the absence of] the light?

————

We're in a theater accidentally showing some old bygone flic only ever meant to entertain. A single tear is brought to the eye of a single audience member. She puts her phone away and just watches the movie.

iii

We're up north (the day after the big turn, 1968). Ben's son and daughter burst out their front door to hug their daddy. Ben is overjoyed. His wife lets a bit of a grin slip from her otherwise pensive demeanor.

iv

No, you're not in a science fiction serial! It's Earth, 1969, and there are men walking on the moon as we speak!

EPILOGUE

JULY 20, 1969

That's one small step for man, one giant leap for mankind...

"Now let's ditch this cargo and get the hell out of here."

"Amen."

The oak trunk landed at the astronaut's feet. It kicked up a bit of moon dust hardly the slave to gravity.

The astronauts had already headed back to Eagle and in seconds were outta there. Escape velocity outta there.

The padlock on the trunk began to vibrate. The frequency of its oscillation was increasing. The lock shook faster and faster and faster until its shackle didn't just break free from the body, it was ripped away and sent flying!

The disintegration of the lock dislodged the hasps forming the brass cross. The trunk itself was now vibrating.

Boom!

The lid blew off launching itself all the way to the dark

side of the moon. The trunk was wide open. Inside it was Harrow! The head of Harrow to be precise. His eyes shot open. He glowered, those eyes darting around. He appeared to be scheming. His wheels were definitely turning. He had to get off this dreary satellite, regain his empire. But—

"I bid you, Velcome."

Walking up to a now despondent Harrow was the shiniest pair of patent leather shoes you'd ever seen. Even in moon dust. Hands reached down to the severed head, positioning themselves just over its ears. The hands began to lift.

The Count held Harrow real close to his visage, almost like he was deliberately occluding something. "You like?" he said in some sort of glee and he let Harrow ease back beyond him to see over his shoulder.

It was the HelCorp complex in all its glory... only, on the moon.

The Count must have had his fill of Harrow having his fill. He set the head of the imposter onto the oak trunk, teeing it up, making sure to face the... *face* away from him.

He gave his right shoe a bit of a buff despite its already impossible shine. Satisfied, he took a few steps back.

"I'm sure you will find this part of my domain more inviting."

He marched forward picking up speed. That shiniest shoe pulled back pendulum-like then burst forward connecting with Harrow's noggin, booting it all the way across the moon like a soccer ball!

The Count tilted his head, gave a bit of a sideways nod. Not a bad punt. He glanced over to his roommate. Barbara smiled in approval. They turned, started to walk back in the direction of that lunar temple.

The part of the Count that was Thumpy came alive,

those streaking ribbons announcing him. The right hand of the Count reached out to Barbara.

She took it in hers.

ABOUT THE AUTHOR

Gerald Simon Jameson is an author *not* famous for his reclusiveness (he's that good) but massively read none-theless (if Gerald Simon Jameson *is* his real name, which it isn't). He publishes both through solicitation and commis-sion, only ever communicating via anonymous letter drops, sending hardcopy manuscripts, and receiving hardcopy requests for all sorts of notes and missives (we just wait for an X on various mailboxes all over the continent to emerge, notifying us of a pickup or a Y for drop off...). For all we know, *Dracula vs Night of The Living Dead* is his debut novel, his first under the name 'Gerald Simon Jameson', or some imposter's. It was worth publishing, though.

www.ingramcontent.com/pod-product-compliance
Lightning Source LLC
Chambersburg PA
CBHW020912130726
47904CB00006BA/1845